ABOUT THE AUTHOR

Rachael Lucas writes novels for adults and teenagers, including the Carnegie nominated *The State of Grace*, which was selected as an Outstanding Book for Young People with Disabilities by IBBY. She lives on a beautiful stretch of coastline in the north west of England with her family and two very enthusiastic spaniels. When she's not writing at the kitchen table with a cup of coffee by her side, she's out walking the dogs on the beach or in the nearby pinewoods.

Keep up with Rachael on Instagram @rachaellucas, join her for chats and news updates on Facebook at @rachaellu-caswriter, and get a free short story by signing up for her newsletter at rachaellucas.com

The Winter Cottage

Rachael Lucas

PRAISE FOR RACHAEL LUCAS

Full of festive comfort and joy

— ALEX BROWN

I loved it - a snuggly hot chocolate of a book

— HOLLY MARTIN

Wonderfully warm, brave and wise

— MIRANDA DICKINSON

A perfect cosy romantic treat

— CATHY BRAMLEY

A romantic, atmospheric read about fresh starts and second chances

— TASMINA PERRY

Cover by dmeachamdesign

For Jude, with all my love.

PROLOGUE

Of *course* the door was rusted shut. After travelling this far, and arriving – unhinged with jet lag and feeling like a zombie – at Applemore Cottage, it felt like her dad was having one final joke on her. Rilla could imagine him chuckling to himself as he stood to one side, watching with amusement as his eldest daughter battled to make her way inside.

Rilla wiggled the key again hopefully, and then shoved at the door with her shoulder. It wasn't giving an inch.

'Ow,' she said, out loud.

A single magpie hopped onto the branch of the rowan tree which sat in the middle of the overgrown lawn and cocked his head at her thoughtfully.

'Oh great. That's just what I need.' Rilla pushed a lock of hair back from her face and – ever superstitious – gave him a fleeting salute. *'Morning, Mister Magpie, how's your wife?'*

The magpie looked back at her and blinked his beady eyes.

Well, this was just perfect. She'd been deposited in the

1

back of beyond with a jumble of bags and a mobile phone with no service, and now she was not only locked out, but there was a bad-luck omen standing in the garden giving her the eye. A few spots of rain began to fall, to add to the injustice of it all.

Rilla stepped back, gathered herself and looked at the cottage for a moment.

'Please let me in,' she said, feeling faintly ridiculous.

Green paint was peeling on the cottage door and windows. Late roses still bloomed, climbing up a trellis and hanging from the wooden porch, their pale pink petals clinging on despite the autumn chill. The garden was shaggy and overgrown, the grass desperately in need of a cut. To one side of the cottage, the vegetable patch had clearly been left to grow wild – there was a huge pumpkin, half-hidden by overgrown foliage, and a tangle of beanstalks clambered up a faded bamboo wigwam. Rilla felt a wave of sadness at the thought of her dad planting the seeds, knowing he would more than likely not be around to see them come to fruition. She gave a heavy sigh and threw herself at the door once more with a shout of desperation.

'Urgghhhhhh!'

The door still didn't budge.

Rilla leant her forehead against it and rubbed her shoulder. Now she was locked out, jet-lagged and bruised.

'It helps if you unlock it.'

She spun around. Standing at the end of the path, one hand on the stone gatepost, was a tall, dark-haired man. He was tanned and outdoorsy-looking in a blue jumper, jeans and sturdy work boots. He rubbed a hand across the dark scruff of his beard, looking at her with an expression she couldn't quite read, then cocked his head slightly to one side, as if he was trying to place her. For a fleeting moment,

Rilla wondered if the magpie had taken human form, then realised that sleep deprivation and jet lag were tipping her into insanity, and being locked out of the cottage was the final step. And now – bad-luck magpie or not – there was a man, *mansplaining*.

'It *is* unlocked.' Rilla pointed crossly at the Yale key which was jammed in the lock, and which she'd managed to twist round with more than a little bit of force and the determination that only came with desperation.

'It is,' he nodded, thoughtfully, and put his hand into his pocket, 'but you'll find it a hell of a lot easier to get in if you have the main key as well.' He strode down the path and lifted one of the stone flower pots which sat by the door. Underneath was a large, rusted metal key. He straightened up, handing it to her with an amused expression.

Rilla took it and then folded her arms. 'Nobody said anything about there being two keys.'

'Ah.' He looked slightly uncomfortable. 'When David left – well, when he went into hospital – it was all a bit rushed. We were left to sort out a few bits and bobs, and this key – well, it must've just got lost in the whole getting-everything-sorted. Sorry.'

Rilla looked at him for a moment, arms still folded. Her face, which was her giveaway, was clearly making a very bad job of trying to look neutral. 'I was told there'd be no problem getting into the cottage.' She sounded prickly and cross, because – well, she was. And tired, and fuzzy-headed, and feeling a million feelings that she'd been keeping neatly locked away in a box in her head until now, when she was standing at Applemore Cottage for the first time in well over a decade. And this *annoying* man was getting in her way. All she wanted was to get inside and collapse on the sofa and

3

sleep for about a hundred years. It wasn't that much to ask, was it?

'Are you trying to suggest I've locked you out?' He seemed amused, a small smile curving at the corners of his mouth.

'Have you got something to hide?'

He looked at her, a fleeting expression of something she couldn't quite read passing across his face. 'Nope, nothing to hide, no hidden agenda. Just one of those things.'

'Hrmm.' Rilla glanced at the key, still feeling suspicious, and put it in the lock, shoving hard once again with her shoulder. The door swung open, and she half fell, half swung into the hallway of the cottage. A pile of letters lay on the mat. 'Okay,' she turned to say. 'Sorry, I didn't mean to—'

But the man was gone, like the magpie before him, and she was standing in the hallway of Applemore Lodge, completely alone.

CHAPTER 1

'So, what's this about?'

Lachlan Fraser looked out of the window of his shared flat. He'd been living with his friend and business partner Gus for the last four years, and in that time not once had he got bored of looking out across the stretch of houses and buildings that looked down towards the slate grey waters of the Firth of Forth. Edinburgh was his favourite city in the whole world, and he was lucky to live there. Or he had been. He turned away from the view.

Gus rolled up the sleeves of his blue and white striped shirt and took a cursory glance at himself in the mirror. As fair as Lachlan was dark, even now in his mid-thirties Gus's attempts at growing anything other than a pale fuzz of stubble were laughable. Not that his extremely expensive girlfriend, Lucinda, seemed to mind. Lachlan groaned inwardly thinking about it. Flat sharing had its down sides, and lying in bed at 2 a.m. with a pillow over your head trying not to listen to your best mate and his pretty much live-in girlfriend in bed was definitely one of them.

'Mate?' Gus broke into his thoughts.

Lachlan stifled a yawn – he'd had about four hours' sleep, and the prospect of today was not a pleasing one. 'It's the house.'

'By house,' Gus said, arching a sardonic eyebrow, 'I assume we mean enormous turreted castle in the Highlands?'

'It's not a castle,' Lachlan began, for the hundredth time. 'It's a—'

'Yeah, yeah, whatever. You've got *turrets*. QED.'

'Doesn't everyone?' Leaning into the joke, Lachlan threw one of Lucinda's expensive coffee mats at Gus's head. It flew through the air like a frisbee and narrowly missed his ear. Gus, with the lightning reflexes of an ex-rugby player, shot out a hand and caught it.

'House. Castle. Okay, what's going on?'

'We've had the calculations through for the death duties.' Lachlan sighed.

'You do realise you give yourself away with that phrasing.'

'I do?' Lachlan said, confused.

'Inheritance tax, that's what the rest of us plebs call it.'

'Death duties, inheritance tax – whatever. The thing is, we've got over two hundred grand to materialise out of nowhere.'

'Excellent.' Gus sat down at the kitchen table and extended his long legs so his feet were balanced on top. 'Well, you can sell an old master or something. You've got loads of paintings hanging in the hall. One of them must be worth a bob or two?'

'You'd be surprised.' Lachlan thought about the shabby, once-grand hallway of Applemore House. The painted walls – once deep burgundy, now faded to a dusty dark pink

– had a series of rectangular shapes where the burgundy paint could be seen. Each one marked the story of a financial disaster in the Fraser family – they'd sold off pretty much anything that was worth anything. Now all that hung on the walls were some distinctly un-PC stuffed animal heads (one of which, last time he'd been home, was bearing some unseasonal Christmas baubles hanging from its antlers) and a selection of portraits of distinctly unglamorous ancestors, glowering down at them in kilts and shooting gear.

'Right. Well, assuming you don't have a spare two hundred grand kicking about, and knowing that we absolutely do not, what the hell are you going to do?'

Lachlan picked up his phone, seeing a message from his sister Charlotte. He swiped it away and turned the screen face down on the table.

'Honestly? I don't have a clue.' He wasn't being completely honest with either himself or Gus. He knew exactly what to do – the trouble was doing it was going to make him the biggest shit on the planet.

'You must have some idea.'

Lachlan hesitated. 'Remember Felix Lowther? Friend of mine from university?'

'Vaguely.' Gus frowned, thinking. 'Massively tall, skinny, golf guy?'

Lachlan nodded. 'That's the one. He's an estate agent now up in Perth. Sells country houses and estates and that sort of thing.'

Gus's mouth fell open as he realised what Lachlan was saying. 'You can't sell it.'

'Oh for god's sake,' Lachlan said, putting his head in his hands and finding himself laughing. 'Don't *you* start.'

'It's your heritage. It's the family seat. It's—'

7

'A massive, crumbling, impractical, financially ruinous—'

'Castle,' said Gus, triumphantly.

'You are not helping.' Lachlan took his head out of his hands. He looked at the stack of beer cans on the table. 'Is it too early for a drink?'

'It's half nine. The answer is very definitely yes. Plus we can't start drinking the proceeds – that way madness lies. Or alcoholism.'

'Yeah, I know. I was only joking.' Well, half joking, thought Lachlan, reaching out and looking at one of their new can designs. He turned it around in his hand thoughtfully.

'So you're up shit creek with a massive debt and a castle you can't sell—'

'I can sell it,' Lachlan said, reasonably, 'In fact, I'm going to be speaking to Felix later this week.'

'Right. Well, bags I come and be a fly on the wall when you tell the three sisters you're making them homeless.'

'Cheers, mate.' He really didn't want to think about that.

'There has to be a solution that doesn't involve turfing the girls out on to the street. I mean, Charlotte would be all right – she's tough as old boots. But you can't expect Beth to just move her entire business, lock, stock and flower barrel when she's spent all that time getting it up and running.' Gus wasn't telling him anything he didn't already know, but Lachlan found himself shifting uncomfortably at hearing the words out loud.

'And we haven't even got started on Polly.'

'Ah, sweet Poll.' Gus had always had a bit of a big-brother fondness for the youngest of the family. 'What's she up to now?'

'Not a lot,' said Lachlan, 'but she's doing whatever it isn't under my roof. Well, our roof.'

'She'd better not stay still too long, or she'll get soaked. Is it still leaking?'

'Very much so.' Lachlan groaned. A leaky roof was just one of the many issues.

'This conversation,' Gus said, getting up and removing another of the cans from Lachlan's hand and looking at him reprovingly, 'is not really going anywhere good.'

Lachlan scrunched up his face and looked at his friend. As soon as the words were out there, it was a thing, and there was no going back.

'I think what I need to do is head up there for a bit, see what I can do to sort things out and—'

'And leave me with a brewery with no brewer.'

Lachlan winced. 'Ye-eah.'

'How did I know where this conversation was headed?' Gus groaned.

Lachlan and Gus had been friends for years. In the same year at Edinburgh University, they'd been part of the same crowd, hanging around the bars and restaurants where everyone seemed to know everyone. Lachlan had left university with a degree in Geology and not much more than a conviction that he had no desire whatsoever to do anything in his life with anything to do with geology, which was a bit unfortunate. What he loved, though, was cooking. He took a job working in his friend's bar, and somehow managed to end up running the place before he knew it. He had a nose for good food and good beer, and a knack of choosing interesting craft beers from small independent breweries. It was no surprise to everyone, therefore, that he and Gus – who was a scientist and worked for one of the research labs that was tied to the university – decided that they'd start a little side hustle and set up a little micro-brewery. Their first few beers were a surprising success – the odd explosion notwithstanding – and before long, both of them had taken the plunge, given up their jobs, and thrown their savings into setting up their own little brewery. Five years later, it was flourishing.

Hedgepig Beers were well reviewed, and Lachlan's ability to carefully balance the ingredients needed to make a consistent, reliably good beer meant that they had a reputation which was spreading rapidly. Gus – effervescent and outgoing – was a whizz with the social media and marketing, and their name was growing every day. The last thing they needed was for one half of the partnership to exit stage left and disappear up to the Highlands, where transport links were terrible and the mobile phone reception even worse.

'What you're saying,' Gus sighed 'is I need to find a temporary replacement for you.'

'The irreplaceable.' Lachlan grinned.

'Watch it, ego,' Gus parried back. 'Nobody's irreplaceable.'

'Exactly what I hoped you'd say.' Lachlan looked at him triumphantly. 'Backed you into that one, didn't I?'

'Right, fine.' Gus shook his head. He picked up one of their cans and looked at it thoughtfully, reading the ingredients. 'How hard can it be?'

'It's not,' Lachlan said. 'You've watched me doing it a million times. You're a bloody chemist, for god's sake. You should be able to do it standing on your head.'

'I might try doing it the right way up to start with,' Gus

replied drily. 'Maybe we can get Lucinda to do the marketing stuff? She's utterly fed up in that temp job.'

'Maybe,' said Lachlan, trying to sound non-committal. Gus's girlfriend was charming, extremely expensive and very focused on getting what she wanted. Of late, her primary goal had been to oust Lachlan so she could move in – well, Lachlan reflected, she'd be happy to hear that he was heading up north – but she was always trying to come up with ideas for them to make more money, expand the business and make it bigger. Lachlan and Gus had spent a lot of time calmly pointing out that the nature of the beer that they made meant that scaling up wasn't necessarily a good thing. He sighed thinking about what would happen to Hedgepig with Lucinda's feet well and truly under the business table and then put the thought out of his head. He had to focus on what was going on at Applemore and then he could work out the rest. Right now, there was the small matter of £200,000 to find…

'I'll speak to her.' Gus brightened at the thought. 'She's going to be well chuffed, you know that.'

'She will.' Lachlan suppressed his misgivings and decided to focus on the positives. 'Thanks, Gus, I really appreciate it.'

'No probs,' Gus said, getting up and dropping a hand on his shoulder. 'You get home and deal with the whole death, debt and dereliction side of things. I'll keep everything going until you get back, and then it'll be like you never left.'

Lachlan privately suspected that was extremely unlikely, but he didn't say anything. He had bags to pack, and a mountain of brewery-related stuff to sort out before he could head back to the Highlands. He looked up at Gus and gave him a nod of thanks.

'You'd do the same for me,' his friend said. At least they were completely on the same page when it came to that.

A couple of days later, Lachlan was loading the last of his bags into the back of his battered old Golf. Gus was standing on the step of the flat, arm round Lucinda's waist, looking thoughtful.

'Don't be gone too long,' he said, giving Lachlan a high-five. 'I'm going to miss my drinking buddy.'

Lucinda patted Gus on the stomach. 'You might get your rugby-playing six-pack back if you don't have Lachlan to go out drinking with,' she said crisply. 'Don't rush back too quickly.'

Lachlan, who knew that she wasn't completely joking, gave a slightly thin smile. 'I'll be back before you know it. You guys can always come up and visit? It's ages since you've been.'

'I'd love that,' said Lucinda, who was very taken with the whole country-house thing. Lachlan privately thought she would be less taken with the peeling paint, extremely temperamental hot-water boiler, and damp-infested cellar but there was a schadenfreude side to him that rather liked the idea of seeing her face when she got there.

'I mean it,' he said, doubling down. 'Give me a chance to get organised, then come up for the weekend.'

'Ooh,' cooed Lucinda, turning to Gus, 'I'll need to get some new clothes. Perfect opportunity! Apparently they change three times a day at Balmoral – I was reading about it in *Hello* magazine when I was at the hair salon the other day.'

Gus looked directly at Lachlan and lifted an eyebrow. 'You still changing three times a day at Applemore?'

'We've cut it down to twice,' Lachlan deadpanned. 'The washing machine wasn't keeping up and dry-cleaning your dinner suit is a complete pain in the backside in the middle of nowhere.'

'There you are, baby,' Gus said, laughing. 'You won't need that ball gown after all.'

'Pity,' replied Lucinda, looking put out.

'I'm sure you'll find an opportunity to wear it,' said Lachlan, laughing. He tossed his keys in the air and caught them. 'Right, that's everything.'

'Give me a bell when you get there so I know you've not emigrated to Peru or something to avoid facing the triple threat of the sisters and their wrath.'

'That's a genuine possibility.' Lachlan winced at the thought. 'They're going to be extremely unimpressed, I suspect, with whatever I come up with. It's not surprising, really, given it's their home.'

'Did you speak to Felix?' They'd been so busy getting last-minute plans organised with the brewery that now, just as Lachlan was preparing to leave, they had lots of things left unsaid.

'I did, yeah.'

Lachlan had rung Felix, who'd been so keen to talk that he'd jumped in his extremely expensive and whizzy convertible sports car and driven down from Perth to Edinburgh the next day. Over a delicious lunch (paid for by Felix, who wouldn't hear of going Dutch), Lachlan had explained the financial predicament that he was in, and Felix had assured him that a place like Applemore would be completely lapped up by rich Americans, who were buying up vast tracts of the Scottish Highlands and doing up the castles –

or country houses – at a rate of knots. Lachlan had swallowed back a faint sense of nausea at the thought of his family home being redecorated with fifteen shades of expensive tartan wallpaper and tried to think about the good side to all of this

'I'm going to have a chat with him once I've had a decent chance to look over the place and see what needs to be done.'

'Sounds like a plan.'

Lachlan headed for the car and climbed in. Lucinda hovered on the step of the new town flat, clearly desperate to get back inside – it was cold for late September, and the wind whistled up from the Firth of Forth and chilled their bones.

'You two get inside. I'll give you a shout later in the week, let you know how it's going.'

'Drive safely,' said Lucinda, giving a tiny wave.

Gus rapped his hand on the roof of the car in farewell and they headed back inside.

Lachlan – suspecting with a pang of regret that things were never going to be quite the same – turned the key in the ignition and left the city behind.

CHAPTER 2

The hallway smelled of wood fires and old newspapers. Rilla flicked on a light switch and realised as she did that the place hadn't been touched since her dad had gone.

Picking up a pile of letters from behind the door, she made her way into the kitchen. Sitting on the big scrubbed wood table was the clay fruit bowl they'd bought on a trip to Greece when they were children. She ran a finger along the edge of it, then pulled out a chair and sat down. She'd been travelling for hours, and the jet lag was making her feel distinctly fuzzy around the edges. Her eyes drooped shut. Maybe if she just rested them for a moment, she'd be able to deal with everything…

'Helloooo?'

Rilla jumped awake, putting both hands on the table and pushing herself up with a start.

'Is there anyone in there?' The voice was sharp, but with the familiar lilting Highland accent Rilla had missed for so long.

'Um – I – yes, hello.' She made her way out into the

15

RACHAEL LUCAS

hall, where a short woman with close-cropped grey hair and a pair of outsized tortoiseshell framed glasses was standing, looking pensive.

'Well, look who it is. Little Rilla Clark.'

Rilla frowned and peered at the woman, before apologising with a brief laugh. 'Sorry, I don't mean to be rude...' How on earth did you say *it's very nice that you know me, but I can't place you at all* without sounding awful?

'Joan Grant.' The woman smiled then, and her face lit up. At that moment, Rilla recognised her.

'Joan!'

'The very same. You've no' changed a bit, but I'm unrecognisable at the moment. You had a bit of trouble placing me, didn't you?'

'Only for a moment,' fibbed Rilla, 'and only because I've just woken up at the kitchen table and I've no idea what time it is here, but in my head it's bedtime.'

'That's exactly why I'm here.' Joan looked at the bags piled up in the untidy hallway. 'When I heard from Ray that you'd arrived by taxi, I thought "well, that lassie's going to be completely worn out after a journey like that", so I came straight over to see if we could get you a spot of supper and a comfy bed.'

'Oh – there's a bed here.' That sounded ruder than she meant it to. 'I mean, I just sort of assumed I'd sort it out and get to work on the cottage in the morning.'

'Your dad's place has been lying empty for months. If I'd had my way and I'd known you were coming back, I'd have been in and given it a good going-over, but...' She paused for a moment. 'Well, I didn't want to be getting under people's feet and there's been a lot of stuff going on around the estate of late, and... Well, I'll tell all once you've had a rest. You must be exhausted.'

Rilla nodded weakly. 'A bit.' The snooze on the table hadn't helped. If anything, she felt worse – it was ridiculous that someone who travelled around the world as much as she did was always so utterly wiped out by jet lag, but travelling west to east was an absolute killer. She felt seasick and nauseous and slightly like a helium balloon that might just float off into the sky if she wasn't pinned down by something.

'Right. Have you a wee bag with enough things for tonight?'

Rilla nodded.

'Okay then, we'll deal with the rest of this in the morning. Now, let's get going.'

Rilla climbed into Joan's car, feeling like she was about twelve years old. She fastened her seatbelt and put the keys to the cottage in her bag, then sat back with her head against the headrest. Her eyes were so heavy, it took everything she had not to doze off as Joan drove.'Where do we start?' Joan tapped her pink varnished nails on the steering wheel as she waited at a junction for a tractor and trailer to rumble by. 'Your dad would be awfully pleased you were back here, you know that, don't you?'

Rilla nodded.

'It's a terrible shame he didn't get to spend his retirement up here as he planned. He was a good man.' Joan shook her head. 'And cancer is a terrible thing. Terrible.'

'Terrible,' agreed Rilla.

'I've had a wee brush with it myself,' explained Joan, putting a hand to her hair. 'Hence the new do.'

Ohhh, Rilla realised, that's why I didn't recognise her. The last time she'd seen Joan, who was the village stalwart and a great friend of her dad's, she'd had long auburn hair. This new close crop made her look completely different.

17

'New hair – I quite like the grey, surprisingly – and I've got these specs now, which I'm no' a fan of, and there's a fair bit more of me than there was the last time I saw you.' She patted herself on the stomach.

'You look great,' said Rilla, rallying. 'I love the glasses on you. They really suit your face shape.'

'Do you think?' Joan looked slightly mollified.

'Definitely.'

'Well, that's awfully nice of you,' Joan beamed.

Ten minutes later, they rumbled up the stone drive to Joan's cottage, which sat on a hill overlooking Applemore Bay. The September evening was chilly and smoke curled from the chimney, making Rilla shiver with tiredness and cold as she remembered how exhausted she was.

'Come on in,' Joan said, lifting her bag out of the boot, 'and I'll make you a spot of supper before you head off to bed.'

'This is really very kind of you,' Rilla began, as she was bustled in through the door of the cottage and into a spotless sitting room where plump cushions sat on their points on neat, new-looking sofas.

'Not at all. I was a great friend of your father, and he'd do the same for one of mine if he was still here.'

'Well, he'd make some tea,' Rilla said, smiling ruefully, 'but I doubt he'd stretch any further than that.'

'Aye, well, catering was never his strong point.'

'When I think back to summers spent up here, I remember a lot of Pot Noodles and the occasional Fray Bentos steak and kidney pie.'

Joan chuckled. 'Well, I've got a nice Scotch broth and some fresh bread, and I made some fruit cake earlier. That'll give you something to sleep on, and then in the morning we'll have a think about what you're going to need to do to get that cottage habitable.'

'Oh I'm not staying long,' Rilla began, but Joan had disappeared into the kitchen and could be heard happily clattering cutlery and plates, singing to herself. Rilla was too tired to pursue the point, so she just sat down and waited. If she'd thought about it, she probably ought to have offered to give Joan a hand, but…

'Oh, look at you, sleepyhead.'

Rilla's eyes snapped open again. 'Oh god, sorry.' She looked up at the clock on the mantlepiece. It was quarter past five. She didn't have the brainpower to count back and work out what time it was in Maine, nor to work out just how many hours she'd been travelling from her sister's house in Marblehead to Boston to Edinburgh, then all the way up to the Highlands by train and then taxi. All she knew was that she absolutely must not, not, not fall asleep in the bowl of soup that Joan was brandishing, her expression kindly and hopeful.

'How's your little sister doing?' Joan asked.

'Sally?'

Joan nodded.

'Oh she's good, married and living in New England with her husband. He's an investment banker or something along those lines. Wears a suit, makes a lot of money.'

'Your dad said she'd married well. Said she was like her mother in that regard, where you definitely took after him.'

'Scruffy and slightly chaotic?' Rilla smiled, picking up a piece of the home-made bread Joan had put on the side plate.

'Ach, he always had a soft spot for you and you know it. He was so proud of all your travels. It was just a shame you didn't get to spend so much time together in the last few years.'

'I know.' Rilla felt a shot of guilt and shame. She'd kept in touch by email and FaceTime calls, telling him about her adventures. 'You just always think there's going to be more time for stuff, don't you?'

'Absolutely.' Joan put a hand on her arm. 'But don't you go feeling bad. He loved hearing about your adventures, and who was to know that he'd be taken from us so soon?'

Rilla felt her lower lip trembling. God, now she was in danger not just of falling asleep in the soup but of blubbing into it as well. She curled her fingers into fists and jabbed her palms with her fingernails, her patented method of stopping herself from crying. It worked.

Half an hour later, Rilla was tucked up in Joan's spare room, her clothes folded neatly on the chair at the end of the bed, and a cup of tea ('just in case you decide you want it') sitting on the bedside table. For a moment, she felt like getting into bed had cured her of her jet lag and that she could get up, head back to the cottage and get to work on clearing everything out, but a second later and she was gone.

The next morning, Rilla woke at eleven. For a moment she couldn't think where on earth she was – the last bed she'd slept in had been in Sally's pristine, neutral-toned spare room. This one had pink walls, and she was covered with a duvet which was decorated with huge, splashy hibiscus flowers. On the walls there were prints of Highland scenery, and on the top of the bedside table there lay a slightly frightening-looking cerise pink embroi-dered doily thing, which looked like it had been rescued from 1964.

Rilla sat up, noticing the cold cup of tea, and rubbed

her eyes. How on earth had she slept for – she counted on her fingers – fifteen hours? And in a strange house, too.

She climbed out of bed and pulled on her clothes, wondering where the bathroom was. She'd gone last night but been so out of it that she couldn't quite remember which of the doors it was, and she didn't want to accidentally walk into Joan's bedroom or something like that.

'Aha,' said Joan, as if she'd been summoned by Rilla thinking of her. 'There you are. I bet you feel better for that sleep?'

Rilla nodded. 'Yes thank you. Much.'

Joan pointed towards a door. 'There's fresh towels in the bathroom and there's a toothbrush if you need one in the packet on the windowsill. Anything else you need – shampoo and all that stuff – is just in the shower. Help yourself. I'll get some breakfast on for you.'

Rilla, who'd been thinking she'd just slope off back to the cottage, put a hand to her stomach in surprise as if to contain the huge rumbling squeak of hunger it made. 'That would be lovely. Thanks.'

She washed all the airplane and travel smells off, replacing them with Joan's shampoo and Marks and Spencer body wash, and emerged downstairs feeling more like she had in what felt like days.

It was funny, Rilla reflected, as she sat at the table waiting for Joan to bring through breakfast, that she seemed able to accept the offer of help from someone who was a relative stranger. There was something about Joan's uncomplicated kindness which made it easier than the vague sense of not-quite-good-enough guilt she always felt when staying with Sally, where she felt like she had to offer to babysit the children every five seconds to make it all right for her to stay there… something Sally would say of course was completely in her own head, but it probably came from their mum, and her strange, slightly detached parenting style. Where her dad had been loving but chaotic, her mother was brittle, constantly worried what other people thought and critical. It made family visits so exhausting that Rilla tried to avoid them as much as possible. No wonder she'd spent so much of the last ten years travelling the world to avoid it all.

'You'll be looking forward to seeing the Fraser lot when you get to the cottage, I'm guessing?' Joan surveyed her over the top of her mug of tea.

'Are they still around?' She'd been wondering on the journey – would they be there? Would they even remember her? It had been so long.

'Oh yes, they're all floating about, one way or another. Of course, you'll not know that Hector Fraser passed away not long after your dad?'

Rilla shook her head.

'Losing the two of them so close together – it was a real blow. And now young Lachlan's in charge, not that you'd know it. He's still spending most of his time down in Edinburgh. Lucky the girls are around to keep the place going. An estate like Applemore doesn't run itself.'

Rilla chewed her toast thoughtfully. When they'd been growing up, spending summers in Applemore, she and Sally had often played in the woods and down by the bay with the Fraser children, who were all around the same age. Lachlan, a couple of years older, had tended to keep himself to himself more, but Beth, Charlotte and Polly had been happy to charge around covered in mud from head to toe and get into all sorts of scrapes. Spending time in the middle of nowhere seemed to give them a chance to carry on being children far longer than they would have in the city, and the adventures they'd had had always reminded Rilla of *Swallows and Amazons*. They'd camped out, built boats, accidentally set fire to the hay shed – she made a face remembering that, and how lucky they'd been that the girls' dad, Hector, had come along at exactly the right moment to put it out, bellowing at them with a temper that accompanied the red hair he'd passed on to two of his three offspring. In fact, thinking about it, that had been the last summer. After that, relations between her divorced parents had become acrimonious. Rilla's mother had made it impossible for her and Sally to make it back to Scotland for the holidays - the year after that she reorganised things at the last minute so they ended up spending time with their dad in Edinburgh and not up in Applemore. There had been a lot of that sort of thing, really.

'Can I get you anything else?'

Rilla jumped. 'Sorry, I was in a dream.'

'Not surprised, darling, you must be exhausted still. Let me know when you're ready and I'll give you a run back up to the cottage in the car. But there's no rush.'

'That would be amazing, thank you – and thanks so much for this, Joan. I really appreciate it.'

'Least I could do.'

'Let me help you with the dishes, at least.'

'I won't hear of it. I've got a dishwasher for that sort of thing.' Joan laughed and whipped the plate and cup away from under Rilla's nose before she could make a move.

'Of course, the jungle drums will have activated, so you'll have no end of visitors popping by, I expect,' Joan observed, sagely, as they made their way along the winding road towards Applemore. They passed a field of cows, huddled together under a tree that was just starting to show the faintest hint of colour in its leaves. 'You've missed a bonny summer. Still, we get lovely winters up here too.'

'I…' Rilla opened her mouth, then shut it again. For whatever reason, Joan had got it into her head that she was planning to spend the winter up here in the cottage, and she didn't have the energy to explain that wasn't the case. It was easier to just nod and smile. 'I suspect this'll seem a lot easier to tackle now I've had some sleep.' Rilla looked at the cottage as Joan pulled the car to a halt.

'Are you sure you don't want a hand today?'

Rilla shook her head. 'It's really kind of you, but I just want to potter about a bit. I don't think I'm going to start blitzing the place straight away.'

Joan nodded. 'Aye. And you'll want to have a bit of time with your dad's stuff, too, no doubt. It's all still there, I think. It's such a shame that he finally got his dream of moving up here full-time and then it was taken away. You never know the minute, do you?'

Rilla frowned, not recognising the turn of phrase.

'I mean, you don't know when… Well, we never know what's in store for us, do we?'

'Dad would have said "when your time's up, your time's up",' said Rilla, laughing.

'He would that. He didn't hold much truck with senti-mentality, really.'

'He did not.' Rilla gave Joan a kiss goodbye. 'Thanks again. It's so, so kind of you.'

'I'll pop by in a couple of days if you like, see how you're getting on. Here's my landline number.' She scribbled it down on a piece of paper and handed it over. 'I suspect the phone's still on – but if it's not, the mobile reception is pretty terrible around Applemore. The best way of getting a signal is to climb a bit of a way up Achiltie hill there.' She pointed to a hill that sloped up beyond the road that curved away from the road. 'You can always pop up and check your messages.'

Rilla, who was used to being in far-flung places with no internet access, was far less worried than most people would be. She waved goodbye to Joan and headed inside the cottage. The sooner she got things cleared up, the sooner she could get out of Applemore and find herself in another part of the world...

Lying in bed the next day under a slightly musty-smelling duvet with a cup of black tea – Rilla really needed to get to a shop, and soon – she thought maybe the answer was to make a plan. Rilla didn't have a clue where to start. Maybe a list. Several lists, in fact. The cottage was a jumble of everything she remembered when she thought of spending time with her dad, but a million times more chaotic. It seemed like the sensible thing to do would be to hire a skip and that way she could just dump it all in there, but did they even do skip hire all the way up here? Maybe she could just sort through the stuff and work out what could go to a charity shop and what could be – she made a face at the thought – recycled? Put on a bonfire? There was a lot of random stuff, but the idea of setting it alight seemed a bit drastic. She heard her dad's voice in her head, telling her that it was only stuff – ironic that he had such a laid-back approach to belongings when he had a house stuffed to the brim with random things that might come in handy. Anyway, whatever the answer was, it wasn't going to be found by drinking disgusting black tea in bed. She decided to pull herself together, get up, get out and head for the village of Applemore.

Rilla threw on some clothes and tied her hair back in a sketchy sort of topknot. Looking through the dust on the mirror in the hall, she realised that the travelling and jet lag had left her with bruised shadows under her eyes and a slightly vampire-like pallor. Her freckles stood out like tiny pinpricks in a face which seemed to have lost any of the late summer tan that she'd caught back in Sally's garden. Hopefully a bit of exercise and fresh air might help. It was sunny, at least, which took the chill off the air – but it was definitely quite a lot colder than it had been in New England. Autumn was making her presence felt. Rilla decided to pull on her dad's old woollen Guernsey sweater – it was miles too big for her, but rolling up the sleeves, she decided there was something quite nice about wearing it – like having him with her for moral support.

Her dad's old bike was leaning against the wall of the dining room, trapped behind two huge cardboard boxes full of ancient copies of *The New Scientist* which dated back to the dark ages. She was already aware that every time she walked into a room she was making a mental list of what was going to go where, once she worked out what to do about it all. There was just so *much* of it. She shoved them out of the way and breathed a sigh of relief. In doing so, she'd revealed the tell-tale little black box of a Wi-Fi router... thank goodness for that. She pulled out her phone, which she hadn't even thought to try connecting, and linked herself up. A moment later, a stream of message notifications came through – they could all wait, she decided, except for Sally. Checking her watch, Rilla realised that Sally would probably be asleep but that she'd still want to know she'd made it there in one piece.

Am here, she typed, *it's pretty much as chaotic as you'd expect. Kisses to the children (and you)*

Rilla looked around the room. Her dad had been a professor of genetics at the University of Edinburgh by day and an inveterate fiddler and inventor of things by night. When she was little, she'd thought he was the closest thing a person could ever get to being Wallace, the inventor of The Wrong Trousers. Disappointingly, he'd never quite managed to create anything quite as exciting, but he was constantly fiddling about with circuit boards and bits of wood and plastic, never happy doing nothing. She half-expected the bike to have some sort of weird mechanical contraption attached or for flames to shoot out of the wheels. As she lifted it over the boxes and wheeled it down the hall, it was a relief to discover that it seemed to be a perfectly ordinary – if slightly too big for her – battered old pushbike.

Cycling down the lane towards Applemore, Rilla was surprised how much the landscape had been etched in her memory. Behind her, the huge shoulders of the hills seemed to act as a backdrop. Ahead, the early-morning sky was still streaked slightly pink from the sunrise and the distant Isle of Skye was etched against the blue. White-painted cottages were dotted here and there, and the long stone farmhouse stood surrounded by pine trees, two chestnut horses grazing in the field nearby. And there was the hand-painted sign for the dairy farm, and the field dotted with black and white cows, surrounded by thick hedgerows which were groaning with berries.

The silence was almost overwhelming. Rilla stopped the bike at the crest of the hill and listened for a moment, realising that in fact it was anything but silent. The birds were deafening – gulls circling overhead, and the hedges bustling with activity. One of the cows mooed mournfully, and in a field somewhere out of sight, she heard sheep bleating. The one thing there wasn't was any traffic. The place was completely devoid of any sign of human life. It was slightly spooky – even when she travelled to far-off places, there were usually people around, working in the fields or walking to and fro. But here there was not a soul to be seen.

Rilla pushed off on the bike, coasting down the hill towards the village. The sea came into view, and then the wide sweep of white sand that was Applemore Bay, and her heart soared. It was lovely to be back, even for a short while. No wonder her dad had wanted to spend his retirement here.

Applemore village was just as pretty as she remembered. The road followed the coast, hugging it tightly until it curved away as she passed a row of white-painted fisherman's cottages. They had colourful doors, and outside each of them neat hanging baskets swung gently in the sea breeze. Pots of still-bright red geraniums gave the front steps a jaunty appearance.

Rilla hopped off the bike and walked along, pushing it by the handlebars, taking it all in. Where the old post office had been, there was now a cute little bookshop – the window jammed with piles of books and colourful posters. There was a sign on the door announcing that it was closed from Monday to Wednesday, but that books were still available to order online. Rilla made a mental note to come back and treat herself to something nice to read later in the week.

There was a new – or new to Rilla, at least – nursery school on the corner of the main street. Cheerful pastel-coloured bunting hung in the windows and over the front door. Over the fence, she could see lots of tiny children dashing about playing some sort of game, chased by a pretty woman with a blonde ponytail. The sign outside announced that they had been rated Excellent by Ofsted, and that the principal was Poppy Harris. It lifted Rilla's heart to see such life and vitality in the middle of the village, especially when she was feeling as jet lagged and jaded as she was.

Two doors along stood the vet surgery – an expensive-looking Range Rover parked outside. A woman with red hair and a serious expression was sitting at the reception desk. She looked up, seeing Rilla peering inside, and her face was transformed as she smiled a welcome. Rilla felt a bit awkward for having been so nosey and gave a slightly shy wave of greeting.

It was funny how familiar it all felt after such a long time – she could remember walking along this street with Sally and the Fraser sisters, pocket money clutched in their hands, planning what they were going to buy from the little village stores.

And there it was. The wooden door was a faded green and the swinging signs announcing they sold ice creams and newspapers hadn't changed in all those years.

Rilla put a hand on the door and paused for a moment before she went inside.

CHAPTER 3

'It's a truth universally acknowledged that a young man in possession of good fortune must be in want of a—'

'Cup of coffee,' said Lachlan Fraser, fixing his younger sister Polly with a shut-up look.

'Just saying.' She made a face.

'Well, don't.' Lachlan's tone was mock stern, but his youngest sister knew perfectly well that he didn't mean it.

He watched as she hitched herself up onto the kitchen counter beside the huge, temperamental old Aga which had definitely seen better days. Much like everything in Applemore House, thought Lachlan, looking down at a sheaf of invoices that had arrived in the post that morning. It would be easier to set fire to the place than deal with all of this. In fact, that was tempting.

He'd arrived back at the house two days before in a rain storm which seemed to echo his feelings about being there. Water had dripped down his neck as he'd hefted his bags out of the boot of the car, and he'd tried to have a shower to warm up, only to discover that the ancient boiler was on the blink again. He'd ended up poking around with a spanner and his father's depleted toolbox, trying to figure out what was going on. By the time he'd sorted it, Polly had knocked up dinner on the Aga and he'd skipped the shower in favour of a night of catching up with his youngest sister. They'd drunk a bottle of red wine and when he'd gone to bed, he was so tired that he didn't even notice the wind whistling through the crack in the ill-fitting window. That was a plus, he thought, smiling wryly to himself. Got to focus on the positives.

'I'm simply pointing out,' Polly said, waving an arm airily in the direction of the paperwork that was strewn across the big table that dominated the kitchen, 'that all this could be solved if you just teamed up with Arabella.'

'Teamed up?' Polly's idea of focusing on the positives was positively terrifying.

Lachlan sat back in his chair, folded his arms behind his head and put his feet up on the table. For a moment, he cast his eye around the shabby, dusty kitchen. Once upon a time, it must've been grand, but not in his memory. They'd grown up accustomed to the shabby, cosy state of the place. Now, it was desperately in need of… well, a coat of paint would be a start, but it would be a bit like that old saying about putting lipstick on a pig. Unfair to pigs, really, Lachlan thought, they were quite cute. This place just felt like the biggest, most unwieldy millstone around his extremely unwilling neck.

'I reckon arranged marriages were all the thing amongst the gentry in the old days.' Polly shrugged. 'Just saying.'

'If you don't stop saying *just saying*, I'm going to commit some sort of terrible crime.' He stretched both hands in her direction, making a strangling motion. 'Just saying.'

Polly giggled. 'Arabella Roxburgh is perfectly nice – if a

bit horsey – and extremely single. She's also blooming *loaded* and she's going to inherit the whole Lochbrannoch estate when her parents pop their clogs. That can't be long away. Just -' she stopped, grinning.

'Okay. Let's start with the facts.' Lachlan groaned, shaking his head. 'You do realise that most parents don't actually die until they're ancient, right? Just because ours shuffled off this mortal coil in their early sixties doesn't mean the Roxburghs are going to oblige by doing the same. So that's one thing to begin with. Then there's the minor detail that I don't find her *remotely* attractive, which is another—'

'You could *grow* to love her,' Polly said, helpfully.

'Dad used to say that about red cabbage, and you know what? I never did. You're all right. I'm quite happy as I am, thank you. Arabella's a perfectly nice girl, but I have no desire whatsoever to combine our households.'

A vision of their dad, who was a hopeless, but determined, cook popped into his head. After their mum had left, he'd had to learn to juggle running Applemore with keeping four children fed, clothed and safe. Thank goodness for Joan, their housekeeper, who'd arrived every morning and kept the place running with a grim determination, despite low funds and a general air of chaos.

'I'm sure the entire female population of Edinburgh will be happy to hear you're planning on staying single.'

Lachlan groaned. His little sister was utterly convinced that – as the heir to Applemore, and living in Gus's trendy flat in Edinburgh – he had a far wilder love life than he did. The truth was that despite various short flings, he'd stayed quite resolutely single. He had his reasons, not that he was going to shatter her illusions by sharing them. 'You are impossible, and you are also very wrong. I'm not seeing *anyone*, as it happens. Not that it's any of your business.'

'Perfect timing for you and Arabella,' Polly teased in a sing-song voice. She was impossible.

'I am not having an arranged marriage to save this place, no matter how much you might want it to happen,' Lachlan said, shaking his head in despair. In a way, he wished he had Polly's sunny optimism – or was it blind faith? Whatever it was, the truth was that she somehow expected him to sort out the million and one problems that were befalling Applemore House, and – he let out a slow exhalation of breath – somehow, he knew he'd have to find a solution.

As if she could read his mind, Polly stuck her tongue out at him, making him laugh despite himself. At twenty-five, she was the youngest of the four Fraser siblings, and she'd always been the baby of the family. He watched her as she scrolled through her phone now, the tip of her tongue poking out as it always did when she was concentrating. She'd spent the last few years working as a nanny for a family in London, but when their dad died, she'd headed north back to Applemore and seemed to be showing no signs of going anywhere. Lachlan suppressed a sigh. It would be much easier if everyone wasn't so attached to the bloody place.

'Where's Beth?'

'Said she'd be along in a bit. She's just taking the babies for a walk to get them to sleep in the pram.'

That just left Charlotte. If he could get them all in the same place at the same time – you'd think, given everyone was currently living in or around the Applemore Estate, that that would be a simple task – he could sit them down and talk about his plan. He picked up the phone and checked WhatsApp.

He tapped a quick message. *Are you en route?*

Will be in two. Just got to check one of the cottages – apparently there's a leak in the bathroom.

Charlotte was – thank goodness – the one he could always rely on. Closest to him in age, at thirty-three she was resolutely single and completely focused on the holiday cottage business she'd built up over the last few years, converting various old farm-workers' cottages from the estate into chic, appealing escapes which were booked out pretty much solidly all year round. It was the most financially viable – no, the *only* financially viable – element of the estate, and it was run in Charlotte's typically efficient, no-nonsense manner.

When their mother had left, she'd taken over as the woman of the house, and she'd grown up fast. Capable and efficient, she took a cool, sensible view of life. Her latest plan was to build a series of log-cabin-style houses along a stretch of wooded land that hugged the beautiful coast, with a narrow strip of private beach and sunset views to die for. Lachlan narrowed his eyes, thinking. They'd be a massive selling point if… well… He quailed inwardly at the thought of trying to explain his plans.

And then there was Beth's flower farm. She'd spent the last few years building it up, taking the overgrown walled garden behind Applemore House and digging it all out, renovating the cracked glass of the old greenhouses. Now in summer, it was a riot of colour, and her beautifully crafted hand-tied arrangements were a hit at weddings and events. Maybe there was a way she could keep the place going if…

Talking of Beth – Lachlan craned his neck, hearing the crunch of gravel. There she was, marching along pushing a dusty, three-wheeled double buggy. Her dirty blonde hair was tied up in an untidy bun, with long tendrils falling across her face. As he watched, she pushed one back with the back of her forearm. It fell across her eyes again almost instantly. It was funny – she'd had that same habit since she was tiny. Even back then, she'd always been happiest grubbing about in the garden. She paused for a second, bending down to pull up a couple of handfuls of weeds that were poking up through the stones of the sweeping driveway. It made him smile despite his worries – the place needed a massive overhaul, and there she was taking the time to pull out wild thistles.

'Shh,' said Beth a few minutes later as she walked in, motioning towards the door. 'I've parked them in the boot room. Hopefully they'll keep quiet for a bit, at least.'

Mabel and Martha, the springer spaniels, looked up from their bed by the foot of the Aga, beating their tails in welcome.

Beth picked up the kettle which was sitting empty on the range and waggled it hopefully. 'Why does nobody ever bloody refill this?' she said, shaking her head and moving over to the kitchen sink. 'You know, if you just topped it up, it would mean the next person making a cuppa wouldn't have to wait ages for the water to heat up.'

'Because we're not obsessed with drinking our body weight in tea every day?' Polly made a face. 'We could always get a proper electric kettle,' she added, helpfully.

'No thanks.' Beth shook her head. 'Anyway. Coffee. I need the caffeine hit. I've been up half the night with teething twins. Lachlan? Want one?'

'Please.' He looked down at the papers on the table. Now that the time had come for the family meeting he'd tried to organise, he was starting to feel uncomfortable. The weight of this sort of responsibility was exactly why he didn't like the mantle of head of the family that he'd inherited, along with the house.

'Have I missed anything exciting?' Beth opened the cupboards and found three mismatched mugs, then fetching the milk from the fridge.

'Nothing much.' Polly swung her legs, still sitting on the counter like a child who'd been parked out of the way. 'Ooh – actually, yes. You'll never guess who's back and staying at the cottage?'

'Which cottage?' Beth raised both hands in query. 'Do I get a clue?'

'I thought you'd have heard already. You know what the jungle drums are like round here.'

Lachlan sat back, amused despite himself at his little sister's nose for village gossip. 'Go on.' He rubbed at the spikes of beard on his chin – really, he ought to get around to a shave and a haircut at some point, but that could wait until he was back home in Edinburgh. Hopefully it wouldn't be too long now.

'Rilla, David Clark's daughter.'

Beth frowned for a second, thinking. The kettle started to whistle on the Aga and she took it off, pouring water into each mug and stirring thoughtfully. 'Oh my god, after all this time?'

'Apparently she's here to sort out his things. Rilla's the older one, isn't she? Sally was the younger one who nearly drowned.'

Beth raised both eyebrows skyward. 'I'd forgotten that. My God, we haven't seen them for…' She counted on her fingers, 'It must be like – fifteen years? Longer?'

Lachlan didn't say anything. He picked up his pen and

tapped it against the table, letting the conversation carry on without him.

'I think I must've been really small.' Polly slid off the counter and headed for the fridge, staring into it for a long moment before breaking off a piece of Parmesan and shoving it into her mouth. 'I don't remember that much about them – she was nice, I think, the brown-haired one. Was that Rilla?'

Without thinking, Lachlan glanced up for a moment at his sister. 'Yes.'

Polly eyed him for a brief moment, but he dropped his gaze, picking up the papers and shuffling them.

'Stop eating that cheese. It's supposed to be for the carbonara I'm making later.'

'Sorry,' said Polly, not sounding it in the slightest. Honestly, it was like living with a teenager.

Lachlan checked his phone again.

Charlotte had sent a message. *Ten mins*

He got up and let the dogs out for something to do. Claws clattering on the parquet floor of the hall, they hurtled through the huge wooden door and out onto the drive. He watched as they zigzagged around the sweep of gravel and weeds, disappearing into the rhododendron bushes, tails wagging furiously. He liked that his dad had been so resolute that they shouldn't be docked, even if Jim, the estate's ancient retired gamekeeper, was appalled.

A moment later, with a blare of loud music and a splattering of gravel as she hurtled up the drive, Charlotte arrived.

'Sorry, sorry. What's all this about anyway?'

'Just fancied a cup of coffee with my sisters,' Lachlan lied, knowing perfectly well that she'd give him a look that said she didn't believe him for a second. 'Do I have to have an excuse?'

'Hrmm,' Charlotte gave him a dark look and pocketed her phone. 'You coming?'

'Two secs. I'll just get these two in.' He motioned to the bushes, from where could be heard crashing and the occasional bark.

'Mabel's got a scent,' Charlotte commented.

'First time for everything. They're clueless, these two.'

'They're house dogs, not workers,' Charlotte said over her shoulder, as she headed inside.

'Just as bloody well.' He whistled, and the dogs emerged. Martha had a long strand of faded goosegrass tangled in her curly, floppy fringe. He reached down and pulled it out. 'Come on then,' he said, heading back into Applemore House. 'Let's get this over with.'

Inside, they were discussing the reappearance of Rilla at the lodge house.

'God, that makes me feel ancient. Remember we used to spend all summer playing weird *Swallows and Amazons* games?' Charlotte had taken off her fleece waistcoat and was rolling up the sleeves of her shirt. 'God, it's hot in here today.'

'I'd forgotten that time we nearly drowned her sister Sally in the loch when we nicked that boat…that must be fifteen years ago?' Beth snorted with laughter. 'I remember getting bollocked by Dad for it. We were grounded for about two weeks in the middle of the nicest summer we'd had in years.'

'Fifteen years. Bloody hell.'

'It's eighteen years.' Lachlan, who'd been silent until now, rubbed his nose and tried to look casual.

'How'd you know?' All eyes turned on him.

'I remember.' He didn't add that he'd waited the following summer, determined that it would be the year he was brave enough to say more than two words to Rilla, who he'd always liked, with her wild curly hair and freckles and infectious giggle. But, of course, they'd never returned.

Charlotte and Beth exchanged a look, which he ignored. He gathered up the pile of papers and shoved them to one side, stretching his arms out and drumming his fingers on the table for a moment.

'Right.'

'Right.' Beth arched an eyebrow. 'We've been gathered here today for…?'

'I've been looking at the figures – I've spoken to my uni mate, Andrew. He's an accountant. Basically, this place is the world's biggest white elephant. It's falling apart –' he motioned to one of the kitchen cupboards, which was hanging drunkenly on one hinge '– and it needs rewiring, new heating, a new roof, a new… well, you name it. It's on the way out.'

'Tell us something we don't know.' Charlotte took a mouthful of coffee.

'Yeah, this isn't exactly news. We all grew up here.' Polly rolled her eyes.

'And it was falling apart then. Dad's been gone for six months, and we need to work out what we're going to do with it.'

'Well, we'll just have to patch it up,' said Beth. 'I mean, think of the state of the farmhouse when Simon and I moved in. It was a complete mess.'

Beth looked away for a moment, an odd expression on her face. Polly clocked it too, Lachlan noticed, but neither of them said anything. A moment later, she seemed to have shaken herself out of it.

The old farmhouse where Beth lived with her husband Simon had been rented out to a tenant farmer for decades, and not once in that time had anything been done to it. Their father was an easy-going, laid-back character – which had been great for the tenants, who all paid a peppercorn rent for their farms and estate houses, but not so great when it came to property maintenance.

'It's not quite the same as doing up this place. Plus it's not… I mean, I don't…' he faltered, coming to a stop. How on earth did you explain to three clannish sisters who felt passionately about the family home that you desperately just wanted to get shot of the place?

The clock on the wall whirred and clicked in the silence, almost groaning with the effort of marking the hour. Out in the hall, the grandfather clock chimed a moment later. Not one of the clocks in Applemore kept accurate time. It was just one more thing that needed fixing in this place.

'Oh come on, Lachlan.' Charlotte surprised him. He'd thought of the three sisters, she'd be the one practical enough to see where he was coming from. 'This place has been in the family for years. Years and years.'

'What're you going to do? I mean it's not like you're going to sell it, is it?' Polly looked at him as if the idea was completely unimaginable. She wrapped a possessive arm around the dogs, as if grounding herself.

'You might like it if you gave this place a try.' Beth gave him a shrewd look. 'You can't play party boy in the city forever. You're thirty-five. It'll start looking a bit tragic, like you're Simon Cowell or something.'

'Simon Cowell?' He shot Beth a look. 'Seriously? I've got a life in Edinburgh. A job. Friends.' Oh, for god's sake. He could feel himself weakening against the triple-pronged onslaught of the sisters, which was exactly what he'd been worried about. It had always been hard to put up a fight against the three of them.

'You've got a micro-brewery, which you could quite easily relocate.' Polly scrambled to her feet.

'Yeah, because it's going to be really handy delivering beer to the pubs of Edinburgh and Glasgow when I'm all the bloody way up here.' He shook his head.

'There are pubs here,' protested Charlotte.

'The Eagle and Feather is hardly my target market,' he groaned.

'There's a nice gastro-pub opened down the road in Oban.' Beth stood up, a split second before an unholy scream emitted from the boot room. 'There we go. I knew they wouldn't stay asleep.'

'How does she do that? She got up before they even made a noise.' Polly looked on with interest as Beth headed out of the door, pulling her hair loose from its band and retying it in a ponytail as she went.

'Motherly instinct. It's a bit creepy, if you ask me,' said Charlotte.

'Anyway,' continued Lachlan, feeling like he'd lost his audience, 'as Polly already knows, I have no intention of relocating the brewery. Gus is taking over the reins, with Lucinda giving him a hand—'

Polly, who'd always had a bit of a thing for Gus, rolled her eyes. 'She'll have your beer plastered with candy-pink labels before you know it.'

'Don't start.' Lachlan, who privately was concerned that she was going to do just that, gave Polly a warning look.

'Just as long as you promise you're not going to sell this place.' Polly crossed her arms.

'I'm with Poll on this one,' said Charlotte, who had the decency to look a bit shame-faced. She was practical

41

enough to know that Applemore was a massive commit-ment, but even she was hampered by the strange pull of the estate. It was weird that he was the only one who seemed to have skipped that feeling, and yet he was the one person who – completely responsible for the place – really needed to feel it.

Charlotte glanced down at her phone, tapped out a brief message, then stood up, pushing her chair back from the table with a screech of metal on wooden floorboards. 'I need to go. The plumbing guy is coming to see if he can sort this leak. We can talk about it later. Another time?'

The screeching from the hall was increasing in volume. Beth popped her head round the kitchen door. 'Sorry, guys. These two are totally overtired and they've not had anything like enough sleep. I'm going to take them for a run in the buggy, see if I can get them back to sleep again. If not, at least they'll sound less blood-curdling in the great outdoors. See you later!'

Lachlan opened his mouth and shut it again.

Polly puffed out a breath and stretched her arms high above her head. 'I think this brings this Extraordinary Family Meeting to a close, don't you? Sorry, Lachlan, but unless you've got any other business – see what I did there? – I'm going to keep Beth company. If she can't get them to sleep, I'll play with the babies while she does flower stuff.'

And with a cheerful wave, she was off, following in Charlotte and Beth's wake.

Somehow, the kitchen was empty, and Lachlan was standing there with nothing more than a table strewn with unwashed mugs to show for it.

Reaching down to ruffle the curly ears of both spaniels, he pocketed his phone and decided that maybe the answer was to go for a walk himself and have a think about things with a business – rather than an emotional – head.

Outside, the dogs dashed off into the undergrowth. The sky had cleared and was a fair pale blue, untroubled by clouds. He turned to look at Applemore, casting a critical eye over the house. It was almost comically pretty – all turrets and secret hidden windows, flanked on either side by trees which gave it the look of a fairy-tale castle in minia-ture. It had been built 150 years ago by one of their ances-tors, who'd clearly had the foresight to realise that while it was important that the place looked outwardly imposing, the inside had to be a home. So once you made your way out of the huge, grand hallway – where stuffed animal heads hung, slightly dusty and faded, alongside old oil paint-ings, and a dark red carpet lined the stairs which led up to a galleried hall, and above that another gallery (the number of cobwebs increasing as one climbed the stairs) where there was an entire floor which was mothballed and neglected – there was in fact a cosy sitting room filled with battered, dog-hair-covered sofas and an oak coffee table strewn with books and coffee cups, and beside that a library with a huge grand piano and shelves of foxed, leather-bound books and piles of their mother's ancient *Vogue* magazines, which looked down through a clearing in the woods towards Applemore Bay.

Applemore house stood in thirty acres of land, mostly overtaken by woodland and the ever-present rhododen-drons, and would make some well-off family with ideas of grandeur the perfect holiday home. Or it would, if he could sell it. His estate agent friend Felix had pointed out that rich Americans loved that sort of thing, and that if he put it on the market as a fixer-upper, they'd get a reasonable price. 'But,' Felix had said, shrewdly, 'if you were to get the place into decent order, you'd make a couple of hundred grand more.' And that would be enough to give each sibling a decent chunk of money which might just be enough to cancel out the guilt he'd feel at selling on their heritage.

Lachlan tried to picture the house being photographed by one of Felix's hotshot property photographers. It looked imposing, he had to admit, surrounded by mossy, lichen-covered trees. The gravel of the driveway had migrated somewhere, leaving bare earth in places. The windowpanes were ringed with ancient paint which peeled and cracked. He reached over and pulled at a piece, revealing the wood underneath. It wouldn't take that much to sand all that down and give it a lick of paint. Perhaps if he gave himself the winter to try to get it sorted, he could put it on the market when the rhododendrons were in bloom and the woods were aflame with purple flowers. That would give the girls time to get used to the idea.

Lachlan set off down the drive, resolving to walk the perimeter of the estate and get a feel for exactly what had to be done.

CHAPTER 4

'Morning,' said a young girl with red hair from behind the counter. 'Lovely day, isn't it?'

Rilla nodded. 'Gorgeous.'

'Glad the rain's gone.' The girl went back to looking at her phone.

Somewhere beyond the thick floral curtain that hung behind her, Rilla could hear a quiz show on the television and an elderly voice shouting, 'That's not the right answer.'

The girl looked up again for a moment, meeting Rilla's eye. 'My granny. She's addicted to that programme.'

Rilla picked up a basket. As well as the usual newspapers, magazines and bags of logs for tourists who rented holiday cottages, there was everything you could possibly need. White baby onesies hung on coat hangers beside rolls of electrical wire. A shelf held boxes of screws and fencing equipment. A faded box contained a coffee maker which looked like it had been there since the 1990s. Rilla stood for a moment, taking it all in. There weren't many shops left like this – this one looked like it hadn't changed a bit in the eighteen years since she'd been there last, and probably not for twenty years before that.

'Is there anything in particular you're looking for?' The girl's accent was soft and lilting – Rilla had forgotten how it sounded, and it felt like home. She half-expected her dad to wander into the shop and offer to buy her an ice lolly.

'Oh! Sorry. I just need some bits and pieces.' Rilla shook herself. 'Just thinking. I should have written a list.'

'Fair enough,' said the girl, putting her phone in the back pocket of her jeans and pulling the curtain across to make her way back into the adjoining house. 'Give me a shout if you can't find anything.'

Rilla pottered around with her basket and filled it with milk, a loaf of plastic-wrapped white bread, some eggs and cheese, a packet of bacon and some chocolate. Her phone started buzzing insistently in her back pocket, and she paused for a second, pulling it out.

Thought you'd like to see this! Missing you!

Sally had messaged on WhatsApp, sharing a photo of the kids. They were sitting on the painted front step of the house, holding a chalkboard which announced 'Back to School'. No doubt it would be gathering hundreds of likes on Sally's Instagram page.

Rilla shook her head, smiling. It felt like a million years since they'd been sitting on the porch together, but it was only a few days. Standing by the counter, grabbing the opportunity of some mobile phone signal, she checked her other messages – a handful of friends asking how it was going, one of her ex-employers asking if she'd be interested in doing some teaching work in China for the winter, a bunch of pictures taken by her friend Ella in Boston who was madly in love with someone new... Rilla sighed at that and shoved her phone back in her pocket. And here she was, in the middle of nowhere, with nobody. Anyway – she straightened her shoulders – she was happy that way. The truth was that most of the time she was quite content with her own company – but sometimes she wondered what it would be like to have someone to share it all with.

There was a clatter and the bell above the door rang out, alerting everyone that a new customer had arrived.

'Morning,' called a crisp, slightly upper-class sounding voice.

'Oh hi, Charlotte,' said the girl coming back to her place behind the counter.

Rilla – standing behind a shelf of pasta and rice – caught a glimpse of a tall, slender woman wearing a checked shirt and jeans. She looked familiar, somehow. Her long, strawberry blonde hair was tied back in a ponytail. Rilla, who'd always had a hopeless memory for faces, tried desperately to recall who she reminded her of, but couldn't.

Picking up a bottle of wine and some crisps, she stood for a moment trying to think if there was anything else she needed. The cottage was in desperate need of a really good clean – she threw a couple of bottles of bathroom cleaner and floor wash into her basket and headed for the counter.

Standing by the counter, a box of washing powder in her hands, the woman – Charlotte – frowned, as if she was trying to place Rilla. She frowned briefly before she spoke. 'Rilla? It is, isn't it?' She laughed, looking uncertain. 'If it's not, I'm going to look a bit clueless.'

'It is.'

'Of course it is. It's Charlotte – Charlotte Fraser?'

Of *course*. The cheekbones were more pronounced now, and there was a feathering of fine lines around her eyes – she was tanned, despite the autumn weather, and clearly spent lots of time outside. But how could she not have realised it? . It was the strangest feeling to be standing here in front of her after everything that had happened. Rilla felt a rush of emotions she couldn't quite put a finger on – but the predominant one was happiness. 'Charlotte! Hello.'

Putting down the box of washing powder she was holding, Charlotte wrapped her in a surprisingly tight hug, then pushed her out to look her up and down. 'Rilla. How strange and how lovely. We were just talking about you. It's been years. Years and years.'

'Eighteen.'

'I know. Well, to be more specific, Lachlan knew. Who knew he was such a mine of family information?'

How funny that Lachlan should remember. An image of the Fraser sisters' tall, dark-haired, slightly aloof elder brother popped into her head and she felt herself going slightly pink at the memory of how much she'd liked him as a teenager. And it was lovely that Charlotte said *family* – that was something that Rilla had always felt. The Frasers had been like family to her, at a time when she'd felt unmoored and out of place with her mother and her new stepfather. They had always been a kind-hearted, friendly bunch who didn't stand on ceremony despite owning a huge chunk of the land in the peninsula. Their dad had been a lovely man – it was a funny coincidence that he'd passed away within months of her dad, when they'd always been such good friends.

Charlotte shook her head. 'This is so amazing. You two were here all the time, then you just – went. I always worried it was because we nearly drowned your sister at the lake that time, but your dad said it was… well, he said it was complicated?'

'Yeah.' Rilla chewed the inside of her lip briefly. 'That's

a good word for it. Families are complicated.' That was a bloody understatement.

'You're not kidding.' Charlotte rolled her eyes. 'Oh, this is so lovely. You're staying at the cottage? Are you here for a while?'

'Yes, staying at dad's place.' She remembered that the lease was up in three months and wondered if they were desperately waiting to reclaim it and felt a bit uncomfortable.

But Charlotte was as stolidly cheerful as Rilla remembered. 'Of course. God, I'm dim. How's it going? It must be a bit chaotic in there. Your dad was always a bit...' She stopped, as if realising what she was saying. 'Well, it's been a while, hasn't it?'

'It's a bit dusty. And a bit cluttered.' That was the understatement of the century.

'Sorry about your dad. He was lovely. He and dad were such good friends.'

Rilla didn't add that she'd always thought that Hector Fraser, head of the family and the Applemore Estate was far, far more eccentric than her own dad. He'd always called her Rilla of Green Gables, which confused anyone who hadn't worked out the origin of her name.

'I expect you heard? Pops passed away at the beginning of the year. Cancer.' Charlotte looked downcast for a moment. 'Such a crappy way to go, don't you think? At least it was quick. We can say that for both our dads, can't we?'

Rilla nodded. 'I'm sorry.' She put a hand out and touched Charlotte's arm in sympathy. 'Your dad was a really nice man.'

'He was. I'm glad I got to spend as much time with him as I...' Charlotte began, then petered out. 'Sorry. That was tactless. I know you didn't get to see as much of your dad as he would have liked.'

'Or as much as I would have. I thought I had forever.'

'We always do,' Charlotte said. 'Anyway, enough doom and gloom. Will you come and see us? The others would love to see you – and, weirdly enough, we're all actually in one place, for once. Even Lachlan.'

'I'd like that.' Rilla lifted her basket onto the counter, where the girl began ringing things through the till.

'Excellent. What are you doing today?'

'Today?' Rilla tried not to squawk. She'd been half-expecting Charlotte's invitation to be one of those vaguely polite mentions people do then never follow through with.

'I'm at a loose end for once in my ridiculously busy life. Are you in the car?'

'No, I came down on Dad's old bike.'

'Shove it in the back of the pickup, and I'll give you a lift. We can head up to the house and say hello. No time like the present, and all that. Beth's probably not around – she's got baby twins, so she's basically a slave to them. They're adorable, but exhausting. Give me two secs, I'll just get the stuff I came in for while you pay.'

A few moments later, Rilla found herself sitting in the passenger seat of Charlotte's pickup truck, thinking to herself that it was a blessing in disguise that she'd been offered a lift. The hill she'd happily freewheeled down would have been an absolute killer to cycle back up, especially while trying to balance two bags of shopping. She'd updated Charlotte on Sally's life and the edited version of what she'd been up to – which always made her life sound quite glamorous, with all the travel and adventure – by the time they made it to the cottage.

Charlotte pulled over. 'Let's drop the bike off. I've had a brainwave.'

It was funny, Rilla reflected, that the people they were at fifteen still showed through. Charlotte had been – well, some people might have said bossy, others confident, back then, too. Rilla had always been a bit wary of getting out of her comfort zone, preferring to do things by herself and work them out rather than mess up in front of the others. That hadn't really changed much.

'Your dad's car was in the outhouse, if my memory serves me correctly. I reckon we could give it a jumpstart, get it going. That way you wouldn't have to trawl around Applemore on a bike in the middle of winter.'

They climbed out of the car.

'Oh, I'm not going to be here all winter,' Rilla began, but Charlotte was rooting about in a box under the passenger seat.

'Here we are. I knew I had the jump leads. Now is the car still there, or has it been magicked away by fairies or teenage joyriders?' Charlotte tugged on the big wooden door of the stone building which sat just to one side of the cottage.

'D'you get a lot of teenage joyriders round here?' Rilla looked on, amused.

'There's a first time for everything,' Charlotte said, breathlessly. 'Aha! There we are. Although, to be honest, I can't imagine many teenagers wanting to joyride in a Nissan Note, can you?'

The car seemed surprisingly unscathed by its extended rest. The keys (thank goodness there were no opportunist thieves on the peninsula) were in the ignition, and while the battery was completely flat, it only took ten minutes to get the engine running again.

'Now what we need to do is leave it running for a bit, and then you need to get down to Ullapool and go to the garage and get a new battery. I can't imagine that one'll keep going for long. In fact, why don't you follow me up the drive and you can park it and leave the engine running while we say hello to whoever is home?'

'Okay,' said Rilla, feeling slightly non-plussed. A moment ago, it seemed she'd been quietly on her own, planning how to get a skip – there was no point clearing the place out if she didn't have somewhere to put it all – and making plans to clear the cottage. Now she'd been organised into visiting the big house with Charlotte and an assortment of Fraser family members. It was nice, if a little bit surprising.

Rilla followed Charlotte up the drive that forked off to the left of Applemore Cottage. In the old days, the cottage had been home to the gamekeeper who worked on the estate – but that was before the Fraser family had sold off a few hundred acres of land to cover inheritance tax. Before her dad had moved in, it had stood empty for some years. She glanced up at it in the rear-view mirror before it was obscured by trees – standing empty again, she thought. Perhaps it was happier that way.

The driveway up to Applemore House was pitted with potholes and overgrown with shaggy rhododendron bushes. Grass grew up the middle of the cracked, worn tarmac. It was all strangely familiar and yet she remembered a gardener working every day, driving around in a beaten-up old Land Rover Defender, chopping down trees for firewood. Now the woodland seemed in danger of encroaching the drive and spindly young growth was pushing up between older, established trees. It felt a little like a fairy story, and Applemore was the castle in danger of being choked forever beneath a wild and magical forest. Rilla shook herself, laughing at her overactive imagination.

A moment later she was brought back to earth when they turned a corner and the turreted splendour of Apple-more House stood before her.

Charlotte pulled her car up to a halt just before Rilla and waited as Rilla unfolded herself from her seat, standing for a moment with her hand on the top of the door, just taking it all in. When she'd remembered her childhood summers playing in and around the big house, she'd created an image of it in her head as a solid, grey version of the famous Disney castle, so it was a surprise to see how dilapidated it looked. The old summer house which had been built onto the side of the house decades before had panes of glass missing and a tangle of wild roses bursting out through the gaps. Buddleia sprouted at an improbable height, self-seeded in the crow-stepped gables. The herbaceous border beneath the kitchen window was choked with weeds, thistles turning to faded brown and scattering their feather-light seeds to the wind. The bricks that made up the winding path that led round the back of the house and into the woods were cracked and mossy. But the tall poplar trees stood on either side of the house, like old, distinguished sentries who hadn't given up their post, and the overall impression, was of tattered, faded grandeur. Rilla felt a thrill of excitement at being back after so many years.

'We'll leave it running for half an hour, that ought to do it,' said Charlotte, giving the bonnet a proprietorial pat.

'I've just thought - it won't be taxed or MOT-ed or anything,' Rilla said, starting, realising she'd been standing gawping at the house for longer than she should. She closed the car door, leaving the engine running.

'And if you want to get technical, it's probably not

insured either, unless you've got insurance for a car back – wherever home is?'

Rilla shook her head, feeling rootless. 'No car.' She didn't add *no home*, but the truth was – she didn't have one. Most of the time it didn't worry her.

'Right, well,' Charlotte rubbed her hands together. 'Don't stress about the car – you're on private land all the way from your place to ours, and we can sort out tax and insurance and stuff online.' Used to taking charge, Charlotte beckoned her to follow. 'Let's go inside and see who's about.'

Rilla's stomach felt like it was filled with a small army of butterflies wearing army boots with nerves at the thought of seeing everyone again. She followed Charlotte through the boot room – the smell of wellingtons and leather oil and dusty geranium plants instantly pulling her back through time – and into the kitchen. It was as big as Rilla remembered, but much shabbier. Everything looked as if it needed a shake up to bring it to life. A bloom of damp spread across one wall, and the plaster had come away from a corner so the wooden lathes could be seen poking through, as if the house was baring its bones.

'Hello-ooo,' called Charlotte, opening the fridge and pulling out a glass bottle of milk. 'Where is everyone?' She pulled out her phone. 'I'll use the power of the family group chat to summon them. I wonder where Lachlan's gone? The dogs aren't usually far from his heels.'

Charlotte busied herself making a pot of coffee.

Rilla sat perched on the edge of the long bench which took up one side of the big kitchen table, looking around at a room that had once been familiar.

'So Lachlan's living here now?'

'Lachlan?' Charlotte snorted with laughter. 'Well, that's

the idea in theory, but he's not exactly keen, between you me and the gatepost. He needs to step up and take his responsibilities seriously, if you ask me. This place isn't going to run itself.' She sounded very much like the bossy Charlotte of old at that moment and it made Rilla smile.

Rilla, who'd spent her whole life being accused of avoiding any sort of responsibility, felt a twin sensation of admiration for Lachlan – who clearly wasn't toeing the family party line – and slight guilt that her family were probably saying the same thing about her.

Charlotte excused herself, saying she needed to pop to the loo.

'Hello,' said an unfamiliar young woman with long blonde hair, a few moments later.

Rilla stood up, putting out a hand in greeting. 'Hi, I'm—'

'I know who you are,' the girl said, laughing. 'But I'm guessing you can't remember me?'

Rilla frowned, and then something clicked into place. She remembered an elfin child with a permanently grubby face and feet to match, never more than a few metres from her rotund welsh pony Edward. 'Polly? Oh my god. The last time I saw you, you were tiny.'

'The last time I saw you, your sister was being dragged in from the lake on a dinghy after my big sister…' she paused, giving a returning Charlotte a dig in the ribs, 'tried to drown her in the bay.'

'Oh yes. My mother loved that,' Rilla explained, real-ising as she did that they were looking at her with shocked expressions. She giggled. 'Not that Sally did her worst impression of a mermaid, but that my dad had officially messed up enough that she could justify stopping us coming here for the summers.'

'Ahhh,' Charlotte and Polly exchanged a look. 'We wondered what made you stop coming. I always felt guilty that it might've been my fault.'

'It was just a silly accident,' Rilla said, shaking her head. 'Sally was fine. But my mother didn't want us coming here – she was – well, she still is – one of those people that likes to draw a line under stuff. The trouble with it is, we didn't get a say.' It was funny that she was able to talk about it freely with the Frasers, even after all this time, where the subject was always skirted around when it came up with Sally.

'That's a bit shit.' Polly made a face.

'Polly,' hissed Charlotte, giving her younger sister a reproving look.

'Well, it's true.' She looked unrepentant.

'She's right.' Rilla nodded. 'I loved coming here. It was the only time we got to actually feel free – we could do whatever we wanted and mess about and Dad didn't ever tell us off for coming home covered in mud or having midnight picnics or any of the stuff we used to do.'

'Midnight picnics,' Charlotte said, dreamily, her serious face lighting up. 'Oh god, do you remember the time we had one in the barn at midsummer? I still think of that every midsummer's eve. We really did have a dreamy childhood.'

'Apart from the no money and terrible clothes thing,' Polly pointed out, waving an arm around the kitchen, 'and the growing up in a house where the roof leaked and there was ice on the inside of the windowpanes in winter?'

'Details, Poll,' Charlotte said, laughing. 'I've just had a message from Beth, she's up to her eyes in baby sick and nappies and can't get away, but says she can't wait to see you and she's glad you've moved into the cottage and she'll catch up soon.'

'I haven't…' Rilla began, again, then closed her mouth. Charlotte was a bit of an unstoppable force. It was easier to just let her think she was moving in than that she was only here for a short-term visit.

They spent a lovely couple of hours reminiscing over some of the scrapes they'd got into as children, and Charlotte dug out an old photo album and found some pictures of them all making dens and dressing up for ridiculous complicated games they used to play down by the river.

'Can't imagine children nowadays doing all that stuff, can you?' Charlotte passed a photograph of them all covered in mud, standing in a stream.

'I think we were pretty weird even then.' Beth shook her head, laughing.

'Weird, or lucky?'

'Lucky.' Rilla grinned. 'I wouldn't change it for anything.

'S'not fair,' Polly grumbled. 'I missed out on all the fun back then, and now I'm missing out on all the memories, too. I hate being the baby.'

'Shh, baby,' said Charlotte, patting her on the head, laughing.

Rilla glanced up at the clock. She'd had a lovely time, but she didn't want to outstay her welcome.

'No sign of Lachlan,' Polly noted a few minutes later, as Rilla was climbing back into the car.

'He's probably sloped back to Edinburgh hoping none of us will notice.' Charlotte tutted.

'Bloody shit.'

'Thanks so much,' Rilla said, turning on the ignition with fingers crossed that the battery would still be working. 'For the coffee, and the cake, and for making my sides hurt with laughing.'

'Mine are aching too. It's got to be as good as Pilates, don't you reckon?'

'Definitely.'

'Right. Don't forget, anything you need - printer, paper, anything like that - just whizz up here. I'm sure there's loads of stuff you need to sort out. But at least we've sorted out car insurance and all that malarkey.' Charlotte dusted her hands together in a *that's sorted* sort of motion.

'And a skip,' said Rilla, relieved.

'Oh, I love a therapeutic clear-out,' said Charlotte, dreamily. 'If you need any help…'

'I'll shout. But you can pop round any time.'

'I will.' Charlotte stepped back, giving a wave. 'See you soon.'

Back at the house, Rilla discovered a note through the door from Joan, who'd 'popped by to see if she needed a hand with anything' and who'd written down some local information on a neat little note.

That was the motivation she needed – fired up after having a chat with Polly and Charlotte (she had to admit to herself that despite thinking she wanted time alone, it was nice to spend some time with people), she got to work, deciding to be brutal. Her dad hadn't been sentimental, and so neither would she be.

She worked through the night, sorting things into piles: there was junk, of which there was quite a lot and which made her mutter *sorry Dad* under her breath as she dumped it in black bin bags and piled it outside the front door. There was recycling – the skip company had instructed her to put all that in boxes and they'd take it away in the morning if she had it ready to go. And then there were all his clothes. Not that he had that many – her dad had always been a functional rather than a fashionable dresser – but, oh, how it made her heart ache.

She stood for a long time with her nose in the wardrobe, breathing in and inhaling the familiar scent of oil and the woody aftershave he'd always worn. She straightened her shoulders, hearing his voice in her head. *They're only things, my love*, he'd say. And so she took them off the hangers and folded them neatly, putting them into bags for the charity shop. She kept the huge woollen jumper – it was like having a hug from him, and it felt like he was close by.

She was almost done. She looked at his bedroom – the bed stripped and bare, the cupboards empty. How strange that a whole life could be erased so easily. She leant back against the door, closing her eyes for a moment, then turned, realising she was leaning on his dressing gown which was hanging from a peg. It rustled slightly as she lifted it up – inside one of the pockets, there was a wedge of folded, white writing paper, soft with age. Rilla unfolded it, carefully.

Darling boy,

Just a brief note to tell you how much I loved our weekend away together. I hope you'll get this on Monday when you get back to Edinburgh and it'll lift your spirits after what you think is going to be a tricky day at the lab. I'll be thinking of you.

Always,
Your best love.

Rilla gazed down at the neat writing. She frowned, turning to the next letter.

Sweetest boy…

And the next –

My love,

There must be about twenty of them. All written in the same beautifully neat hand, all on the same expensively laid white writing paper, all folded carefully and clearly read and re-read so many times that the edges had become soft and fuzzy with age. No name on any of them. It had never occurred to Rilla that in the years since her parents had split her dad would have met another woman... She shook her head, smiling to herself. It was nice, she decided, to think that he hadn't been completely alone all this time. He'd had his friendship with Hector Fraser, and of course he'd always been close to Joan, but – well, this was clearly something different. Whoever it was, he'd taken the secret of her to the grave.

Heading downstairs, Rilla banked up the fire and dozed on the sofa, aware that the skip hire company would be arriving bright and early.

'All right, love? You got someone to give you a hand with this lot?' The driver took one look at the pile of boxes Rilla had stacked by the back door of the cottage.

She shook her head. 'No, but it's not that tricky.' The good thing was she didn't have to deal with any of the furniture – shabby and battered as it was, all of it belonged to the house and therefore to the Fraser estate. She just had to get rid of her dad's belongings, and in doing so say goodbye for the last time. An unexpected wave of grief hit her and she felt her knees go wobbly.

'You okay, there?' The man looked at her with concern.

'Fine,' she said, taking a deep breath and putting on her best brave smile. 'Just tired.'

He gave her a brief nod of acknowledgement, then loaded up the boxes of recycling. 'That's one less thing for you to do, love.'

'Thank you.' Rilla was feeling distinctly fuzzy-headed. Maybe she'd just sit down on the sofa and have a quick five-minute nap before she got to work. She pulled a blanket over herself and curled up...

She woke to a sharp knocking on the window.

'Hellooo?'

Rilla scrunched her eyes closed hard, then forced them open. Outside, her face pressed against the glass, was Joan, covered from the rain by a blue polka-dotted rain mac.

She motioned to the leaden sky. 'Are you busy?'

'No! Come in, quickly,' Rilla said, leaping out from the depths of the sofa. A wave of just-woken-up nausea washed over her and she exhaled slowly, making it to the front door of the cottage just as Joan arrived in the hallway in a flurry of raindrops and fuss about wet coats and not making a mess.

'Honestly,' Rilla took Joan's coat, hanging it on one of the pegs on the rack by the door, 'a bit of rain can't make this place look any untidier.'

But Joan wasn't paying attention. She was standing to one side, looking down the hall towards the sitting room, as if lost in thought. A moment later, she shook herself, as if remembering that Rilla was there, and rubbed her hands together briskly.

'Right then,' she said, almost too brightly. 'Gosh, it's funny being back here without David, isn't it? What needs to be done?'

Afterwards, Rilla would have sworn there was a tear

glistening in the corner of Joan's eye, but if there had been, the moment had passed before she'd felt she could ask – and it wasn't her place to pry. Whilst Joan headed off to the kitchen, Rilla was careful to put the letters she'd found safely away in the side pocket of one of her bags. Whoever had written them – and she was beginning to wonder – wouldn't want to know Rilla had seen them.

CHAPTER 5

By the time he'd made it back from his walk around the grounds of Applemore the day before, Lachlan had missed all the excitement of Rilla turning up. He'd had no reception when the first message arrived from Charlotte, telling the family group chat that she'd bumped into Rilla and brought her round for a coffee and was anyone going to join them, followed by another from Beth apologising and saying she couldn't make it. Polly, he assumed, had been at a loose end as usual, because she'd been full of excitement when he got home later that afternoon. A new person was a huge novelty in Applemore, and Polly was clearly very taken with Rilla. He'd played it cool, being quite dismissive and offhand about it all – but the reality was he'd replayed the moment when she'd stood on the doorstep looking tired, cross and even prettier than he remembered over and over again in his head. The last thing he needed to be thinking about, though, was Rilla. He had far bigger concerns, like Polly... she was his biggest worry.

At the moment, she was basically just floating around,

doing not very much at all, and as the de facto head of the household, and with no parents left, he somehow felt responsible for his baby sister in a way that made him feel slightly alarmed. How on earth did you galvanise a slightly flaky twenty-five-year-old into doing something with her life? God, it was all bloody hard work. But it wasn't going to get sorted if he didn't do anything about it.

His thoughts turned unbidden back to Rilla. Funny – she'd clearly not recognised him at all – perhaps it was the two-week-old beard, or else he'd aged so much with all the bloody family stress that he was completely unrecognisable. She, on the other hand, had looked exactly as he remembered her – only prettier. He'd wanted to reach out and tuck the stray curl that had escaped from her ponytail behind her ear as she'd stood there on the doorstep. She'd clearly been worn out from travelling – it was a long way from the airport in Edinburgh all the way up here, even without the journey back from the USA. He was jolted by his thought by the weather, as a gust of wind howled down the chimney.

Rain was hammering against the windowpane of his bedroom and pooling on the windowsill where the ancient sash windows didn't quite close properly. Lachlan hauled himself out of bed, threw on some jeans and a T-shirt, went downstairs and made a coffee in the kitchen. There was a string of messages from Gus – always a night owl – who'd been messing about with recipes for new beers and was determined that he'd be fine making a go of the brewery single-handed while Lachlan wasn't there. That just meant that he needed to focus a) on finding something to do to make some money while he was up here and b) on how best to get the place into some sort of order so in six months' time when winter was over, he could get Applemore House on the market with Felix and get the hell out of Dodge and back home to Edinburgh.

The kitchen was quiet – Polly wouldn't be up for hours yet, and Charlotte and Beth wouldn't drop by until much later. Yesterday as he'd been out walking, he'd realised that the best course of action was to take some photos of the place and send them to Felix. That way – rather than having to drive all the way up here – he'd be able to give a realistic idea of the sort of price that Applemore might raise. Lachlan felt faintly guilty about it. If he was honest with himself, he felt horribly guilty. But there wasn't really a solution. He sat down and opened his laptop.

Between that and brewery work the morning flew past. Polly headed off to Inverness for the day, which gave him a chance to take a load of photographs of the interior of Applemore without causing suspicion. He felt awfully disloyal doing so, but as he typed up a brief description of the various parts of the house, he put his feelings to one side. Being practical was the answer. There was no room for sentimentality.

'Hello stranger,' said a cheerful voice. Lachlan was sitting at his favourite table in the window of the Applemore Hotel. He'd finished work, realised he was ravenous and decided the best cure was one of the Applemore's steak pie and chips special lunchtime deals.

Harry, who owned the hotel, had recently taken over from his parents when they'd retired. He'd gone to primary school with Lachlan and they'd grown up together, messing about on boats in the bay and getting into scrapes.

'Harry. How's it going? Weird being back?'

Harry pushed back his red curls from his forehead, nodding emphatically. 'It's a bit of a change from Sydney.'

'That's the understatement of the decade.'

'Well, I couldn't leave the olds in the lurch when they were retiring.'

'You got time to join me for a drink?' Lachlan asked.

Harry glanced across the bar. Apart from Lachlan, there were two older women sitting with a pot of tea and some scones, and three walkers dressed in practical hiking gear, their rucksacks balanced against the wall. 'Yeah, we're not busy. It's that time of year.'

Harry went over to the bar, poured two pints of beer and returned, placing them on the table before sitting down. He put his chin in his hand and looked at Lachlan, one eyebrow lifting slightly.

'So.'

'Here we are.' Lachlan lifted his glass slightly. 'Here's to us, and all that.'

'Indeed.' Harry took a sip. 'Who knew we'd end up back here, duty-bound?'

Lachlan groaned. 'You planning your escape?'

Harry shook his head, laughing. 'I've done my travelling. Seen the world, worked in Sydney on the boats, had my adventures.'

'And now you're happy to settle down here?' Lachlan looked at his friend with surprise.

'I don't know if I'd say happy so much as—'

'Resigned?'

'It's not that either. You must get it – now your dad's gone, you've got to deal with the house and estate and all that stuff.'

'Mmm.' Lachlan was non-committal.

'There are worse places to end up,' Harry indicated the little harbour. 'I mean, it's not exactly slumming it, living in the prettiest part of the Highlands.'

'Oh god, I know.' Lachlan looked outside. A woman

with a bright purple coat was being dragged along the pavement by an extremely overenthusiastic, extremely scruffy springer spaniel. He laughed.

'I've got lots of plans for this place, anyway. Starting with a Hallowe'en party at the end of the month. You got your costume ready?' Harry smirked.

'I have not.' Lachlan shook his head. 'Aren't we a bit old for fancy dress?'

'You're never too old for fancy dress in my opinion. We had an amazing night last Hallowe'en in Sydney – stayed up all night, had a hangover for days. You can bring the girls along, they'll bump the numbers up a bit.'

'I'm not sure Beth'll be able to escape from the babies for a party.'

'Can't believe she's got twins,' Harry shook his head. 'I missed a trick there.'

Lachlan looked at his friend in surprise. 'You and Beth?'

Harry made an enigmatic face. 'A gentleman never tells…'

'Seriously?'

'You know we always got on.'

'I did,' Lachlan said, 'but I had no idea there was anything between you. Weren't you seeing some Aussie girl, anyway?'

'Meghan? Yeah. Ended it when I came back. You can't have a relationship with someone who lives thousands of miles away.' Harry took another sip of his drink, moving slightly as a fair-haired young lad put Lachlan's food down on the table. He pinched a chip, waving it for emphasis as he spoke. 'To be honest, I was looking for an excuse to finish it. She was definitely hitting the point where she was slowing down every time we walked past a jewellery shop, if you know what I mean.'

Lachlan nodded. 'I do.' He'd seen it in friends, but he'd never quite got to that stage himself.

'I definitely *do* not. I'm not the marrying type.'

'Maybe you just haven't met the right girl.' Lachlan speared a chip. The woman outside had stopped on the other side of the road and was looking confused. The dog was bouncing vigorously. For some reason, she was using what looked like a man's belt as a lead, with the end of it wrapped tightly around her palm. She caught Lachlan's eye and gave him a slightly wild-eyed look, then hurried across the road, the spaniel orbiting around her. She did not look like a dog person.

Harry looked at him thoughtfully. 'Maybe I did, but she married someone else.'

Before Lachlan had a chance to reply, there was a crash as the door into the hotel opened and the woman lurched in, holding on for grim death.

'Help!' she gasped.

Lachlan and Harry looked at each other and tried not to laugh.

Fifteen minutes later, the woman had gone, and Lachlan's steak pie lunch was inside the extremely skinny, scruffy-looking spaniel.

'I'll take him along to the vet, see if he's microchipped. Someone must've lost him somewhere along the way,' Lachlan suggested.

Harry glanced at the bar where the young lad from earlier was washing glasses and looking on with interest. He checked his watch. 'If you don't mind – I need to get on before the dinner-time rush starts. I've got a delivery coming in half an hour and I need to get organised.'

'No problem.' Lachlan scratched the dog behind the ears. On closer inspection, it turned out that he was wearing the belt as a makeshift collar – there was nothing to identify him at all. But he was clearly well bred and quite young – someone must be missing him, somewhere.

The Applemore vet surgery was situated on the main street, behind a brightly painted blue wooden door with a horseshoe nailed onto it for luck. Inside, there was an assortment of chairs and an old-fashioned counter which hadn't changed since Lachlan was a boy and had visited with his sisters and their assortment of pets. It was run by Fiona MacEwan, a no-nonsense woman in her mid-fifties who treated everyone with the same brisk, cheerful manner whether they were clients or animals.

'What have we here?' She emerged from the back office, wiping her hands dry on a paper towel. 'Ah, Lachlan. I heard you were back up. For good, is it?'

'Something like that,' he hedged, not really wanting to get into that conversation.

'And this is? Not one of your dad's dogs – is this yours? He could do with a few good meals. And a decent clip, come to think of it. He looks like he's been through a hedge backwards. Hello, my boy,' she said, kneeling down to inspect the dog.

'He's not mine.' Lachlan briefly explained how he'd ended up with the dog, as Fiona ran a practised hand over him.

'A good couple of kilos underweight, but…' She listened to his heart through the stethoscope she had hanging around her neck. 'Other than that, he seems in relatively good health. Let's scan him, see if we can find a chip.' She beckoned for Lachlan to follow her through to the examination room.

They lifted him up onto the examining table and she ran a scanner across the back of his neck, shaking her head.

69

'Well, that's unusual. Nothing. Down you go, lad,' she said, lifting him back onto the ground. 'I'll have a quick check on the missing dogs page – they're usually pretty hot on the case, although he looks like he's been on the run for a couple of weeks.'

There was nothing – lots of missing and stolen spaniels, but none with his particular markings – with his smear of white across his muzzle, the dog was quite distinctive.

'So,' Fiona said, crossing her arms and looking at the dog. He flopped down on the tiled floor and looked back at them, hopefully. 'I guess the question is – what shall we do with you?'

'I'll take him for now,' Lachlan heard himself saying. 'We can work out what to do with him from there.'

'Glad you said that,' Fiona, looked relieved. 'Janice who runs the rehoming place is completely full – I know that for a fact because I was in there yesterday. You won't notice an extra bod around the place, the size of Applemore. Glad to be back?'

Lachlan nodded.

'Right. Well,' Fiona glanced up at the clock. 'Afternoon surgery starts in ten minutes and I've got to get over to the dairy farm before dinner tonight, so if it's okay with you…'

Lachlan took the hint. How on earth, he wondered, had he ended up leaving with a new dog in tow? This was definitely not what he'd planned for his return to Applemore.

CHAPTER 6

Joan had worked wonders. With two pairs of hands to get things sorted, the cottage was basically clear. They'd filled the skip and together Rilla and Joan had sorted everything else into bags and boxes. Once she'd kept her dad's voice in her head, telling her to just bloody well get on with it, she'd found it easy to just jettison everything. There were a few bits and pieces she'd decided to hold onto – in the bedside table, she'd discovered an old album full of photographs of herself, Sally and her dad, which had made her cry and laugh. They'd had a magical childhood up here in Apple-more. It was a shame that her mum hadn't been able to see that the adventures – even with the resultant accidents and disasters – had given them something most children didn't get to experience.

After Joan had left, Rilla had eaten lunch and drunk about three cups of tea – a habit she'd caught from her dad and never lost – as she'd gone through his desk. In a way, it was a bit like having one last visit with him, she'd thought, picking up a newish-looking notebook and flipping through the pages. His writing made her catch her breath once again – neat and precise, and always with the same fine-point black ink pens. This book wasn't full of scientific notes and diagrams, however, but what looked like plans of some sort. She peered at it closely. It was a plan for a camper van, by the looks of it. There was a bed, with a little kitchen unit alongside and a cute little table with two tall chairs. A sketch showed a little space under the bed where a cabinet for a gas canister sat, alongside a set of batteries and a very precisely planned-out electrical system. That was funny – he'd always talked about travelling round Europe when he retired, and he'd loved hearing about her stories of the places she visited whilst teaching English to students. It was a pity that he'd never managed to make it. Poor dad – Rilla sighed, closing the book. She'd done enough for today. Her nose was full of dust and she felt like she was getting cabin fever to go with the jet lag. Maybe if she wore herself out with a walk, she'd manage to actually get some sleep tonight.

Something about back here was throwing her completely. If she could just stay awake until eight tonight, she'd have a decent chance of making it through the night and sorting herself out.

Rilla stood up, stretching until her back cracked, and looked out of the window. The rain had stopped. She could have a wander about, poke around and make sure her dad hadn't left anything in the old outhouses. In the old days, she'd loved spending time out there with her dad, watching him build things out of old scraps and pieces of leftover wood. He'd had faith in her abilities in a way that her mother never did – she'd always been hyper-cautious, alarmed in case the girls hurt themselves or (worse still) did something that might embarrass her. Pete, her second husband, was very much a Southern gentleman of the old-fashioned sort. Rilla suspected that since they got together her mother hadn't so much as changed a light bulb. No wonder she freaked out at the thought of Rilla travelling the world with nothing more than the bags she could carry...

A dog barked sharply somewhere in the distance as Rilla stepped outside. The air smelled fresh and damp, with a chill behind it which suggested winter was on the way. In contrast to New England, the trees here were already half-naked, the ground carpeted with a layer of fallen leaves.

There was that barking again – what was a dog doing down here? It must be one of the Fraser pets. Maybe one of the girls was out walking. Rilla peered around, looking to see if she could see anything – but no. It was silent once more, save for the sound of some birds in the trees that surrounded the cottage. A moment later, she thought she heard a whine. This was ridiculous – she was clearly hallucinating with tiredness. Shaking her head, she wandered across the yard to explore.

When her dad had first rented Applemore Cottage – or the Lodge House, as the family called it – the outbuildings had been in use. The gamekeeper kept some of his dogs in the old stone kennel, and she'd loved helping to mix up their feed when he arrived early in the mornings from his cottage up the lane. He was long retired now, and the cottage was one of Charlotte's pretty, cosy little holiday lets. The kennels stood empty, with only a battered old yard broom and a bucket standing in one corner beside a neat stack of metal dog bowls to show they'd ever been in use. If she stood for a moment, she could almost imagine the sound of Sally and the Fraser sisters playing hide-and-seek. George, the old estate manager, had always been to and fro with the cows in those days – but they were gone, too. The dairy windows were opaque with dust and age, and the door was jammed shut. But the carriage house was open – the door lay ajar. For a moment, Rilla fancied she could hear the ghost of one of the old gundogs giving a tiny whine – or was it real?

She looked around the yard, trying to work out where it was coming from – it seemed to be behind one of the old outhouse doors. Tugging at the metal handle, she pulled it open and a scruffy-looking brown and white spaniel hurtled out, looking relieved. It must be one of the Fraser dogs from Applemore House, she was almost certain – although they'd looked a lot more sleek and domesticated than this one, but perhaps it had been off shooting or whatever it was Lachlan did with them.

She knelt down, reaching out a hand gently. 'Hello,' she said.

The dog bounced up to her, tail held high, and sniffed her hand, then ran a circle around the yard and disappeared out of sight. Perhaps they were allowed to run around freely on the estate? She frowned, looking around again.

Anyway, where was she? She'd been investigating the outbuildings...

She pulled open the double stable door that looked directly across into the kitchen window. As a girl, she'd spent hours daydreaming about one day having her own pony living there, looking out at her as she ate breakfast. She'd loved having her own pony in Edinburgh, and her heart had broken the day her mother sold him. Why she'd decided it would be less painful for him to just go 'without protracted goodbyes, darling – he's getting too small for you anyway' was utterly beyond Rilla. For months afterwards, she'd had nightmares about him being sold to someone awful who'd treated him badly, until they bumped into the woman who owned the stables where he was kept, who happily told her that he was living the life of luxury on a sheep farm on the Pentland Hills. It had been cold comfort. Rilla hadn't ever really forgiven her mother for that.

She shook her head, as if to chase away the memory and stepped inside the stables. It was a long time since a horse had set foot (or hoof) in the place. Like everything else in Applemore, the paint was peeling and the overall impression was of faded grandeur. The huge wooden hayrack at the far end of the stable had been stuffed with old cattle feed bags. Spiders had made the place their own, festooning the place with web upon web which were choked up with dust and grime. It must be a weird thing to inherit a place like this. She wondered what Lachlan felt about the responsibility of it all. She looked inside the second of the three stables, where there was a jumble of stuff which seemed to be crammed in as if someone had been playing Jenga with farm machinery. It didn't look like any of it belonged to her dad, so she felt like it was probably safe enough to close the door and leave that problem to the Frasers.

The spaniel reappeared, tail wagging furiously, and started barking at the carriage house – the huge, arch-shaped door wide and tall enough to allow a horse and driver in. Rilla pulled at the big metal handle and it swung open easily. At least one door around here opens easily, she thought, shaking her head with wry amusement, thinking about how cross she'd been when she thought she was locked out of the cottage. Whoever it was that had given her the key must have thought her incredibly rude. Given the size of Applemore village, she assumed that at some point she'd bump into him again and be able to apologise. A moment later, she almost jumped out of her skin.

'Found you!' said a voice, triumphantly. It took a

moment for her eyes to adjust to the gloom, and when she did, she realised what she could see was the outline of a tall, broad-shouldered man. There was a small, subdued bark from the scruffy spaniel, who was now wriggling in his arms.

'Um, hello?' Rilla looked to the side of the door, hoping there might be a light switch. She flicked it on, but nothing happened. A moment later the fluorescent light flickered several times, then came to life.

'Hi.' The man looped a slip-lead around the dog's neck and put him down, giving him a warning finger. 'Don't you move.'

Talk of the devil, Rilla thought. It was *him* again. She tucked her hair behind her ears and resolved to make up for her previous rudeness.

'What on earth are you doing?' He looked at her hair with frank amusement.

Rilla put a hand to her head, coming away with a dusty clump of cobwebs.

'What am I doing? I'm sorting out my dad's things.' She looked at the dog, who was clearly very interested in the conversation, watching them both, his tongue lolling.

'I'm not sure you should be in here…' He indicated the huge, battered old tractor which looked like it hadn't moved for about twenty years. 'There's some pretty lethal stuff, and it's not exactly safe.'

Rilla bristled slightly. 'I'm not sure *you* should be in here,' she said, crisply, 'but here we are.' So much for apologising for being frosty.

Annoyingly, he looked at her with an expression she couldn't place at all. 'You don't think?'

She put her hands on her hips and raised an eyebrow. 'I think you'll find it's *my* house,' Rilla began, and then her voice tailed away slightly. 'I mean, it's my dad's place, but his lease doesn't run out for three months and…' She was babbling, she realised, and it wasn't exactly helping with the air of authority she was trying to convey.

A moment later, he surprised her by stepping forward, looking at her very directly – so she could see his dark chocolate brown eyes, which were fringed with incredibly long lashes, and the tan of his skin which almost hid a smattering of freckles which made him look younger than she'd thought at first and reminded her of—

'Lachlan Fraser.' She put her palm to her forehead, laughing.

'Rilla Clark.' He looked at her, shaking his head. 'Do I really look that different?'

'You've got a…' she motioned to his face, waving a hand in a vague sort of way. 'You didn't have a beard the last time I saw you.'

'This is true.' He rubbed it thoughtfully. 'I had no idea it was such an effective disguise.'

'I was tired,' she said, feeling suddenly shy. He was – she had to admit, despite the fact that he was very possibly trespassing on her father's property – or was she trespassing on his? – very handsome indeed. Which was slightly inconvenient, given the circumstances.

A split second later, he extended his hand and gave a broad smile. 'I'm not actually sure if I'm supposed to shake your hand or hug you at this point.'

She took his hand and he looked at her for a moment, then wrapped an arm around her shoulder. It felt nice. Better than nice, if she was honest. Her face was pressed against the prickly wool of his sweater and he smelled of freshly cut wood and something faintly citrusy. She stepped back, looking at the grown-up version of the boy she'd once had an enormous crush on.

'It's nice to see you back after all this time.' He smiled, showing good teeth.

Rilla felt a vaguely familiar sense of something which she most definitely did not have time for. He was – it had to be said– really very cute indeed.

The last time she'd seen him, he'd been the Fraser sisters' grown-up, always slightly aloof older brother. She'd had a secret teenage crush on him, which she'd put to one side when they'd left the estate for the last time. From time to time, she'd wondered what he was up to and where he was now, but that was years ago. But now here he was, considerably taller, an awfully lot more handsome, and looking at her with the confidence that came with being the owner of an entire estate and a castle, to boot.

She gazed at him for a moment, realigning her memory of the tall, gangly teenager she'd known. He'd filled out, and was standing there looking calm and confident, which was about as far removed from how she felt as humanly possible. She felt derailed.

'I'm sorry I was rude the other day. I was jet-lagged to the point of total brain death. Still am, actually. Sorry.' She could feel herself going pink.

'You haven't changed.' He lifted an eyebrow slightly, mocking her. Did he mean that in a good way? Why did she care?

'You have.' Last time she'd seen him, he'd been a boy. The person towering over her, looking very much in control of the situation, was definitely a man. A man with a runaway – and extremely scruffy – dog.

'So who is this?' Rilla leant down to pat the dog and try to gather herself, aware she was probably going pink – she always did at the wrong moment, and this was definitely not a moment for being overwhelmed by emotions. Even unexpectedly lustful ones. *Especially* unexpectedly lustful ones, she told herself, focusing instead on a tangle of fur and goosegrass on the spaniel's ear. He definitely needed a good grooming. She looked up at Lachlan.

'Ah.' He looked slightly confused and frowned down at the dog. 'I don't have an answer to that just yet.'

'He's an international dog of mystery?'

'No name, no pack drill.'

'If he tells us, he'll have to kill us?'

'Pretty much.'

'Right.' Rilla straightened up. 'You've got a dog with no name?'

'I have two dogs with perfectly good names – you must've met them the other day when you were at the house?'

'Martha and Mabel,' Rilla nodded. 'This isn't one of them.'

'I should think not,' said Lachlan, indignantly. 'I'd be pretty bloody ashamed if one of mine looked like this lad here. No, this is… well, this is mystery dog. I sort of happened upon him this lunchtime.'

'He doesn't belong to anyone?' Rilla's heart melted. She knelt down on the ground, oblivious to the dust and dirt, and petted him some more. He rolled over, inviting her to scratch his belly, and squirmed blissfully when she did. 'How could anyone abandon a dog like this? Or any dog, for that matter?'

'I dunno,' Lachlan said, shaking his head. 'He's a lovely boy, aren't you? But he's not microchipped, there's no record of him on the missing dog register, and we've drawn a blank at the vet surgery. So I said I'd take him home. Trouble is, Martha and Mabel have very much got their paws under the table – they were my dad's dogs, and they're not going to be wildly keen on sharing their bed with this ruffian.'

Mystery dog nudged at Rilla's hand, encouraging her to carry on stroking the soft – extremely filthy – ruffle of fur on his chest.

'I could take him,' Rilla heard herself saying.

'Really?' Lachlan knelt down to join her on the floor. Mystery dog looked extremely pleased with himself and wagged his tail vigorously.

'I mean just to foster him. If you like?' She tried to sound casual.

'You'd be doing me a massive favour. How long are you here for, though?'

'Well,' she felt awkward all of a sudden, remembering that all of this belonged to Lachlan. 'Dad's lease expires on the first of January.'

'Three months.' Lachlan nodded, as if he'd just remembered something. 'Of course.'

'I think he approves of the idea, anyway.' Lachlan looked down at the dog.

'I've always wanted a dog,' Rilla said, as the spaniel climbed into her lap and gave a gusty sigh before closing his eyes and allowing her to continue petting him.

'Well, this would appear to be your moment,' Lachlan replied, getting up. He reached a hand down to help her up.

CHAPTER 7

Rilla stood up. For a moment she kept hold of his hand and he looked at her, thinking how much the seventeen-year-old Lachlan would have relished this moment. She somehow managed to make being covered from head to toe in dust and cobwebs look cute – even though she was filthy, her green eyes sparkled in a face which was as freckled and pretty as he remembered after all this time. She had a smudge of dust on her nose, and he longed to reach out and brush it off, but… she'd let go of his hand and was looking down at the untidy spaniel with an expression he could only dream of.

'Right then,' he began, collecting himself. 'First things first—' He was about to say that they needed to sort out a dog bed, some bowls, dog food and a lead.

'I can't decide,' Rilla said, frowning at him. She wrinkled her nose and then rubbed it so the errant smudge disappeared. 'George? Herbie?'

The dog wagged his tail.

'Hugo.'

He wagged again.

'Hugh?'

He jumped up, putting his paws on Rilla's arm and carried on wagging.

'I think it's a yes for Hugh,' Rilla said, rubbing the fluff on the top of his forehead.

'Hugh, the spaniel.' Lachlan shook his head and laughed. 'That's quite a name. He'd better live up to it.'

'I'm sure you will, won't you, Hugh?'

With that agreed, Rilla acknowledged that there were some other slightly more pressing details that they needed to attend to besides his name.

'I'll nip back to the house and get some bits,' Lachlan offered. 'I'd only just made it out of the Land Rover when he hotfooted it down here. I'd keep him on a tight leash until he gets to know you a bit better – that way, he won't exit stage left the moment your back's turned.'

Rilla looked at Hugh adoringly. 'He's not going anywhere, are you?'

Hugh looked back at her, matching her expression. The only difference was that his tongue was lolling in a slightly gormless fashion and Rilla's was most definitely not. Lachlan suppressed a chuckle.

'Okay, give me half an hour to get back to the house, get the stuff sorted and head back.'

'I could take you in the car if you like?' Rilla pointed to the car that was parked to one side of the cottage.

He'd forgotten that Charlotte – being Charlotte – had organised that for her the other day.

Rilla drove them back to Applemore House, Hugh taking up quite a lot of space in the front footwell. He didn't take his eyes off his new foster parent. It seemed that Rilla was a bit of a hit with him, too. Lachlan opened the window and Hugh hung his head out, ears flapping in the wind.

'I was sorry to hear about your dad,' Rilla said, as she made her way carefully up the drive, manoeuvring her way between potholes.

Lachlan looked out with a critical eye at the grounds. There was a gate hanging off its hinges over there – that would need to be sorted. There was a tenant farmer who rented the land for his sheep, in exchange for keeping an eye on the perimeter. He made a mental note to give him a ring when he got back.

'And yours,' he said in return, turning his thoughts back to their fathers. 'I liked David a lot.'

'Me too. It's been strange clearing out all his things. Sad and nice at the same time?'

He nodded. 'I wish I could do the same, but it'd take more than a skip.' As he spoke, the house came into view.

'It's so pretty, though,' Rilla said, pulling the car up to a stop on the sweep of front drive.

'Pretty awful,' Lachlan joked. She looked at him with surprise. 'I don't mean it. Well, I do – well – it's complicated.'

'I get it.' She dropped a hand onto his knee for a brief moment. 'It's a pretty big undertaking, being responsible for a place like this. I've never been much good at staying in one place for long, so I think if I was you I'd be having a complete meltdown at the prospect.'

'That's a pretty good summary of how I'm feeling.'

Rilla waited outside in the car as he nipped in to pick up the essentials she'd need for Hugh. Both of his spaniels were making their feelings about an interloper very clear, barking and growling at the top of their voices. The irony was that there was absolutely no way they'd do anything to Hugh, but given that he was a flight risk, it wasn't worth taking any chances.

Lachlan scooped up enough dried food to keep Hugh going for a few days, found a spare slip lead and an old leather collar, and collected a couple of metal bowls from the cupboard under the sink in the boot room, where pretty much anything could be found. There was a slight rustling as he pulled them out – he peered down, catching a fleeting glimpse of a tiny brown mouse disappearing out of sight. He couldn't help but laugh.

He was still smiling when we went back outside.

'You look cheerful,' Rilla said, looking at him questioningly. 'Good news?'

'Hardly. No, just laughing at the fact that I've just discovered a mouse nest in the boot room. It's one thing after another with this place.'

'D'you mind if I follow you back down in the Land Rover? There's something I wanted to check in the outbuildings.' For some reason he didn't want to tell Rilla he was making plans to sell Applemore. 'Want to see if something I remember is still there.'

'Of course' She smiled at him, her dimples making her look even prettier than she already did.

God, what a moron he was… now he looked like some sort of lovelorn teenager, following her around. He shook his head faintly.

'No problem,' she said, cheerfully. 'It's nice to have the company, actually.'

'If you fancy it,' he said, 'we could take Hugh for a bit

of a wander on the way back. I need to prop up a fallen gate before the farmer sorts it.' (There – he'd kill two birds with one stone.) 'And it might help him get his bearings a bit.'

'Good thinking.' Rilla glanced at the dog, who was curled up on the back seat of the car.

Hugh seemed delighted to have two people exclusively to himself. He trotted along on the lead, plumy tail wagging cheerfully, nose down and sniffing the delicious and unfamiliar scents of the Applemore Estate. Lachlan walked alongside Rilla, glancing at her in profile. She had yawned several times already.

'You look like you could do with a massive sleep.'

'I need to try to hold off until bedtime. Fresh air will help. Anyway, you can tell me what you've been up to for the last eighteen years.'

'Can't believe it's been that long, can you?'

She shook her head. 'And I still don't feel like a proper grown-up.'

'I don't think we ever will. Your dad once told me that he'd given up waiting for it to happen.'

Her face clouded over as they paused by the gate, waiting as he tied it up with some twine he had in the pocket of his jacket.

'Sorry,' he said, feeling awkward. 'I didn't mean to make you feel sad.'

She shook her head. 'It's okay. You know. I mean, it's shitty, but it's just one of those things. He wouldn't want me moping. Nor would yours, I imagine.'

Lachlan stepped out of the way to let Rilla and Hugh over the little turnstile. 'He wouldn't, no. He didn't have a lot of time for sentimentality. Well, he said that, but he was very attached to this place.' He waved an arm in the general direction of the house and grounds.

'It must've been hard, bringing you four up by himself, don't you think? D'you think he ever wanted to just jack it all in and sell?' Rilla had always had a knack of asking the questions other people held back on.

He frowned slightly. 'Possibly? He'd never have admitted as much to any of us, though. He was all about duty and doing the right thing by the Fraser name, and all that stuff.'

'D'you think that's why he never remarried?'

There she was again.

'I think he was married to this place.' And in one brief moment, Rilla had got to the heart of his problem with Applemore. 'There wasn't room for our mother – which is why she left, I think.'

'Sad, isn't it?' Rilla stepped up onto a bank as the path to the loch narrowed. Hugh hopped up behind her, his eyes not moving from her for a second. He was clearly completely besotted already. Join the club, Lachlan thought, suppressing a smile.

It was weird how comfortable it felt being with her, after all this time. Like stepping back into a friendship he'd missed more than he realised – but with the added bonus of the self-confidence that came with age. The diffident, shy teenage Lachlan would have been tongue-tied and awkward.

'At least our dads had each other,' she continued, pausing to turn and look at him. She put one hand on the low branch of a silver birch and shaded her eyes against the sun which had appeared from behind a cloud with the other. 'I'm glad they did, especially after everything.'

'He missed you and Sally a lot.' David had been a good man – kind and friendly, happy to help out with anything that needed doing in the village. Lachlan had always suspected that he kept himself as busy as he did to keep his mind off the loss of his daughters. 'But he always said it wasn't your choice that you stopped coming.'

'It wasn't.' Rilla's expression was thoughtful.

With silent agreement, they started walking again. The path sloped down between rocks, the pale silver-brown purses of the gorse bushes rattling their seeds as they brushed past them. He was cursing himself for being so thoughtless – why on earth did he think it was a good idea to take her down here of all places?

Rilla paused as the little loch came into sight.

'Oh, it's just as beautiful as I remembered. More so.' She sighed, happily. 'It's funny, this is the first time I've been to the loch since the accident.'

'I'm sorry, I wasn't thinking. It wasn't exactly tactful of me to bring you down here.'

'Unlike my mother,' Rilla said, and there was a slight edge to her voice, 'I don't bear a grudge. Nor do I blame anyone for what happened. We were messing about on a home-made raft, and Sally fell in and broke her leg.'

'She nearly drowned.' The village rumour mill had been rife for months afterwards, particularly after it was clear that David's always-slightly-frosty ex-wife had no intention of letting the girls come back to Applemore.

'It could have been any of us. Would you trade the adventures we had as teenagers for a risk-free existence sitting playing computer games?'

He shook his head, laughing. 'No chance.'

'Well, there you are. You know, Sally doesn't have any hard feelings about it either.'

'I was told she might lose her leg.' Village gossip had a lot to answer for. David, who kept himself to himself when it came to the girls, never corrected anyone. Lachlan had seen him in action on many occasions, smiling quietly to himself. '*Let them think what they want,*' he'd said, chuckling quietly. '*I know the truth. And, in time, the girls will be free to make their own choices.*'

Rilla raised an eyebrow. 'You were? Well, whoever said that had it seriously wrong. She didn't. She's got a bit of a limp, which is more pronounced when she's tired. That's as far as it goes.' Her tone was quite determined, and the snap of her green eyes and the expression on her face made it clear that she'd had this conversation many times before.

'Your dad was a good man.'

'I know. And, most importantly, he knew I knew that.' She sounded incredibly level-headed – the fiery Rilla who'd been as quick to laugh as she was to lose her temper and fight with her younger sister had clearly got herself completely sorted in the years since they'd seen each other last. He was quietly impressed.

'He was always telling Dad about your travels. It made me quite jealous – you've been all over the place.' Lachlan stopped as they reached the edge of the loch, and watched as Rilla sat down on one of the wide, flat rocks they'd sunbathed and picnicked on so many times as teenagers. She loosened the slip lead, letting Hugh off. Lachlan opened his mouth to warn her that he was liable to shoot off at a hundred miles an hour but closed it again as Hugh sat down beside her on the rock, leaning against her slightly, and didn't move a muscle.

'I think my little foster companion and I are going to get on just fine, don't you?' She beamed at Hugh, who wagged his tail back. 'So what have you been up to in my absence?' Rilla poked her tongue out slightly, teasing him. 'Besides missing me, of course.'

He looked away briefly. God, she had absolutely no idea the effect she had on him. After all this time, the flame he'd had burning for her was clearly in no danger of burning out. It was nice to think for a moment that she might be flirting with him, but... he shook himself. This was ridiculous. He'd had countless girlfriends back in Edinburgh – one or two of them serious. He'd contemplated asking one of them – Anna – to marry him, but realised that there was no way he'd lumber someone else with the massive white elephant that was Applemore, nor was he going to subject himself – or the perfectly nice Anna – to the slow disintegration of a relationship that was par for the course as owner of the Applemore estate, if his father and his grandfather before him had been anything to go by. He'd rather stay single. Or – he cast an eye across the loch, imagining Felix taking drone shots and marketing them to enthusiastic foreign buyers – sell the place, and take his chances somewhere else.

'I've got a brewery down in Edinburgh with a friend of mine – Gus. He's running it at the moment single-handed while I work out what's happening up here.'

'What kind of brewery?'

'Craft beers – American-style IPAs, that sort of thing. It's fun to do – well, the brewing side of it is – and we've managed to make a bit of a go of it. It pays the bills,' he said, aware he was playing it down. Hedgepig was actually doing surprisingly well – their little ten-barrel brewery was struggling to keep up with demand, and they were getting a good reputation on the various beer review sites by which companies lived or died.

'I was hoping you might say gin,' Rilla smiled.

'Funny you should say that.' He'd been contemplating it for a while – there was a spring up here on the estate where they got all their water, and it had struck him that if they could get organised with some of the fruit and flowers that Beth grew in the big walled garden, there was definitely something there… or there would be, he reminded himself, if he wasn't planning on selling.

'Have you got something up your sleeve?' Rilla looked interested. She picked up a flat stone and tossed it into the water. Hugh's floppy ears lifted slightly and a second later he'd thrown himself in after it, sploshing in an ungainly manner in the direction of where it had landed.

Lachlan made an indecisive, weighing-things-up motion with his hand. 'It's a possibility.'

'So Charlotte said you're up here for the foreseeable? That's a big change from Edinburgh.'

'You're not joking. Yeah, I've got to try to get this place into some sort of order.'

'If you're stuck for help,' Rilla said, 'I'm here until January. I can always give you a hand. It'll stop me getting into mischief.'

'You've got Hugh to do that,' he replied, realising as he did so that he sounded like he was putting her off. 'Seriously though, I'd love that. You might even be able to inspire Polly to work out what she wants to do with her life.'

'I like Polly,' Rilla said, loyally. 'She's sweet.'

'Oh I love her to bits,' he agreed, 'but since Dad died she's spent the last few months floating about like a spare part. She needs a project.'

'Renovating Applemore's enough to be going on with, I would have thought? It's going to take more than just you to get it into some sort of order.' Rilla put a hand to her mouth, her cheeks flushing pink. 'I mean – not that it's a state or anything, but…'

He liked that she hadn't lost her lack of filter over the

years. 'It is a state,' he agreed, laughing. He stood up, reaching his hand down to hers for the second time. 'But it'll be a hell of a lot more fun not doing it on my own.'

'Deal,' said Rilla, shaking his hand with a mock-serious expression. 'You're on.'

CHAPTER 8

The next week flew past. Lachlan and Polly were making lists of things that had to be done in the big house. Rilla spent her time cleaning the cottage, walking Hugh around the estate, and driving back and forth to the charity shop in the big town ten miles away, dropping off the black sacks full of her dad's things. It was strangely therapeutic – the woman in the shop was kind and sympathetic, not minding when Rilla had a little weep as she handed over the final bag of clothes and a box of his old books. 'Happens all the time, dear,' she said, passing Rilla a paper hanky and patting her on the shoulder. 'But I'm sure you'll be glad to know you're making money for a good cause.'

'I am,' Rilla had nodded, slightly damply. She'd spent some time in Africa doing volunteer work when she'd first qualified as an English teacher, and she was quite certain that her dad would have been delighted to know that the sale of his stuff was going to make a difference. She'd squared her shoulders and headed off for a restoring cup of coffee and a cake in the little café next door, which didn't mind one bit that Hugh sat under her chair, panting and grinning at passers-by.

She got home one afternoon – tired and cold, because the October weather had suddenly shifted and it was feeling distinctly wintry outside – from a walk with Hugh. He'd proved himself far more reliable than Lachlan had expected – walking happily off the lead, scampering ahead of her to investigate interesting smells but always returning, tail wagging, as soon as she called him (with a pocket full of delicious treats). She was glad to see Polly waiting in the little courtyard behind the cottage.

'Lachlan's been over in Inverness getting a load of stuff for the house renovations, and I've been making a list. D'you fancy coming over so we can have some late lunch and I can tell you my amazing plans to transform the house?'

'I'd love to.' Polly's open-hearted enthusiasm was catching. 'I need to bring Hugh with me though – I don't know what he'd do if I left him here in the cottage.'

'Course!' Polly rubbed his head in greeting. 'Don't you look smart? He looks like he's been poshed up a bit?'

'He's been to the groomers.'

'Ah, Kerry's place?'

Rilla nodded. Lachlan had popped by with the number, saying it was where the family had always taken theirs for a tidy-up, and she'd found her way to a tiny cottage just outside the village where a converted garage had been transformed into an all-mod-cons canine beauty salon. Hugh had howled the place down when she'd left, but when she'd returned a couple of hours later – having popped into the Applemore Hotel to try some of the famous steak pie that Lachlan insisted was out of this world (it was) – he'd been his usual tail-wagging, tongue-lolling happy self. Only a lot cleaner, completely free of mats and smelling like lavender. That had lasted about a day, until he'd leapt into the loch on a walk in hot pursuit of a stick Polly had thrown. Now he still looked clean, but he smelled slightly musty, as if he'd been left out to dry on a damp day. Rilla knew perfectly well that after only a week he'd stolen her heart completely and was flatly refusing to think about how she would feel if either his owner turned up, or she had to hand him back over to the dog rescue kennels.

Up at the house, the moment they opened the door, Rilla was hit with the delicious scent of freshly baked bread.

'Oh that is amazing,' she said, her mouth watering instantly. She'd been existing on a pretty scrappy diet of things on toast and a lot of apples and cheese – along with gallons of hot tea – since she got to the cottage.

'Get yourself a brother that makes Tuscan bean soup and fresh sourdough,' Polly said, reaching across the table to pinch a piece of the bread crust.

'Hands off,' admonished Lachlan, laughing. 'Hi,' he said, looking up at Rilla.

She had no idea how he managed to make a black T-shirt streaked with flour look sexy, but – she shook herself. She'd spent the last few days trying not to think about the fact that her teenage crush on Lachlan had grown – as he had – into something rather more adult. He was pottering around in the kitchen in a pair of worn jeans (very nice bottom, she noted, forgetting she wasn't supposed to be noticing) and with a dish towel tossed over one shoulder. He had a way of moving that was surprisingly graceful for someone as broad – and well over six feet tall – as he was.

'This is really lovely of you,' she began, hoping he hadn't noticed the huge growl her stomach made, 'but I've got Hugh in the car and I'm not sure what to do about these two?'

She motioned to Lachlan's two spaniels, who were curled up in a heap of liver and white spots on a blanket beside the Aga.

'I've warned them they've to be polite to guests,' Lachlan laughed. 'And if they're not, I'll banish them to the library. Bring him in.'

There was a cacophony of barking as Rilla opened the kitchen door a moment later, with Hugh in tow. Both spaniels dashed towards Hugh, looking at him with suspicion for a moment or two. Hugh took one look at them and decided the best course of action was to roll over and pretend to be invisible. At this, both Mabel and Martha stopped barking and sniffed him, tails wagging in cautious greeting. A few moments later, they were all milling about quite happily, looking perfectly content.

Rilla sat down on the edge of the big sagging armchair that stood to one side of the Aga and Hugh took her lead, collapsing at her feet with a gusty sigh.

'Well, that seems to be that sorted.' Lachlan took some plates out of the bottom oven where they'd been warming. 'Now, Polly has a plan of action. If you're thinking you have any second thoughts about getting stuck in to help, now's the time to exit stage left at speed.'

'Shut up,' Polly said, laughing and flicking her brother with the dish towel from his shoulder.

They ate lunch – which was delicious – and Polly explained that she and Lachlan had worked out there were levels of work to be done.

'There's your essential "this place leaks" maintenance,' she said, through a mouthful of sourdough, 'and then there's stuff that would be nice to get sorted.'

'And then there's "completely unrealistic pie-in-the-sky plans from Polly who thinks we've won the lottery in secret",' Lachlan continued, laughing. 'I'll take you for a wander and you can see for yourself.'

Polly volunteered to get on with clearing up the kitchen, and Lachlan led on.

'If we start at the top – that's where the worst of the leaks are, obviously – I'll show you what we're looking at. And then you can tell me this is insane and we should torch the place and collect the insurance money.'

'You don't sound convinced by this at all,' Rilla said, as they climbed the two flights of stairs that led up to the second floor. The galleried landings were beautiful, but the red-painted walls had blooms of dark mould on them. 'That's just damp, isn't it? If it's dried out, that'll go.'

'You sound like Poll.' Lachlan paused and poked at the wall. 'I dunno, really.'

They carried on up the stairs to the top floor and looked down at the wide entrance hall below. The rug – moth-eaten and threadbare up close – looked beautiful from that height, the ornate patterns matching the rich shades of the décor.

'I think the secret is to get the place looking half decent and then...' He stopped and bit a thumbnail, looking thoughtful. Rilla wanted to push him, suspecting what he was thinking, but she stayed quiet, and Lachlan left it unsaid.

On the second floor – which she hadn't ever seen when they'd last been there as teenagers – there was a huge, empty room with a tired-looking grey rocking horse in one corner and a fireplace blocked up with a piece of plywood. One wall still had an ancient blackboard fastened to it, and there was a wooden abacus sitting on the mantlepiece.

'This is a bit spooky, don't you think? Like a horror film.'

Lachlan nodded. 'Used to give me the creeps when I was younger. It's the sort of place you half expect to come to life at night. I always thought we'd hear the sound of little children playing and the tune from a music box.'

Rilla shuddered, wrapping her arms around herself. 'Don't say that.'

Lachlan laughed. 'If it helps, I didn't hear any of that even once in the whole time we were here.'

'That helps a bit.' She was still glad to leave the room behind.

There were a series of tiny attic rooms down a corridor – 'Servants' rooms,' Lachlan explained, looking slightly uncomfortable. 'Not that we ever had any growing up,' he added.

'I remember.' Rilla could also remember her surprise at discovering Lachlan's dad – the gruff but affable Hector Fraser – vacuuming the rug in the scruffy, cosy sitting room. 'I did bump into Joan. She was really sweet and gave me a bed for the night when I got here. She helped with clearing up as well – I wanted to say thank you to her for being so lovely.'

'She's an angel,' Lachlan agreed. 'If we hadn't had her as housekeeper god knows what state this place would have been in.'

Rilla put a hand on the silky oak of the banister, worn after years of use, and looked around thoughtfully. 'A bit of paint will help,' she suggested.

Lachlan looked at her and, for a moment, neither of them said anything. Then – faced with the enormity of the task ahead – they both burst into gales of laughter.

'You don't need to do this,' Lachlan said once again,

after they'd poked around in one of the dilapidated old bathrooms.

Rilla was touched by how genuinely grateful he was. But it was pretty clear from the conversation they'd had over lunch that the family was struggling – Polly had let slip that they had a six-figure inheritance tax bill to pay – and it wasn't as if she had anything else to do with her time.

'I like projects,' she said, pulling at the old-fashioned metal chain of the loo. It came away in her hand. 'Oops.'

'On second thoughts,' Lachlan said, laughing.

Rilla looked out of the bathroom window. The view stretched over the walled kitchen garden – where Beth could be seen, digging over a flower bed in a pair of dungarees. Her baby twins were fast asleep in the double pushchair on the gravel path beside her. She had her hair tied out of the way with a headscarf – she could quite easily have been a land girl from during the Second World War.

Turning to look at Lachlan, Rilla smiled. 'I'm serious. Give me a paintbrush and I'll be quite happy. It'll keep me out of mischief. I've got nothing to do until I start my new contract in Paris, anyway.'

'Well,' Lachlan fixed her with his chocolate brown eyes, 'I really appreciate it. Thanks, Rilla.'

There was something about that deep, serious voice that made the hairs on her arms stand up – and when he said her name, well, that made the hairs *on the hairs* on her arms stand up.

She shook herself, mentally, as he said, 'After you,' and motioned for her to go first down the stairs. If she was going to be spending all her time hanging out at Applemore, she was going to need to get a serious grip on herself. Lachlan Fraser was extremely handsome, extremely sweet, and extremely out of bounds.

It didn't help that he kept finding excuses to wander down to the cottage. The next day, Rilla was messing about in the yard with Hugh, throwing a tennis ball for him to catch, when Lachlan appeared looking ridiculously handsome in jeans and a dark blue sweater. The beard, which he'd shaved off the week before, was making a reappearance. The dark stubble only served to emphasise the strong jawline and good cheekbones.

'Did you ever finish looking through the outbuildings for your dad's stuff?'

Rilla put a hand to her mouth. 'Oh god, no. Sorry.' The recycling company had come back the day before, swinging the heavy metal skip onto the back of the truck on thick iron chains. 'If there's anything in there, I can always take it to the tip or something.'

Lachlan started to laugh. 'That's not what I was thinking.' He tipped his head in the direction of one of the bigger outbuildings which lay to the side of the courtyard. 'Did you look in here?'

She shook her head. 'Since Hugh arrived, I've been pretty much taken up with being a dog foster parent.'

'I thought you mustn't have seen it.' Lachlan beckoned for her to follow him. 'You need to have a look.'

He pushed open the door and stepped inside, switching on the light which flickered for a second before illuminating the big workshop. In the middle of the building, a big, white van was parked.

'It's real!' Rilla gasped and stepped forward, putting her hand on the bonnet as if she was greeting an old friend. 'I didn't realise it was actually a thing.'

'I didn't know you knew about it.' Lachlan looked pleased. He pulled open the side door, sliding it back to reveal the plans her father had made come to life, at least in part.

Where her dad had imagined a kitchen, there was still just a wooden carcass, but the bed frame was there, and the table where he'd sketched a chair which looked out of the sliding door and onto... Where had he planned to go? Rilla felt a pang of sadness for the places he'd never visit.

'Last time I saw your dad, he was telling me he was determined to get better so he could go off round France in the summer.'

Well, that was one. So, he'd planned to go to France. Rilla felt a lump rising in her throat and swallowed it back. 'Really?'

'It's not completely finished, but it wouldn't take much.'

Rilla stepped inside the camper van, looking around. There was a little skylight in the wooden panelled roof which opened with a twist of the handle. The walls were clad with pale pine, and a shelf hung – perfectly neat, which was typical of her dad's workmanship – above what would be the little gallery kitchen space. There was even a tiny combined gas hob with a sink, which was so cute it was ridiculous. It was a whole world, neatly packaged into the back of a van. If the doors were closed, you'd never know what was inside. It was easy to see how he'd taken his beautifully drawn plans and executed them. He'd always had an amazing ability to visualise things and just create them. It was a very practical sort of magic.

'You could finish it off.'

'Me?' Rilla looked at him dubiously. 'I'm not exactly the world's best at DIY.'

Even as she said that, she felt a thrill of excitement at the thought. Imagine if she could get the van finished and head off to Paris in her own little travelling house. She could go wherever she wanted then – anywhere her wheels could take her. Her heart thudded and she looked at Lachlan for a moment. He had an odd expression on his face, which cleared after a second. He patted the roof of the van.

'I could help.'

'Really?'

'If you'd like. I mean, you offered to help with the house, so it seems a fair deal.'

'I wasn't saying I was going to rescind my offer of help and just disappear into a workshop like Dad,' she said, laughing at the idea of it. Come to think of it, though, it was a relief that she'd decided at the last minute to keep a hold of his old overalls. They'd come in handy when she was doing whatever needed to be done.

'Look, we're both stuck up here for the next few months. You're here until after Christmas. It'd stop me going out of my mind with boredom, and you might like a bit of company if you're stuck here on your own. When we get bored painting the house, we can come down here and you can show me your prowess with the power tools.'

'I wouldn't get too excited,' Rilla said, eyeing the workbench that lined the wall of the building. 'I mean, Dad let us mess about with a saw and stuff, but I haven't a clue where to start when it comes to making cupboard doors and things like that.' She was already looking at the van, trying to work out what needed to be done.

'I think you're probably doing yourself down.' Lachlan looked at her for a moment. 'I think you can do pretty much anything you put your mind to.'

Rilla felt her heart thudding against her chest again and told herself it was just excitement at the prospect of turning her dad's plans into reality.

'I've got the plans,' she said, climbing down from the van. 'Hang on, I'll go and get them.'

She dashed across the courtyard, leaving Lachlan waiting. Hugh, sensing excitement, hurtled into the cottage with her and grabbed a tennis ball, dropping it at her feet as she flicked through the pages of her dad's notebook. Thank goodness he'd written such precise plans. She hurried back to Lachlan.

'Here. Look.' Rilla flattened the notebook out on the bed frame and leant over, peering at the drawings. There wasn't much space. Lachlan leant over to look, his arm pressed against hers. She was acutely aware of the heat of his body close to hers. Doing her best to look as if she was focused exclusively on the plans, she dropped her head as if scrutinising them and tried to collect her thoughts. This was ridiculous.

'So we'd need to put doors on these cupboards.' He reached out, pointing to one of the drawings. His wrist was tanned and covered with a tracing of dark hair. For a moment, Rilla imagined how it would feel to lift the finger holding the notebook and trace a line along the back of his hand, just to feel the sensation of her skin on his… 'Rilla?'

She shook her head. 'Sorry, I was just thinking.'

'Doors,' Lachlan continued, 'which aren't as difficult as you'd think – I mean, there are hinges to deal with, but we can do that easily enough. And you need to finish the plumbing, but by the looks of it, David's done most of that.' He straightened up and climbed out of the van, opening the double doors at the back. 'Look, there's your water tank, and the pump, and – well, that's impressive.' He gave a low whistle.

'What is?' Rilla had been standing in the van trying to remind herself that she was thirty-three, not thirteen, and that acting like a swooning teenager was utterly insane. She joined Lachlan at the back of the van. 'Ooh, wow.' It looked incredibly technical and very neat.

'Typical David. He's got all the wiring in place, and the plumbing is pretty much sorted. It looks better than the electrical system in our house.'

'Given the state of Applemore, that's not a huge surprise,' said Rilla, wryly.

'Well no, exactly. So there's nothing here that's too terrifying. I'll leave you to have a look at the plans and then we can have a think about when we can get to work.'

'Thanks.' Rilla looked at him for a second and it struck her. 'Did you come down here for something?'

'Oh.' He rubbed his jaw for a moment, a fleeting look of confusion on his fave. 'Yes – I did.' Lachlan nodded.

'I mean, apart from the pleasure of my company.'

'Obviously.'

'Well?' Rilla laughed and shook her head. 'Are you going to let me in on the secret, or is it classified?'

'Ah,' Lachlan said. 'Well – funnily enough, it was thinking about the outbuildings that made me realise you hadn't mentioned the van. And I was thinking about the outbuildings because I was out walking the dogs earlier and racking my brains trying to think of something to do to bring some money in.'

'Besides selling a kidney, you mean?' She made a joke of it, but she knew – from him, and from Polly – just how worried they were about the massive tax bill, and how they were going to afford the repairs.

'Believe me, I've contemplated it,' he said, ruefully. 'But I had the glimmer of an idea… Come and I'll show you. Or rather I'll try to show you.'

CHAPTER 9

Lachlan was torn between admitting the truth about what he was planning to Rilla – unloading the burden of it onto someone who wasn't caught up in the emotion of Applemore and might actually be able to give him advice – and feeling like such a shit for even considering selling the place, that he couldn't work out what to do.

'This way,' he said, tipping his head in the direction of the old dairy on the other side of the courtyard. Rilla fell into step beside him, Hugh at her heels. 'Years ago, and goodness knows why – he was such a character, and he didn't really have much truck with rules and things – my dad decided he was going to brew his own whisky and save himself a fortune.'

'Ooh.' Rilla looked at him. 'That's *definitely* illegal, though, isn't it?'

'It is if you're doing it unlicensed at home, yes. Very much so.' He glanced at her, smiling without realising he was doing so because her face was such a picture of disapproval and intrigue.

'So what happened?'

'I think he got his knuckles rapped by the local police-man, who basically said he'd turn a blind eye as long as Dad didn't try it again.'

'And did he?'

Lachlan laughed, remembering his dad's face when he'd tried his concoction. It was unspeakably awful and completely undrinkable. 'He did not. It wasn't even fit to make paint thinner, it was so disgusting. He tipped it all down the drain. I suspect he probably killed off half the trout in the loch in the process.'

'So what's this got to do with your plans to make a fortune?'

'Ah.' Lachlan paused for a second with his hand on the door of the outhouse that stood next to the dairy. 'Are you all right with me going in?'

'Why wouldn't I be?'

'I'm just conscious that this is still your dad's place, and I'm wandering around with my big size tens helping myself to whatever.'

'It's your stuff,' Rilla said, shaking her head in amuse-ment. 'I have no desire to rummage through eight billion outhouses and then take a load of old farm equipment in my rucksack when I head off on my travels in the new year.'

'No,' he said, opening the door and fumbling for the light switch. He kept forgetting that – lovely as it was having Rilla here, for a million and one reasons – she wasn't stay-ing. This was a flying visit to put some old memories to rest. Unfortunately, it had brought a whole load of other memo-ries to the surface. He'd found himself thinking about her a lot of the time – while he was walking the dogs and making plans for the house. She just seemed to pop up in his thoughts. It was natural, he told himself firmly, that an old friend (emphasis on the friend) should make him feel like that. That was all.

'What are we looking at?' Rilla peered in at yet another building full of random chaos.

'If my memory serves me right, I think my dad left the copper still and all the bits and pieces down here. He said he wanted it well out of the way because even looking at it reminded him how filthy the end product had been.'

He climbed up onto a pile of wooden fence posts that had been thrown in there out of the way at some point. From his vantage point, he caught a glimpse of something shining dully.

'There you are,' he said, and scrambled across the metal spikes of a harrow and a stack of old furniture. A moment later, he'd uncovered it. 'Found it!'

'Right.' Rilla did a thumbs up motion. 'Now all you have to do is work out how to sell it? Is that the plan? Are they worth lots of money?'

He shook his head and clambered back out.

'Oh my god,' Rilla said, her eyes wide. 'You're not planning on making moonshine and hawking it on the black market, are you?'

He burst out laughing. She was still the same Rilla she'd been all those years before – funny and fanciful, with a keen eye for the ridiculous.

'I am not.' He jumped down from the wood pile and brushed down his jumper, which was covered in cobwebs. 'I'm thinking that Applemore Gin could be the secret.'

Rilla looked interested all of a sudden. 'Do you think you'll need a taste tester?'

'I'm sure I will,' he said, laughing at her enthusiasm.

'Excellent. When will it be ready?'

'Nothing happens fast in the drinks business. I need to

do some research, look at costings, work out if we could have a market for it… then we'd need to wait until next spring when Beth's garden is in full swing, and—'

'Oh,' said Rilla, and her face fell.

He cleared his throat. 'Yeah. Well. Maybe we can send you some to wherever you are by then.'

'That'd be lovely.'

The spell of the moment was broken. Lachlan held the door open for Rilla to make her way back out into the afternoon, where the weather had followed through with its threat of rain and the skies were a plum purple, heavy with a brewing storm.

'I better get back,' he said, reaching down to give Hugh a pat.

'I'll see you tomorrow,' Rilla replied.

'I'm just thinking.' Lachlan put a hand on the bonnet of the Land Rover screwing up his face in thought in an expression that reminded Rilla with a jolt of his younger self. 'I need somewhere that can be scrubbed down and totally hygienic. Right now Applemore is basically damp central, but the outhouses are pretty sound. Can I have a look?'

Rilla made an open-handed gesture. 'It's your estate.' She smiled.

'Yeah, I know, but this is still your dad's place.'

'Didn't stop you earlier when you started climbing around in the outhouses.' She grinned at him.

'Touché. Come on, let's have a look.'

He walked alongside Rilla as they made their way across the yard to the little whitewashed stone building that had been the estate dairy years before. She'd pulled her long hair back into a ponytail and was wrapped in a thick jumper which was so huge that it must have belonged to her dad.

'Here we go.' He looked at her.

She stopped in front of the door, hesitating for a second.

'You go ahead,' he said, and Rilla pushed open the door. When they'd been growing up, there had been a little Applemore herd of Jersey cows who grazed the pasture which wrapped around the edge of the estate and who sheltered under the trees of the wood where they'd played as children. It had been years since he'd been in there, but as Rilla stepped into the empty room, it was clear that it was absolutely perfect for what he had in mind. The reality was there was nowhere up at the big house that would do for what he had planned – he needed to be able to keep the place scrupulously clean and tidy, and there was absolutely no chance of that happening at the house – not least because of the slightly worrying damp which seemed to be blooming on every wall, but also the dogs, and the general chaos that Polly seemed to bring with her. Plus, it would be nice to have somewhere to get away, he told himself, watching as Rilla ran a hand along the cool of the marble worktop. The fact that she'd be right next door was purely coincidence.

The room wasn't big – perhaps sixteen feet square – but there was enough space to set up everything he'd need. Gin was big business at the moment, and small independent distilleries seemed to be making a decent living. If he could get it going as a bit of a side hustle while he was stuck up here trying to get the place sorted, then once he'd sold Applemore – because despite everything he'd told his sisters, that was still the plan lurking at the back of his mind – he could always transport the whole shebang back down to Edinburgh and just take it on board with the brewery.

He felt a fleeting pang of guilt at the thought of breaking up the estate, but shook his head, telling himself if he could manage to get it to a point where he could hand over a decent chunk of money to each sister, he'd feel okay about it. After all, Applemore was just a building. They didn't need a heap of granite and turrets to be a family.

'So, you're going to take over the world of gin and I'm going to figure out how to get this van of Dad's sorted.'

'That's the plan.'

'And then you're going to head off to the Maldives with your millions, and I'm going to travel round Europe.'

'Deal.'

'Okay,' Rilla said, rubbing her hands together. 'We'd better get started.'

CHAPTER 10

Rilla woke early, and sat with a cup of coffee working out from her dad's plans what was left to do to finish off the van conversion. He had pretty much every power tool under the sun in his work shed, all lying in a jumble of wires and cordless batteries on top of the workbench. She'd had a little quiet weep to herself, thinking about him pottering away in there, and then pulled herself together. He'd tell her to stop being so soppy and to get on with it, and so she'd squared her shoulders, looked at his plans and decided to make a list. The first thing she needed, she'd decided, was some screws. There didn't seem to be any left at all – just an empty box. There was a piece of wood which was clearly intended to be the tabletop balanced – slightly cobwebbed and dusty – against the side of the wall. She'd measured it twice to be certain. All she had to do was screw it into place, and work out how to put hinges on the cupboards of the kitchen doors. How hard could it be?

She drove into the village, parking on the harbour and walking along the little lane that led to the row of shops. It was picture-postcard pretty, despite the glowering clouds which hung overhead, threatening to spill over. There was a storm forecast, and she shivered, wishing she'd remembered a coat. She pulled her hands inside the sleeves of her jumper to keep them warm.

'Hello my love.' Someone tapped her on the shoulder and made her jump. It was Joan wearing a pair of jazzy purple-rimmed glasses which matched her purple spotted raincoat. She was dressed for the weather, even if Rilla wasn't. 'I'm awfully sorry, darling. I've been meaning to pop up again and see how you were getting on, but my nephew and his wife turned up unexpectedly – they're doing a driving tour of the west coast – and I haven't had a moment.'

'Don't apologise,' said Rilla, putting a hand on her arm for a moment.

'It's the least I could do. How are you getting on? Getting things sorted? I hear from Polly you've not been hanging about.'

'I was getting organised,' Rilla explained, 'and then I discovered Dad was in the middle of converting an old transit van into a camper—'

'Oh yes,' Joan nodded. 'I had a look at that not long before… well, not that long ago.'

Rilla looked at Joan for a moment, wondering how much she'd known about the plans…

'I had no idea he was planning it.' Rilla felt another pang of guilt, thinking about her dad's life up here, wondering if he was lonely. She should have been here for him.

As if reading Rilla's mind, Joan took a hold of her hand and gave it a motherly squeeze. 'Don't you go feeling bad, my love. Your dad knew how much you loved him.'

'Do you think?'

Joan nodded. 'Without a shadow of a doubt. He was awfully proud of you. And Sally, as well,' she added, as an afterthought. 'Anyway, look at you. I suppose you're planning on doing up his van and then you'll be away off travelling the world. He'd love that.'

'I am,' Rilla agreed. She fell into step beside Joan, and together they made their way along the little street of shops towards the tiny general store.

'It's an awful shame,' Joan said, as they paused outside for a moment.

'What is?'

'This.' Joan motioned to the sign in the window.

CLOSING SOON, it announced, in huge capital letters.

'They can't close the shop!' Rilla was horrified. 'Where are we supposed to get bread and milk and things?'

'Tell that to the big supermarket in the town,' said Joan, disapprovingly. 'Since they opened up, the takings have gone right down apparently. Wee village shops can't compete with the likes of Tesco.'

'But not everyone can make it into town. What about the people who don't have cars?'

'Aye.' Joan nodded shrewdly. 'That's exactly my point. There's a bus twice a week, but that's hardly going to make a difference to people from the village, is it now?'

'So what are they going to do?'

Joan shrugged. 'Not much they can do, really.'

Rilla followed her inside the shop. Already the place looked a little bit sadder – the shelves were starting to empty, and the cans of tomato soup and packets of washing powder weren't being replenished. It seemed sad to think of Applemore without the funny little shop stacked from floor to ceiling with everything under the sun that the villagers might need.

Rilla found the screws she needed and decided to buy the whole box in solidarity. She asked the girl behind the counter if they had hinges for cupboard doors.

'Granny,' she shouted through the curtain, 'have we got hinges?'

'Hold on a wee sec,' came a voice. A second later, a grey-haired woman emerged wearing a floral overall. 'Hinges, is it?'

'I was just thinking you'll no' get hinges in Tesco,' Joan remarked to the woman, disapprovingly.

'Aye, well that's a good point,' said the woman, riffling under the counter. 'I'm sure I have some in here some-where. Let me just have a— There you go!' She re-emerged, handing over a plastic-wrapped packet to Rilla. 'How many do you need?'

'I'll take them all,' said Rilla, not sure exactly how many she'd need for the kitchen and the overhead cupboards she still had no idea how to build. The whole van-building expe-rience was going to be a rather steep learning curve. Hope-fully she'd have inherited some of her dad's handiwork skills.

Just as they were leaving the shop, Polly was heading in. She gave Joan a kiss of greeting and Rilla a huge beaming smile. 'So lovely to see you! Can I come and visit you at the cottage soon?'

'Any time,' said Rilla, gratefully. 'And the same goes for you, Joan,' she added, as Joan hurried away, giving them a wave and explaining she had to get back before her nephew and his wife returned from their visit to the beach to spot seals.

'What are you up to?' Polly paused with her hand on the door of the shop.

'Just getting some bits and pieces,' Rilla replied, indicating the handful of screws and hinges she was holding. 'I'm attempting to finish my dad's camper van conversion.'

'Ooh,' Polly said. 'Now I *definitely* want to come and visit. Have you seen all the *hashtag vanlife* stuff on Instagram?'

'A bit,' Rilla nodded. It all looked a bit fancier than her dad's workmanlike but not very instagrammable effort. 'I'm not sure you're going to get me taking photos of myself in a bikini having an outside shower or doing yoga, mind you.'

'No,' Polly giggled. 'I like the idea of going travelling, but I'm not really into all the hippy stuff. I need to grab some bits, then get going before lunch – but I'll come and see you soon?'

'Yes please.'

Rilla strolled back towards the car, taking a moment to soak in the peace and beauty of the village. The sky was lowering but it only served to enhance the beauty of the sea and the surrounding hills, giving the whole place a moody, atmospheric look. The whitewashed shops and houses looked pretty and quaint with their colourfully painted doors and windows. Gulls wheeled overhead, and a fishing boat was heading into harbour – coming home early to avoid the oncoming stormy weather, she supposed. There was a tiny bookshop and a café, the hair salon and a shop selling outdoor gear and camping equipment which was closed for the winter season. It seemed a pity that Applemore was going to lose a shop which actually made a difference to the community, but maybe that was just what happened in places like this.

Later that afternoon, Rilla was trying to get to grips with

a circular saw – she'd been surprised and delighted to discover that somehow the internet had been switched back on at the cottage and was eternally grateful for how-to videos on YouTube – when there was a shout of 'Helloo-ooo' from outside in the yard. She brushed down her sawdust-covered jeans and straightened up, heading outside.

'I know you said any time,' said Polly, wrinkling her nose and laughing, 'and I'm fairly sure you didn't mean *this after-noon*, but I'm going mad with boredom, and I've had a brainwave and I thought you might have some thoughts on it.'

She was standing in the yard holding a brown paper bag and looking hopeful.

Rilla – who was feeling more than a little bit frustrated at her seeming inability to cut a piece of plywood in a straight line – gave a huge sigh of relief. 'Right now I'd be more than happy to stop what I'm doing.'

'Ooh, are you doing the van?' Polly took in the dusty clothes.

Rilla released her hair from its ponytail and shook it out before tying it back up again. Several curls of wood shaving fell to the ground as she did so.

'I'm trying,' said Rilla, making a face, 'but it turns out it's easier in theory than in practice.'

'Can I see?'

'Of course.'

'I brought cakes,' Polly said a moment later as they stood surveying the van. 'I think everything is improved with cake.'

'I completely agree.'

Polly opened the bag and extended it in Rilla's direction. 'These are from the shop. Which is what I've been having a brainwave about.'

Rilla took a huge square of chocolate brownie. It was delicious – melt in the mouth in the middle, with a crisp outside. 'This is gorgeous,' she said, with her mouth full.

'I know. They're made by Anna, who lives in a little cottage by the harbour. I was picking them up when I had an idea, and I thought – well, you're well-travelled and you've been to lots of places.' For a moment, Polly looked suddenly very young. 'And I thought you'd have an unbiased view on stuff. The trouble with being up here is that everyone still sees me as the baby sister, and they forget I have a brain.'

'That must be hard.' Rilla thought of Sally. She'd always been the more assertive of the two and despite being the youngest managed to make Rilla feel a bit clueless and disorganised most of the time.

'It's okay,' said Polly, wrinkling her nose again. 'It's just it means whatever idea I come out with I get patronised and patted on the head, and this one – well, I think this might actually solve lots of problems.'

'Go on?'

The promised rain had materialised at last, and they sat on upturned plastic canisters in her dad's workshop as Polly began to explain.

'So, the village shop is closing,' she said, looking thoughtful. 'And we need to find a way to make Applemore pay. So, I've been thinking – what if we opened a shop? Like a farm shop?'

'Oh wow,' exclaimed Rilla, impressed. 'That's a brilliant idea.'

Polly beamed. 'You see, that is *exactly* why I wanted to talk to you. If I'd told the others first, I'd have got a lecture about my hare-brained schemes and not having any business sense.'

'A village needs a shop,' Rilla said, chewing her thumbnail thoughtfully.

'Our village needs a shop. But it also needs… I'm thinking not just a shop, but somewhere we can sell local stuff, like Anna's cakes and Beth's flowers, and – well, there are loads of artists and craftspeople up here. Right now, most of them sell their stuff in town, but with the increase in tourists because of the North Coast 500 trail, I'm sure we could make it work.'

Rilla thought. The last time that she'd been in Applemore, there had been no such thing as the North Coast 500 – a tourist trail which was populated year-round by visitors in car, caravan and motorhome. It took in the most scenic parts of the Highland coast and was visited by hundreds of thousands of people every year. Applemore was just off the route, but it wouldn't take much to lure tourists in their direction – especially if it was to somewhere as pretty as the grounds of Applemore House. 'I think it's an amazing idea.'

Polly beamed. 'You know what? That is exactly what I needed to hear. Just for once, it's nice not to get put off something before I actually try and do it.'

'Are there rules about planning permission and stuff?'

'No idea,' said Polly, cheerfully. 'I need to work out where we could do it, first of all. But there's a big old barn off the Drover's Track where we could put it, I think? I'd need to check stuff like access, but it would work.'

Rilla rather admired her straightforward way of thinking. She watched as Polly peered inside the van and then climbed inside, standing in the middle of the still half-finished space, miming making a cup of tea, then pretending to sit at what would be the table.

'This is just the most amazing thing ever. You sure you don't have room for a tiny little stowaway?'

Rilla laughed. 'I need to finish it first.'

'Well, if you decide you do, just shout. Meanwhile, I'm going to go home and make some plans.'

Rilla, who was suddenly overcome with tiredness, saw her out and back into her little Fiat 500. When Polly had left, she closed the door on the outhouse and climbed into bed for a nap. Everything else could wait until she'd closed her eyes for half an hour...

CHAPTER 11

'Hello,' said Beth. 'We meet again. Finally.'

Rilla whistled Hugh, who was dashing ahead along the path between the trees that led down to the tiny private beach. He galloped back, his curly ears flapping in the wind. Rilla pulled her coat collar up. 'It's lovely to see you.'

Beth leaned forward, giving her a kiss on the cheek. She indicated her muddy clothes. 'I'd hug you, but I'm disgustingly filthy. Can't believe you've been here weeks already and I haven't had a chance to say hello.'

'You've got quite a lot on your plate,' Rilla said, looking down at the pushchair. Two sturdy, blue-eyed babies looked back at her from within bright rainbow-striped fleece suits. They didn't look like they were troubled by the freezing weather.

'They're no trouble, really. I think they like the fresh air. So, I gather you've been keeping my big brother out of mischief? Polly's been singing your praises.'

'Keeping myself out of mischief, more like. I didn't quite know what I was going to do with myself when I got

119

here. Now, somehow, I've ended up covered in paint at the house.'

Beth gave her an odd look. 'Have you seen inside the walled garden? I assume you'll have had a good look around.'

Rilla shook her head. 'I haven't, no.' It seemed a strange thing to say. She'd known Beth less than the others – where Charlotte had been prone to being bossy, Beth had always lingered a few steps behind, slightly daydreamy. It must have been hard to follow in the footsteps of someone as certain of herself as Charlotte, Rilla thought. 'I've seen it from upstairs when Lachlan was showing me the top floor of the house, but I've never been inside.'

'Oh,' Beth pushed open a gate in the wall, shouldering it slightly as it stuck, 'this gate's always open.'

'No, but it's not my place to wander.'

Beth's expression changed slightly, and Rilla realised that she'd passed some sort of test.

'I haven't been down here before,' she continued. 'But now I've got to walk Hugh,' Rilla indicated the spaniel who was lolloping ahead of them, nose to the ground, tail flagged high, 'and Polly said that the beach walk was lovely in autumn. I've never been there at this time of year.'

'Of course.' Beth looked thoughtful. 'It must be strange, coming back, is it? We all loved you and Sally coming – it sort of diluted the family, if that makes sense? We don't have any cousins, so we didn't have anyone else. And it's a bit weird when you've got a place like this, people can be a bit…'

'Weird?' Rilla stopped as Beth paused on the neatly edged grass path between two mulched flower beds.

'I think people have very decided opinions about the sort of people who live in a place like this. Which means if you don't mix with lots of other people who live in places like this – which we didn't, because Pa was allergic to socialising – you end up just not really mixing with anyone. And when you're a biggish family, it's easy to sort of occupy each other, even though half the time you want to kill each other.'

'I feel like that about my sister and there's only two of us.'

Beth laughed. 'Sally was always a bit... well, she's got a lot in common with Charlotte, hasn't she?'

'She's efficient,' said Rilla, wrinkling her nose.

'Precisely. It doesn't leave you much room to mess up, does it?'

'No.'

'Families are strange, basically.'

'I completely agree.' Rilla shaded her eyes, looking across at Beth's handiwork. 'But you've done an amazing job of this.'

'It keeps me out of trouble,' Beth said, laughing. 'Seriously, though, it's been the most amazing thing. I've got loads of photos of what it looked like before – I had to use a tractor to dig out some of the old fruit bushes that had basically tangled themselves into the walls, and I'm still constantly weeding to keep on top of it, but this last year I've finally started making a profit.'

Rilla looked around at the walled garden. There were huge trellises fastened to the walls, with fruit trees trained along their lengths. An enormous, slightly shabby greenhouse had been repainted with a dusky pale green paint, and when Beth led her inside, she could see rows and rows of tiny seedlings.

'They'll grow better next spring because I've started them off in here. We're lucky, because we've got a bit of a

121

microclimate here on the West Coast, and the walls of the garden heat it up a bit more as well, but it's still good to give everything a bit of a head start. It's always stressful when winters are so unpredictable. Last year was really warm and wet, which worked in our favour, but the year before was so cold that I lost a load of plants – and a fortune. But I think I'm getting the hang of it now.'

'That's pretty impressive with baby twins to look after as well.' Rilla looked down at them. They'd dropped off to sleep, their long eyelashes like half-moons on sweet, round, pink cheeks. 'Does your husband help a lot?'

Beth snorted. 'That's a bit of a sore point at the moment.'

Rilla looked at her old friend, cautiously. 'In what way?'

'We're not… It's – well, we're not exactly getting on at the moment.'

'Oh,' said Rilla, 'I'm sorry. I didn't realise.'

Beth gave a tiny shrug. 'Nobody knows. I don't really know how to tell them, to be honest. I mean, right now Charlotte's so wrapped up in the holiday chalet things she's building, and Lachlan – well, he'd rather not be here at all – and Polly's just Polly.'

Rilla thought about Lachlan, and how conflicted he was about the whole Applemore thing, and about Polly, who'd very firmly been cast in the baby sister role, and how sweet and welcoming she'd been despite only having a sketchy memory of Rilla and Sally from years before, and thought that she'd probably be a good listener if you were going through something difficult. But that was the thing about families – you were pretty much given a role in childhood and it was almost impossible to step out of it when you were an adult.

'Is it just the stress of having toddlers? I remember when

Sally was looking after her two when they were younger, she and her husband Brendan used to argue over the most ridiculous things.'

Beth cast her eyes down, scuffing the grass with her toe. 'No – I mean, that doesn't help, of course – but it's more than that. I tell you what – these two have dropped off, why don't we walk down to the beach, and I'll talk at you, if you don't mind?'

'I don't mind at all.'

They set off for the beach, following the path which led down the side of a field which was edged with a traditional drystone dyke. Every now and again, Beth would bend down and pick up a stray stone, tucking it back into position.

'The farmer had some cattle in here, and they've got a terrible habit of scratching their bums on the stone. Some of this has been here for so long that it's worked loose – it's another one of those things we probably need to get sorted at some point, but I don't want to point it out to Lachlan.'

Rilla noticed she was slightly wary of her brother's response.

'I'm sure he wouldn't mind,' she said, thinking of how easy-going and fun he'd been the last few days when he, she and Polly had been painting the big hall. He'd ended the day with dark red paint in his hair and insisted on taking them both down to the Applemore Hotel for dinner as a thank you for their help.

'Hrmm.' Beth looked unconvinced. 'It doesn't take a genius to work out that Lachlan would rather be anywhere else but here. It's not really a surprise, is it? I mean, it's the ultimate poisoned chalice: *here, have this castle, oh and by the way you owe twenty grand in taxes and it's falling apart.*'

'I think he might be coming around to the idea.' He'd mentioned the gin idea again the other day.

Beth scrunched up her face. When she did that, she looked about twelve, and not at all like a business-owning mother of two. 'I dunno. Seriously, I can see why he has a problem with this place. Who'd want to end up like our Pa, living here alone with only the dogs for company?'

'Why would that happen? I mean he's...' Rilla was going to say something about him being funny, and hand-some, and nice company, and... but she looked away, feeling her cheeks flushing pink.

'I always thought you two might have...' Beth looked at her sideways as they carried on walking.

'Me and Lachlan?' Rilla went even pinker. 'What made you think that?'

'When we were teenagers, I used to watch the way he looked at you. And I got the feeling you liked him, too. And then of course you stopped coming, and – well, he's never had anyone particularly serious.'

'Really?' Her heart thudded wildly.

'Oh, loads of girls have come and gone – the trouble is I think they came up here thinking they'd met the Highlands version of Prince William who was going to inherit every-thing and then they'd soon realise that they were on course for a life in a freezing, crumbling ruin with nobody but sheep for neighbours.'

'I love it here, though. Surely there must've been some people who felt the same way?'

'Oh, I'm exaggerating. I'm sure there have been some nice girls, but they just never lasted. I reckon it's because Lachlan's convinced every relationship's a non-starter because of what happened with Mum.'

Rilla didn't speak. In all the time she'd known the

Frasers, she'd never really heard them talk about their mother. All she knew was that she wasn't part of their lives, and that she'd died somewhere in France. It was all very mysterious.

'She just couldn't hack it,' Beth continued. 'I dunno – now I've got these two, I can sort of understand it a bit. It's weird, but it really changes your perspective. For years I thought your mother had completely overreacted in taking you and Sally away and not letting you come back. I was thinking the other day, though, if I left the babies with Simon and something happened, I don't know if I'd be able to forgive him.'

'What happened at the loch wasn't Dad's fault, though.'

'Oh, I know that, logically – but I don't think this whole parenting lark is particularly logical. All I'm saying is that I can see why Mum legged it – even though she had all of us – and I can see your mum's point of view.'

'Do you wish you'd seen more of your mum?' Rilla regretted the words as soon as she'd said them. It was the most idiotic, ridiculously obvious question.

Beth nodded slowly. 'I do now – at the time, though, I just resented her for leaving us. Mainly I resented the fact that she left and Charlotte saw it as her job to be the one in charge, when she was already far too bloody bossy.'

Rilla laughed.

The path opened up before them and they climbed over a wooden stile, lifting the pushchair over together, and onto the grass of the machair. In summer, this was a carpet of wildflowers which attracted ground-nesting birds and all sorts of wildlife, but by this time of year it had faded to a dull green, close cropped by the sheep that wandered along the edge of the beach, grazing.

Beth parked the double buggy, leaving the sleeping twins

facing away from the wind which was blowing off the sea. Hugh dashed towards the waves, barking with excitement. They followed him, climbing down over the rocks at the edge of the sand, and then stood, looking out at the distant hills of the islands. The sand was as pale white as any tropical beach, and the sea a sparkling azure blue. The only difference, of course, was that the water here would turn your skin a matching blue within about two seconds of jumping into it.

'So, what are you going to do?' Rilla bent, picking up a piece of opaque green sea glass. It was shaped like a heart. She turned it over in her hand, then pocketed it.

'About Lachlan?'

Rilla shook her head. 'About Simon.'

It was strange how comfortable it was being back with the Frasers. Time seemed to have slipped away, and they just settled back to being their old selves.

Beth looked thoughtful. 'I got married because I was trying to make up for all the… well, we didn't have all that stuff.'

'What Sally calls two point four children and a dog?' Rilla asked.

'Exactly. She did the same thing, didn't she? D'you, think you go one way or the other?'

'How'd you mean?'

'Well, look at Charlotte. She's resolutely single. Lachlan – a string of casual relationships, but there's never been anyone serious.'

'So, they're one end of the spectrum and you and Sally are the other?'

'Trying to make the family we didn't quite have when we were growing up.'

'That makes sense.' Rilla looked out at the water. The

sky was as clear as the sea, the pale sun shining down and casting an unseasonal warmth. It could have been early September.

'What about you?' Beth looked at her, her hands thrust into her pockets. A long strand of blonde hair had worked loose from her ponytail and wrapped itself around her neck in a sudden breeze. The weather could change here in seconds.

'I guess I'm at the Charlotte and Lachlan end of the spectrum,' Rilla admitted. 'I travel, which means it's easy to avoid getting involved with anyone.'

'You don't fancy settling down?'

A fleeting image popped into Rilla's head, of walking along this beach with Lachlan and a bundle of dogs running ahead. Her stomach flipped over, and her knees felt a bit weird. For goodness' sake, she was behaving like she was the teenager she'd been back when she used to spend summers here. She shook her head. 'Nope. I've got a million and one countries I want to visit first.'

'Lucky thing.' Beth sighed. 'I wish I'd done a bit of that before I got married. Now I've got no chance.'

'Of course you do. You can go travelling with the family, can't you?'

Beth opened her mouth and then closed it again. For a second, she squeezed her eyes closed, tightly, then shook her head as if trying to clear it. 'I can't go travelling as a single parent with twins.'

'Beth,' Rilla said, looking at her with surprise. She put a hand on her arm, squeezing it gently in reassurance. 'What's going on?'

'Don't breathe a word,' Beth said.

'Of course not.' Rilla moved her hand as Beth pushed the hair out of her face. A moment later, there was an indignant squawk from the buggy as one of the babies woke up, followed a second later by a matching cry of fury.

'Oh god, let me get these two out to potter about and I'll tell all.' She moved over to the buggy. 'You take Edward,' Beth said, handing her a surprisingly heavy lump of toddler. 'I'll take Lucy,' she added, lifting the second baby out, laughing as she kicked his legs with delight at being freed, 'and they can have a play about on the grass.' She looked down at Hugh, who was looking at the babies with concern, his furry eyebrows knitted together. He sat down beside Rilla's feet, tail wagging slowly.

'I don't know if he's okay with children,' Rilla said, looking at him. Hugh looked back at her as if he was faintly insulted at the insinuation he might be anything other than angelic. Never mind how much she'd miss Applemore, she thought, not for the first time, she was going to have her heart broken into pieces when she had to part with Hugh. Fostering a dog really was the worst kind of good deed.

'A-ba!' gurgled Edward, delightedly, lurching towards Hugh. The dog rolled over, showing his belly and making him laugh.

'How old are they?' Rilla was spectacularly bad with things like this. She'd once sent Sally's youngest a chemistry set as a birthday present, before receiving a highly amused WhatsApp message to the tiny apartment in Chile where she was staying at the time, telling her that the thought was nice, but that three-year-olds weren't really massively into chemistry experiments.

'Eighteen months.'

'So they really are still babies.'

Beth nodded. 'Part of me thinks that it'll be easier to deal with at this age. They won't know any different.'

'Beth?' Rilla looked at her, watching as she tried her

hardest to compose her expression. Beth's chin trembled slightly, and she tried not to notice.

'Oh god.' Her face crumpled. 'We're not together anymore. I haven't told anyone. I can't bring myself to admit it. He had an affair. It wasn't supposed to happen, he said, as if that's some sort of consolation.'

'Oh god, I'm so sorry,' Rilla said.

'It's fine. He met her at work.' Beth took a brief breath inward, as if to gather herself.

'It's not fine.' Poor Beth, keeping this to herself out of some complicated sense of pride.

'I stalked her online. She's incredibly glamorous and definitely doesn't have mud under her fingernails and massive eye-bags from waking up with babies at night.'

'Beth,' Rilla began gently, 'that doesn't make you a failure, it makes *him* one. What sort of man does that?'

'A really shitty one.' Beth stooped to redirect one of the twins. They were like tiny, sturdy, wind-up toys. They ran for so long, then she'd pick them up and point them in the opposite direction and they'd beetle off that way instead. It was sweet to watch, but must be exhausting to manage, especially by yourself.

'And you haven't said anything to the others?'

Beth shook her head. 'Too proud, I think. Is that silly?'

'No, I get it.'

'The thing is, everyone said that getting married at twenty-two was ridiculous in this day and age, and I was so determined to prove them wrong that I've just been putting my head in the sand for ages. The truth is, things hadn't been good between us for ages. Even before we had the babies.'

'That explains a lot,' Rilla said, unthinkingly. Polly had mentioned the other day that they hardly ever saw Simon.

'What does?'

'Oh, just something Polly said. I think she picks up more than you realise.'

'She probably does. I think I forget that she's not ten anymore.'

'She's not. She's full of ideas for this farm shop.' Rilla smiled. 'Lachlan seems delighted that she's got a project.'

'I think we all are. She's been a bit directionless.'

'Anyway, enough about Polly. What about you?'

Beth shook her head. 'You know what? I feel so much better for just saying it out loud. I've been trying to act like everything's okay, and hoping nobody will notice, but at the same time desperately wishing someone would ask so I could just stop hiding it. Does that make sense?'

'Perfectly.' Rilla nodded sympathetically. 'So, what are you going to do now?'

'Sort my life out,' said Beth, with a slightly watery smile. 'That's the obvious thing, isn't it?'

'Well,' Rilla was trying to be tactful, 'it would seem to be, yes.'

'At least we can have the conversation now. He tried to talk to me about it the other day and I literally jumped into the car and drove off rather than speak to him. I was one step from singing *la la la* with my fingers over my ears. Mad, isn't it?'

It was easier to offload to someone who was a bit removed, Rilla reflected later, after she'd walked back up from the beach with Beth, who seemed a different person for unburdening herself. She'd resolved to go home and have it out with Simon. Rilla had promised she'd be there for her whenever, telling her the next time she jumped in the car and fled she could drive to the cottage and have a cup of coffee with her instead of parking the car on the harbour and sitting there for hours in the freezing cold.

Back at the cottage, Rilla turned on the television and lit the fire, sitting there all evening with an exhausted Hugh snoring beside her. It was strange that she'd only been back a short time, but somehow Applemore felt like – she didn't even quite want to admit it to herself – home.

CHAPTER 12

'Morning,' said Gus, slurping a coffee and looking at Lachlan through the phone screen. Lachlan was sitting, elbows on the table, his mobile balanced against a pile of books Polly had left lying there from last night. She really was untidy, he thought, brushing a tsunami of her toast crumbs onto the floor, where the spaniels sprang into action, snuffling them up like flop-eared vacuum cleaners.

'How's it going?' Lachlan looked at the kitchen behind Gus. There was a huge bouquet of flowers in a red jug – clearly Lucinda's doing – and a new blind hung at the window. 'I see you've been doing a bit of DIY.'

Gus grinned. 'Hardly. Well, not compared to what you're up to—'

As if on cue, there was a huge bang from upstairs, where a builder had arrived to sort out the worst of the roof leaks. 'It's expensive chaos,' Lachlan agreed. 'I've used my savings to pay these guys to come in and do a patch-up job, because the alternative was waiting for the grant, which would take months, and I don't have months.'

'Not if you want to get it on the market in spring,' said Gus, opening his eyes wide a second later and putting a hand to his mouth as Lachlan made a *zip it* motion with his finger across his mouth. 'Sorry.'

Lachlan shrugged. 'It's fine, the girls aren't here. But they're still hell-bent on keeping the place, and, worse still, Polly's had a brainwave about starting up a farm shop like Jeremy bloody Clarkson, and now she's up to her eyes in business plans and samples of chocolate brownies from little local businesses.'

'That's a good thing, no?'

'Not if I'm then going to turn around and tell them I have to sell the place,' Lachlan said, shaking his head ruefully. He carried on thinking about that while Gus updated him on how things were going at the brewery, only half-listening as he reeled off the orders they'd had, and Lucinda's idea for this, and Lucinda's idea for that, and—

'So anyway,' Gus continued, 'I was thinking about your invite for the weekend.'

Lachlan saw his own expression on the screen and adjusted it quickly. 'Oh yeah?'

'Lucinda's dying to come up and see the place.'

Lachlan looked at the kitchen, where a pile of paint pots and an ancient wooden ladder were stacked against the far wall. 'As long as she's not expecting glamour.'

'Of course she is. But I'll try and set her expectations. What are you guys doing for Hallowe'en?'

'There's a party at the hotel – remember Harry? He's running the place now.'

'Cool. Does that work for you?'

'It's as good a time as any. At least Lucinda will have something to dress up for,' he added, drily.

'She'll be onto the fancy-dress-hire place about three

nanoseconds after I tell her.' Gus smiled indulgently at the thought. 'I might see if I can persuade her to go as a naughty nun or something.'

Lachlan shook his head, laughing. 'I'm going to leave you with that thought and get back to these builders.'

A couple of hours later, he'd finished the grant application. The woman he'd spoken to assured him that it was a sure thing that they'd get the money which would help with repairs – it seemed almost too simple to Lachlan, but she was insistent. He'd just have to take her word for it. Meanwhile – the banging still going on upstairs, and scaffolding climbing up one side of Applemore house – it at least looked as if something was happening, even if it was costing thousands to do the most basic patching-up job. Lachlan looked at his bank balance and then closed the lid of his laptop with a groan of despair.

'What's happening?' Polly and Rilla appeared in the kitchen a moment later, both wearing paint-splattered boiler-suits. Polly opened the fridge and scanned it, hopefully. 'And why is there never anything to eat in here?'

'Probably because I haven't been to the shop yet and you've been painting the gallery.'

'It's looking good,' said Rilla, sitting down on the edge of the chair beside the Aga. 'But it's freezing cold up there on the second floor.'

'Heat's supposed to rise,' Polly said, making some cheese sandwiches. 'But I suppose there has to be some heat in the first place for that to happen.'

Lachlan watched Rilla spread her hands flat and hover them over the lid of the Aga, being careful not to burn her fingers. She had managed to get paint pretty much everywhere – there was a smear of red on her cheek, and a thick ringlet which had come loose from her ponytail looked as if she'd managed to somehow dip it into the paint pot. She looked up for a moment, catching him looking at her and smiling.

'Oh, Gus has sort of invited himself for Hallowe'en weekend.'

'Ooh,' said Polly, going slightly pink.

'With his girlfriend,' Lachlan pointed out, feeling like a bit of a party pooper. Polly had always had a bit of a thing for his friend, ever since he first visited in their first term at uni. 'But we need to get the place warmed up a bit in preparation. There's no way Lucinda will cope with the Arctic conditions you two have been working in. She's a bit of a hothouse flower.'

'What's he like?' Rilla took a bite of the sandwich Polly handed her, still hugging the Aga for dear life. Her cheeks had flushed pink now as she was beginning to warm up, making her look even prettier. He shook the thought away.

'Gus?' Lucinda sat – as she always seemed to do – on the kitchen worktop and looked thoughtful. 'He's funny. Nice. What's *she* like, more importantly?'

Lachlan chose his words carefully. He'd never warmed to Lucinda, thinking she was a bit of a gold digger. 'Very, um, driven.'

Rilla shot him a look and raised an eyebrow slightly. He felt a grin tugging at the edges of his mouth.

'You don't like her,' Rilla said.

'I didn't say that.'

'You don't need to.' She looked pleased with herself.

'Shut up, clever clogs.'

'You two,' said Polly, shaking her head. She hopped down from the worktop suddenly, grabbing her sandwich.

'I'm going to go and see what the builders are doing. One of them is quite cute.'

'So, I take it she's awful?' Rilla said, with a shrewd expression.

'She's not awful. Not completely awful. She's just… well, you'll see. D'you fancy experiencing the village Hallowe'en party? It's the most excitement you'll get round here until the Hogmanay night at the hotel.'

'I'd love to. Are we supposed to dress up?'

'You could just go as an extremely scruffy painter and decorator,' he said, teasing her.

She looked down at the boiler suit she'd borrowed. The arms and legs were rolled up, and she was wearing a pair of battered purple Doc Marten boots. She couldn't look more beautiful if she tried. Not that he was looking, he tried to remind himself. But he knew he was failing completely on that front. The more time he spent in her company, the more he realised he was falling head over heels all over again for the girl he'd known all those years before, but this time it was different. She was a woman, who'd travelled the world, and who knew her own mind. And a woman, he reminded himself firmly, who was planning to leave Apple-more at the beginning of January. She wasn't a permanent fixture.

But he knew what Gus would say – something along the lines of grabbing the opportunity while it was standing in front of him.

'Seriously though,' he said, hearing his voice thickening slightly. 'I'd love it if you'd come.'

'I'd love to.' She looked up at him through long dark lashes. 'It's a date.'

His heart thudded unevenly against his ribcage. He lifted his coffee cup in a toast of recognition. 'Deal.'

Later that evening, when the night had drawn in, Lachlan went outside to let the dogs out before bed. The sky was a velvet blanket scattered with a million tiny stars, the trees whispering in the wind that blew in off the water. Behind the turrets of Applemore House, the scaffolding hidden by the darkness, the moon hung low and almost full, a huge butter-yellow circle untroubled by cloud. Somewhere in the distance, an owl hooted, and he heard the swooping of wings as it flew over his head in search of prey. He wondered how Rilla was doing down there in the cottage on her own, with only Hugh for company. Thank goodness he'd found him – and thank goodness the rescue place hadn't had any room for him. He hated to think of her sitting there alone. At least this way she'd be snuggled up on the sofa by the fire with him for company.

Lachlan gave a heavy sigh. Who knew he'd be jealous of a scruffy rescue spaniel?

'So what I'm thinking,' Polly said the next morning, standing in the outhouses behind Rilla's cottage, 'is we can clear this place and turn it into a shop, and then there's room for parking here –' she waved her hand around the courtyard – 'and round the back, and it's already got power and a sink – albeit a slightly dodgy ancient one – and I can just get some shelves and stuff and, hey presto, a farm shop with no major outlay. And then I'm contributing and not just being a drain on resources.'

Lachlan had to hand it to her – she'd done her home-work. She'd written a plan with projected incomes, found out what she'd need to get the place ready and even made a long list of potential suppliers.

'And I'll not just be making a difference to us, I'll be making a difference to the local economy. I reckon Dad would be impressed with that, don't you?'

'He definitely would have.' Her enthusiasm was infectious. 'So what sort of timescale are you looking at?'

'Well,' Polly leant back against the wall, folding her arms and looking thoughtful, 'I can't see any reason why we can't be ready to open in time for Christmas. It's seven weeks until the tenth. We could have the place looking amazing and have a little opening do.'

Seven weeks to get this place from dusty farm building to fully functioning farm shop seemed a bit ambitious to Lachlan, but he wasn't going to quash his little sister's enthusiasm. Her eyes were sparkling, and she was desperate to get going. He felt a lurch of guilt at the thought that if he sold the place, he'd be quashing her plans completely.

'I'm meant to be heading over to Inverness the Monday after the Hallowe'en party with the trailer to pick up some wood and stuff. You could come along and sling whatever you need in the back.'

'Seriously?' She looked delighted at the prospect.

'Seriously. You've worked your backside off with Rilla painting the gallery, it seems only fair I do something to help with your plans.'

'You are bloody brilliant,' Polly said, reaching out a hand and giving him a high five. 'It's a deal.'

He couldn't quite look her in the eye.

They wandered back out of the outhouse. Rilla, whose curtains had been drawn when they pulled into the courtyard, peered out at them from the kitchen window. She waved and opened the window to shout hello.

'Morning, you two. What are you doing up and about

at…' she checked her watch, 'eight in the morning? Are you insane?'

'No,' said Polly, cheerfully, 'I've been showing Lachlan my grand plans for the shop.'

'And does Lachlan approve?' Rilla looked at him with an amused expression.

'I do,' he said, nodding.

'I'd invite you in for a coffee,' Rilla said, 'but I'm in pyjamas and I look like I've been dragged through a hedge backwards.'

Lachlan, who privately thought she looked adorable, didn't say anything.

'It's fine,' replied Polly, reassuringly. 'I'll come by later so we can have a fancy-dress conference. D'you have any idea what you want to wear to the party?'

'Not a clue,' confessed Rilla.

'How about you, Lachlan?' Polly turned to look at him.

'I was thinking I might go as a slightly impoverished owner of a slowly disintegrating castle.'

'Very funny.' Polly rolled her eyes.

Rilla giggled. 'I think you should wear a kilt in that case.'

'That's not fancy dress round here,' laughed Polly. 'Although I can't remember the last time I saw my big brother wearing one, come to think of it.'

'It's in Edinburgh,' he said, cutting her off at the pass. The last thing he wanted to do was spend an evening in Rilla's company wearing a kilt and feeling more aware than he ought to that he was – as all good Scotsmen should be – wearing nothing underneath it.

'I'll have to find you something else,' said Polly.

'Only you could manage to make a perfectly pleasant offer sound vaguely threatening.'

Rilla snorted with laughter again. 'She does, doesn't she?'

'Watch this space,' Polly remarked. 'I'll come down later. Give Hugh a kiss from me meanwhile.'

CHAPTER 13

The night of the Hallowe'en party was upon them in what felt like hours, not days. Rilla had left Hugh up at the big house with the other two dogs and had last seen him ensconced quite happily on a cushion on the big armchair next to the Aga. The phone rang just as she'd climbed out of a hot bath.

'Hi stranger,' said Sally.

'Morning,' said Rilla, realising it must be early for her sister. She could hear the shrieks of her niece and nephew in the background. 'I take it you guys are going trick or treating later?'

'They sound like they're hyped up on candy already, don't they?' Sally sounded mildly frazzled. 'This is the longest day of the year for parents after Christmas Eve. I've already had to mop up tears.'

'I think alcohol is the secret.'

'For me or for them?'

'Probably a bit of both. Can't you lace their breakfast cereal with whisky to calm them down, or something?'

'I think the authorities frown on that sort of thing these days,' said her sister, laughing.

'In that case, I'd just get stuck into the gin. Tell anyone who asks it's medicinal.'

'Believe me, I'm tempted. I assume you will be getting stuck in later?'

Rilla wiped the steam away from the bathroom mirror with her arm and rubbed moisturiser into her cheeks. 'I think I might. I'm feeling a bit nervous, for some reason.'

'That's because you've got a hot date.'

'It's not a date,' Rilla said, wiping the mirror again. It had steamed up almost instantly. 'We're just going together. I mean, Polly's going to be there, and Charlotte – even Beth might be coming.'

'How is she?' Rilla had shared what was happening with Sally, figuring that telling her sister who was thousands of miles away wouldn't do any harm.

'She's okay. I think Simon's looking for a new place in Glasgow.'

'She still hasn't told the others?'

'Nope.' Rilla combed her hair and rubbed in some conditioner in the hope it might tame her curls.

'She's going to need to at some point, or they're going to wonder why their sister is suddenly a single parent and their brother-in-law is living 150 miles away.'

'I think she's worried that Lachlan's got enough on his plate.'

'Families,' said Sally.

'Exactly,' Rilla agreed.

They chatted for a while – the phone on speaker, balanced on the windowsill – as Rilla applied her make-up.

'Right,' she said, putting on a second coat of mascara, 'I'm done.'

'What are you dressing up as?'

'Guess.' Rilla lifted her hair, trying to decide if she should pin it up or leave it loose around her shoulders.

'A nun. A sexy waitress. A...' Her sister paused for thought.

'It's a Hallowe'en party, not a sex club,' said Rilla, laughing. 'I always forget that it's more about fancy dress than spooky stuff over there in the States. I'm going as a witch. Polly found an old black dress of her mum's in the wardrobe.'

'That sounds... sensible.' Rilla could imagine Sally's expression. Sally would have knocked some gorgeous outfit up on her sewing machine, trimmed it with marabou feathers and would manage to look like a complete knock-out. 'I assume it looks better than it sounds, given you're going on a date.'

'It's not a—'

'Yeah, yeah,' said Sally, laughing. 'Take a photo and send it over when you're dressed. I want to see for myself.'

Rilla decided to have a glass of wine for Dutch courage – suddenly the prospect of a night out in the local hotel where everyone knew everyone else felt slightly terrifying. Standing in the kitchen, she looked at her reflection in the window. It wasn't often she made a real effort to get dressed up and it always surprised her that she scrubbed up all right. Her hair was curling down past her shoulders in ringlets, and she'd applied a lot of the dark eye make-up that Polly had lent her for a witchy look – hopefully the lighting at the party would be subdued or she was going to look a bit like she'd applied it with a shotgun. She snorted with laughter at the thought, and was just examining her black-painted nails when a loud rap at the door made her jump.

Rilla pulled open the door. Lachlan filled the doorway,

one arm propped up against the wall. He was dressed in battered jeans, a faded grey T-shirt and a black leather jacket. In the gloom of the evening, he looked vaguely threatening, and very alpha male. Stubble darkened his jaw, and he pushed back the dark tangle of his hair, looking at her with undisguised admiration.

'Wow.' He gave a low whistle.

Rilla was too taken aback to speak. He looked utterly gorgeous. But—

'What are you?' she asked, cocking her head slightly to one side in scrutiny.

Lachlan laughed and shook his head. 'I told Polly nobody would get it.'

'It is fancy dress, isn't it? I'm not…' Rilla looked down at her outfit, feeling extremely overdressed all of a sudden.

'You are most definitely not.' He shook his head, his eyes sweeping over her in a way that sent a heat through her entire body.

'I'm Michael, from The Lost Boys. I couldn't face dressing up as a skeleton or being the fourth Frankenstein's Monster of the evening, so I thought I'd go left field.'

Rilla lifted an eyebrow. 'Well, it's a look.'

'Is that a good thing?'

She nodded. 'Definitely.'

'Glad to hear it. I promise not to bite you,' he added, lowering his voice slightly.

Rilla felt the hairs on the back of her neck stand up and a jolt of desire, which threw her completely, causing her to step back into the hallway and make a joke of it. It seemed the only way to handle the way she was feeling. 'Watch it or I'll cast a spell on you,' she said, pointing the piece of cane she'd painted to make a wand at him.

'I think you already have,' he said, shaking his head. 'You look amazing.'

'Not too much?' Rilla brushed at the velvet of her dress.

Lachlan reached forward and caught the edge of the cloak she was wearing, flipping it so it was the right way around. His fingers grazed the skin of her shoulder blade and she caught the faintest scent of his aftershave. A breath caught in her throat.

'Definitely not too much.'

What she hadn't told her sister – she'd always felt a bit self-conscious about dressing up, because she spent so much time wearing her traveller gear of loose trousers, flip-flops and a vest top – was that the dress Polly had unearthed for her was a slinky black velvet number which clung in all the right places. It had a narrow waist and a swirling ice-skater-style skirt which came to just above the knee. The neckline was a sweetheart shape, which Rilla was going to spend all evening tugging up to avoid showing too much cleavage, but the overall effect was – well, she had to admit it looked good. They'd found some black ribbon and made a choker which she'd fastened around her neck, and Polly had lent her a pair of knee-high black suede boots. Together with a cloak of black satin which they'd made out of an old night-dress, the whole outfit worked quite well. It certainly seemed to be having an unexpected effect on Lachlan, who was gazing at her with undisguised admiration.

'Right,' he said, seeming to shake himself. 'Shall we go?'

'Where is Polly?' She looked outside, seeing the Land Rover in darkness.

'I haven't a clue,' he replied, laughing. 'I don't generally take my younger sister as a chaperone when I go on a date.'

Rilla felt her stomach tighten slightly with excitement.

They left the house, Rilla locking the door, and headed for the Land Rover.

'I didn't realise…' she began, as he opened the door and stepped back to let her inside, with old-fashioned manners.

'Didn't realise what?' He stood for a second, his arm slung over the top of the door as she fastened her seat belt. Suddenly she seemed to be all fingers and thumbs, the seat belt catch slipping out of her hand as she tried to fasten it. Her heart was pounding.

'Oh, nothing,' she said, shaking her head.

He looked at her, a strange expression crossing his face for a moment, and closed the door.

They drove down the hill towards Applemore village. The darkness here was so intense that she still hadn't worked out how people found their way around at night, but Lachlan drove confidently down the winding country lanes, knowing the roads like the back of his hand.

'You ready for this?' he said, turning briefly to look at her.

'A village party?'

'No,' he laughed, 'the third degree you're going to get from my friend Gus's partner. She's been desperate to hear all about you since they arrived this morning.'

'She hasn't frozen to death yet, then?'

He gave a bark of laughter. 'No, we've gone through about half the log pile keeping the place warm. She thinks the house is "sweet", apparently.'

'You should show her the haunted nursery at midnight. That'd freak her out.'

'You're evil,' he said, laughing again.

'I am,' she agreed.

The Applemore Hotel had been transformed for the night. The front door was decorated with an archway of black crepe paper roses, and inside the lighting was atmospheric – pools of red light spilled across the carpet, and the air was misted with dry ice.

'Harry has done a good job,' Lachlan said, stepping back to let Rilla into the bar. Music was playing and the place was surprisingly crowded.

'Where have all these people come from?'

'Oh, they don't let us out often up here, so when there's a party, everyone makes the effort. And makes the effort to get dressed up.' Lachlan nodded a greeting to a green-faced Frankenstein's Monster who was leaning with one elbow on the bar, waiting to be served. 'Evening, Fergus.'

'The disguise isn't that good then,' said the monster, chuckling.

'It's great.' Lachlan nodded to the tall man behind the bar dressed as Count Dracula. 'What would you like, Rilla?'

After she'd decided on a gin and tonic, Lachlan ordered their drinks and they stood at the bar for a while, chatting to Harry and watching as people milled around, catching up on village gossip and laughing at the fancy-dress outfits they'd chosen.

'Look at you,' said a voice from behind Rilla. She turned and saw Charlotte dressed as a mermaid, her long blonde hair tumbling down her shoulders, for once not tied up out of the way. Her tail was a work of art, iridescent fabric scales sewn on in a patchwork effect.

'You look amazing,' Rilla exclaimed.

'Pulled out all the stops,' Lachlan agreed. 'I had no idea you had such sewing talent.'

'I thought I'd make an effort for once,' said Charlotte, looking slightly embarrassed at the attention.

'Well, it was worth it,' said Lachlan.

Charlotte looked delighted. 'Thanks.'

They stood by the bar with their drinks, Harry chatting to them when he wasn't serving. He wasn't dressed up – instead he was in black jeans and a black T-shirt with The Applemore Hotel monogrammed in a near font on the left side. He could have been serving in a cool bar in a city pretty much anywhere.

'He's determined to drag this place into the twenty-first century.'

'If it kills me,' Harry said, laughing. 'Which it probably will, given this place.'

'Oh I don't know,' Rilla, took a sip of her gin and tonic, 'I've been to some pretty parochial places. I think Applemore has a lot going for it.'

'I agree,' said Harry. He nodded at Lachlan. 'Tell this bloke. I'm trying my best to persuade him to stay here and keep me company, but he's determined to head back to Edinburgh as soon as he gets half a chance.'

Rilla looked at Lachlan, who gave him an odd look.

'I'm here, aren't I?' he said, lightly. 'Shall we go and find a seat?'

The first couple of drinks went down quickly, Lachlan asking her about her travels around the world and telling her about the brewery. The band was playing, but not so loud that you couldn't talk, and the place was beginning to fill up. Rilla excused herself to go to the loo.

'Hello!' Polly appeared behind her in the mirror. 'I've just got here. How's the date?'

'It's not a date,' Rilla said, laughing. But her stomach flipped over disobediently as she remembered Lachlan sitting outside waiting for her.

'I'm joking. Although you two do make a nice couple, if you don't mind me pointing out the obvious.'

'I'm going to Paris in January,' Rilla said quickly. She ran her fingers through her hair, untangling her curls.

'And Lachlan's desperate to leave Applemore,' Polly agreed. 'But that doesn't mean you can't...'

'Shush,' Rilla said, laughing as she applied more lipstick. Polly was sweet, but she was young and idealistic. Lachlan was... well, it didn't really matter what he was. She wasn't looking for a relationship, no matter how neat it might seem to his younger sister.

'Just saying,' said Polly, disappearing into the loo. 'Oh and brace yourself,' she shouted over the door, 'Gus and Lucinda are on their way.'

By the time Rilla returned from the loos, Lachlan was no longer alone. Sitting beside him, burly in a white dinner jacket and a Phantom of the Opera mask, was a tall, broad-shouldered man who had his hand on the leg of a pretty, very petite blonde girl who was dressed as a fairy. Both Lachlan and Gus stood up as she returned.

'Rilla, this is Lucinda, and my friend Gus, her partner.'

'I can see why Lachlan's too busy to take my calls,' said Gus, laughing. 'I'd be distracted if you were hanging around helping with the painting.'

Lucinda shot him a look.

Rilla slid a sideways glance at Lachlan, who rolled his eyes. It was going to be one of *those* evenings, she could tell.

'Hello, Rilla,' Lucinda smiled prettily. 'Lovely to meet you. Isn't this sweet? Quite a difference from my usual nights out.'

'I quite like it,' she said, feeling she ought to defend Applemore.

'Oh gosh, me too. It's just... different.' The way she said it sounded like she'd rather be anywhere else.

Rilla sized up the situation and decided the answer was probably more gin.

'Shall we get some drinks?'

'Very good idea,' agreed Lachlan, taking her hand. A crowd of rowdy young farmer types had just arrived and the place was suddenly much noisier. He held onto her hand as he led her towards the bar, then turned to face her, letting it go in an instant as if he'd realised what he'd done. 'Sorry,' he said, shaking his head. 'It's just—'

'Don't apologise,' said Rilla, who could still feel the dry warmth of his palm in hers. She glanced down at his hand. The urge to pick it up and lace her fingers through his was strangely irresistible. Probably the gin, she told herself.

'Two more?' Harry looked up, throwing a tea towel over his shoulder.

'Please. Make them doubles. We need something to get through the evening.'

Lucinda was one of those people who managed to turn every conversation around to herself. Once she'd held court on her previous job and the failings of her employer, she went on to explain to Lachlan what she thought he could be doing from up there in Applemore to make the brewery more profitable. Eventually she went to the loo, and Lachlan sat back against the wall, pretending to mop his brow.

'I feel like I've gone five rounds with Tyson Fury,' he said, laughing.

'She's very driven,' said Gus, fondly.

'Like a rottweiler,' observed Lachlan, murmuring in Rilla's ear as Gus got up to get them more drinks.

The band was playing a mixture of cover versions now, and people – fuelled by several drinks – were starting to dance.

'Shall we?' Lachlan tipped his head towards the dance floor.

'If it means I don't have to get a lecture on the reasons why I should stop working as a language teacher and set up my own highly profitable chain of language schools, I'm in.' Rilla pushed the chair away from behind her so quickly it squeaked on the wooden floor.

Gus returned with drinks. 'Where are you two off to?'

'I'm going to wow Rilla with my dancing skills,' Lachlan said, laughing.

'Well, that'll be the death of anything,' Gus replied, shaking his head. 'I'll see if Lu wants to join you when she gets back.'

It seemed easier to stay up dancing than it was to go back and make more stilted conversation. Eventually, though, the music slowed and the band took a break.

Rilla put a hand to her forehead. 'I'm melting.'

'Shall we get some air?' Lachlan suggested.

'Think we can grab our drinks and sneak out without them noticing?'

'Better still, you wait out there and I'll get Harry to pour us another couple.'

Gus and Lucinda were several drinks in and she was tucked under his arm, still talking, gesticulating in the direction of the band. Probably explaining to Gus what she'd do to make them more of a success, Rilla thought archly, as they made their way past without being noticed. She headed outside into the crisp autumn air. The sky was ink black and threaded with stars. In the distance, she could see the regular flash of the lighthouse which stood on the edge of the rocky outcrop at the entrance to the tiny harbour. A couple walked past, arms round each other, laughing quietly. Inside, the band was starting up again, the guitar player testing a couple of notes as a warm up.

Rilla pulled the thin material of her cloak around her shoulders – it didn't take long before she was chilly, and Lachlan had taken a while to be served at the bar.

'Here you are,' he said, coming outside with two drinks. 'Are you cold?'

'A little bit.' She took the drink and sipped it. The ice touched her lip.

Lachlan took off his coat and, putting his drink down on the stone window ledge, draped it around her shoulders. 'Is that better?'

'Much.' It smelled of him, and she could feel his body heat on it.

'Did you ever think we'd be here?' he asked, suddenly.

'At a Hallowe'en party?'

'No,' he laughed, shaking his head. He was only in a T-shirt now, and she could see the lines of the muscles on his arms. Hauling huge barrels of beer around was clearly a pretty good workout.

'You mean here in Applemore?'

He nodded. He reached forward, tucking the stray curl that always fell into her face back behind her ear. 'Here in Applemore, together.'

She took another sip of her drink, looking at him over the top of her glass. 'I think teenage me would be pretty impressed.'

'I think teenage me would be astounded. I never plucked up the courage to tell you that I liked you back then. I was going to, then the accident happened and you never came back.'

Rilla looked at him.

He gave her a thoughtful look, his dark eyes burning into hers. 'What d'you think you'd have said if I had?'

'I'd have said I liked you, too.'

He dropped his gaze and looked across the harbour into the distance, a smile playing on his lips. 'Really?'

'Really.'

Lachlan shook his head. 'Really.'

'I spent a lot of time daydreaming about you back then.'

'Ditto.' He reached forward, taking Rilla's glass out of her hand and putting it down beside his on the window ledge. 'I think I owe it to my teenage self to do this.'

'Ditto.' Rilla could feel her heart thumping hard against her ribcage. That moment before someone kissed you, when you knew it was about to happen – it was the most exhilarating feeling. She reached out a hand and caught his. 'I would like that very much.'

Lachlan put his other hand to her waist, drawing her close. She could feel the heat of his body through the thin material of his T-shirt. The leather coat slid off her shoulders and onto the pavement and she didn't even notice. Lachlan's fingers were laced in hers, his dark eyes gazing into hers with undisguised longing. She tipped her face up towards him, and a moment later his mouth was on hers, and she forgot how cold she was, forgot who was walking by and didn't hear the band beginning the final set of the evening. What felt like moments later, Lachlan pulled away with a groan as Gus and Lucinda came through the door.

'I *told* you they were a thing,' Lucinda, sounded pleased with herself.

'Thanks guys,' said Lachlan, shaking his head in amusement, not letting go of Rilla's hand. 'Talk about killing the moment.'

'I think we'll leave them to it,' said Gus, taking Lucinda

firmly by the hand. 'Polly says she'll give us a lift back – she's not drinking.'

'That's a thought,' Rilla, looked at Lachlan. 'How are we getting home?'

'Well,' he looked at her thoughtfully, 'we could walk, which would be romantic but might end in hypothermia, or we can hang on here until the end of the evening and Harry will drop us back, or—'

'Or we can be practical and get a lift home with Polly, Gus and Lucinda.'

'That's about the size of it.' Lachlan curled a hand around the back of her neck, drawing her back towards him. Lucinda and Gus had wandered across to the harbour and were looking out to the velvety black of the sea. He dropped a kiss on her forehead. 'You can come back to the house for a drink if you like.'

Rilla thought for a moment. Hugh was there, in any case. She could invite Lachlan to the cottage, but the fire would have gone out and the place looked like a bomb-site after she'd spent all evening getting ready. 'Yes please.'

'You'll just have to put up with a ribbing from Gus and the third degree from Lucinda.'

'I can cope with pretty much anything,' Rilla said, laughing. 'Particularly if it means you'll kiss me again.'

'I think that can be arranged.'

He drew her into his arms.

CHAPTER 14

Polly drove them home in the Land Rover. Gus sat in the front seat and Lachlan sat with Lucinda and Rilla squashed in beside him on the back seat. Lucinda prattled away for the whole journey. Lachlan reached out in the darkness and closed his fingers over Rilla's hand, feeling the softness of her skin against his. God, he wanted everyone else to bugger off.

'Let's have a drink when we get back,' Gus said heartily.

Lachlan glared at the back of his head, as if he could send him a telepathic message. It did absolutely nothing.

'Oh god, yes please,' said Polly, as they pulled onto the Applemore drive and started bumping their way down the potholes. 'This designated driver lark is absolutely no fun. I am dying for a massive drink. There's a bottle of Prosecco in the fridge with my name on it.'

Rilla turned to look at him. In the gloom, she could probably just about make out the rueful smile on his face.

Polly pulled up outside Applemore and everyone climbed out.

'We'll let the dogs out,' Lachlan said quickly, taking Rilla's hand in the darkness. 'I'll grab you a coat,' he offered, lowering his voice.

'I think we should probably grab some boots, too. I'm not sure these heels are up to dog walking.'

'I wasn't planning on taking you far,' he said, laughing, 'but I'll grab you some wellies.'

Inside, Polly wasted no time. She had music playing from the speaker in the kitchen, and the bottle opened before he'd even managed to rouse the sleepy dogs and persuade them to leave their comfortable bed by the Aga to go outside and get some fresh air. Gus and Lucinda had their feet under the table, Gus pouring hefty measures of the single malt he'd brought up with him.

Rilla was waiting in the porch, looking ridiculously pretty in her witch garb and a pair of green Hunter wellies. He passed her a Barbour. 'That'll keep you warm.'

'It's a look,' she said, echoing her comment from earlier that evening. 'Not sure it's quite as sexy as your Lost Boys outfit, mind you.'

'I don't know.' Lachlan took her hand and spun her around, lifting her long hair which was caught under the collar of the waxed jacket. He caught it in his fist, pulling gently so her mouth tipped up to meet his. 'I think it's extremely disturbing.'

'You do?' Rilla's mouth was almost on his. He could feel the curve of her smile against his lips.

'I definitely do.'

Five minutes later, the dogs – who had taken matters into their own hands and rushed outside to investigate the night air – returned, milling around and getting under their feet. So much for the plan to take them for a walk.

'We could just stay out here,' he said, dropping a kiss on her temple.

'I think they might notice.' Rilla lifted a hand, running a finger along the stubble of his jaw. His breath caught in his throat. God, he wanted to take her to bed, not to go and make conversation. Why the hell did Gus have to turn up this weekend of all weekends? With one final kiss, Rilla followed the dogs through to the kitchen, with Lachlan following reluctantly behind her.

Fortunately, the whisky took its effect on both Gus and Lucinda within the hour.

Yawning, her neatly painted nails fluttering up to cover her mouth, Lucinda said, 'Gosh, I can't believe how much the country air tires me out.'

'Oh, it's definitely a thing,' Lachlan said, catching Rilla's eye.

'Absolutely,' agreed Rilla. 'When I first came back, I was absolutely flat out every night.'

'No you weren't,' said Polly, looking up from her phone. 'You couldn't sleep for ages because you had jet lag, don't you remember?'

Lachlan shot her a look.

Polly opened her eyes wide for a moment, then caught on. 'Oh, silly me – you did sleep a lot, you're right.'

'I did,' agreed Rilla. 'You'll feel loads better tomorrow after a good ten hours.'

'I'll even make you my famous full breakfast,' said Lachlan, giving Gus a look.

Finally – God, he was slow on the uptake sometimes – Gus seemed to get it. 'Come on, gorgeous,' Gus took Lucinda by the hand. 'Take me to bed or lose me forever.'

'I thought they'd never leave,' Lachlan said, collapsing against the Aga with a burst of laughter.

'I can't believe Gus has found someone so bossy,' said Polly, sounding surprised. 'I always liked him, but his taste in women is *terrible.*' Polly sneezed three times in quick succession. 'I think I must be allergic to her.'

'Perhaps you should go to bed,' said Lachlan, staring at his sister pointedly. Why was everyone he knew so completely bloody clueless?

'Oh I will in a moment,' Polly replied. 'I'm just reading this thing on Instagram about farm shops.' She was completely oblivious, but Lachlan couldn't wait one more minute.

'You don't mind if we leave you to it?'

Polly shook her head, absently, and sneezed again. 'Not at all. I banked up the fire, if you're going to the sitting room.'

The logs were burning merrily on the grate. Pools of low light gave the room a warm, welcoming atmosphere. On a night like this, you could easily forget just how dilapidated Applemore was – it looked warm and welcoming and homely.

Rilla stood for a moment, looking at the fire.

'I've had a lovely evening,' she began.'

'It's not over,' he said, going over to the table in the corner where the drinks were kept. 'Shall we have one more?'

'I'd love that.'

He tipped some whisky into the heavy crystal glasses that had been in the family for years and brought them over to the sofa, putting them down on the table.

Rilla sat down on the edge of the sofa, looking up at him. She looked impossibly beautiful, her eyes highlighted with dark make-up. He'd kissed off all her lipstick earlier but her cheeks were flushed pink. He knelt down in front of her.

'I've waited a long time for this.'

'Me too.'

He unfastened the cloak she was still wearing, tossing it over the edge of the sofa and running a hand up the soft skin of her arm. She arched forward, pulling him closer, her hands sliding inside his T-shirt, her fingers warm against his skin.

'Lachlan,' Polly said, bursting into the room a second later, 'I was thinking about our trip to Inverness on Monday...'

He let out a groan of frustration and fury.

For a second, Polly didn't seem to realise what was going on, then she put her hand to her forehead and closed her eyes, backing out of the room. 'Oh my god,' she said, 'I'm so sorry,' and she closed the door.

'I think perhaps we're safe now?' Rilla reached out a finger and traced a finger along the inside of his arm.

'I wouldn't bet on it,' Lachlan said, shaking his head and laughing.

'Shall we go to bed?' Rilla looked at him, and he realised that she was worried the answer might be no.

'I thought you'd never ask,' he said, laughing. He stood up, taking her hands and drawing her into his arms.

Lachlan woke the next morning, half-expecting to discover that it had all been a dream. But no – Rilla was there, fast asleep in his bed, the witchy make-up washed off after they'd had a shower at 2 a.m., giggling and shushing each other. It had been exactly the night he'd always imagined it would be with Rilla – everything she was, in fact – sweet, sexy, funny.

He let out a long, slow breath of frustration. He wasn't going to admit to himself what he already knew in his heart… there was no point. Rilla was leaving for Paris in January, and he had a life back in Edinburgh, not to mention the minor detail of a house he still hadn't worked out how to sell.

He shook his head. Maybe, just once, he'd enjoy something for what it was without overthinking it.

Rilla stirred.

'Morning,' he said, brushing her curls back from her forehead.

'Hello.' She reached up, catching his shoulders with her hands. 'Come here and kiss me.'

He made the promised breakfast, but it was later than he'd planned.

Polly's sneezes turned out to be the beginnings of a nasty cold. It was clear on Monday morning that she wasn't going to be well enough to travel to Inverness to buy the things she needed for the farm shop, but Lachlan was delighted when Rilla said she'd love to come along instead. He hitched the trailer onto the back of the Land Rover and set off early, Polly having left Hugh up at the house for the day again. He'd settled in remarkably well with Mabel and Martha, and felt like part of the family. Nobody wanted to talk about the day – which would possibly come – when his owner would return and reclaim him.

'I've made us coffee,' Rilla brandished two travel mugs. 'And bacon rolls.'

'You're a star,' he said, kissing her. She climbed into the passenger seat. She'd stayed until late afternoon on Sunday, helping him to make a Sunday roast for everyone and saying goodbye to Gus and Lucinda when they finally left at four.

'I thought she was never going to let him leave,' he'd said as they closed the door afterwards.

'She did seem quite keen to hang around,' Rilla had agreed.

'I think – given she was expecting Balmoral – she quite liked it.'

'How could she not? It's lovely.' Rilla had looked up from the carrots she was chopping as she said that. She'd been wearing one of his old shirts and a pair of Polly's jeans, her hair tied up in a ponytail. She looked as if she belonged there, sitting at the huge, scrubbed table, the dogs snoozing on the cushion beside the Aga. For a moment, he'd found himself wondering if – no. He'd shaken his head. Rilla was a traveller – she had a constant hunger to explore new places and a fear of putting down roots. She'd told him that herself.

'D'you ever think it's funny that Sally is so different to you?' He paused at the junction on the way out of Applemore, waiting as a tractor chugged past with a load of black-wrapped silage bales on a trailer.

'Sometimes I think we're two sides of the same coin. I think she reacted to our family stuff by putting down roots. I went the other way and was determined to keep myself separate.'

'Yeah,' he reached down and took the coffee mug from the holder. 'That makes sense.'

'You're not like Polly or Charlotte or Beth,' Rilla said, looking at him.

'No. Beth's like Sally. She's quite happy with the whole family thing.'

Rilla looked away for a second, gazing out of the window. 'Mmm,' she said.

'What does "mmm" mean?'

'Nothing,' Rilla picked up her mug and examined it carefully. 'I think we all have more to us than meets the eye. That's all.'

He frowned slightly, wondering if he should check up on Beth when he got home. She'd been pretty low-profile for the last few weeks.

'D'you think Charlotte is quite happy up here?' she asked.

'She's a workaholic. I wonder if she'll wake up one day and realise she's spent so much time making sure she's financially secure with the holiday-cottage business that she's forgotten to have a life. It was nice to see her at the party the other night.'

'She looked amazing.'

'She did, didn't she? She so rarely bothers that you forget how pretty she is when she does. I think she's always felt responsible for everything because she was the oldest girl and it all sort of fell on her after Mum left.'

'I wonder what happened to me?' Rilla gave a rueful smile.

'What d'you mean?' He glanced across at her.

'I'm the oldest girl.'

'You never seemed like it, though. I mean, Sally always seemed like she was about forty-five even when she was twelve. She's just that sort of person.'

'She did cut loose and have two margaritas the night before I left for the airport.'

He laughed. 'I take it all back. She's clearly a secret party animal.'

'I wouldn't go that far.'

They drove on for a while in silence, Rilla looking out of the window at the scenery.

'It's so beautiful up here. It's such a long time since I was here, I'd forgotten – Oh! Look!'

A huge red stag stood to the left of the road on a rocky outcrop, watching as they drove past.

'Isn't he gorgeous? I don't think I've ever seen one so close before.'

'Unusual to see one so close to the road. The speed the lorries come down here, he'd better be careful or he'll end up being knocked over and bagged for someone's dinner.'

'Do people do that?' Rilla looked horrified.

He laughed. 'It has been known. To be honest, if you hit something that size you'd probably write off your car, so you'd be better off avoiding it and buying a haunch of venison from the butcher. Talking of which, there's a really lovely place down by the river in Inverness – I thought we could go there for lunch?'

'I'd love that.' She reached across, putting a hand on his thigh.

He dropped his hand onto hers. It might be nothing more than a short-term thing, he told himself firmly, but that didn't mean he couldn't enjoy it.

CHAPTER 15

It was a long time since Rilla had visited Inverness. They parked on the edge of the city and walked in, leaving the pickup and the trailer out of the way of the throngs of tourists that still seemed to be everywhere despite the November chill.

'So what are you after?' Lachlan took her hand. 'I mean, besides lunch.'

'I only came along for the ride,' she said, teasing him.

He grinned. 'You can help me, then. I need to sort out this paint order and pick up some of the wood we need for the repairs in the hall.'

'D'you think once it's done you'll feel a bit less torn about it?'

'How'd you mean?' Lachlan stopped, turning to look at her as they waited to cross the road.

'Well, it doesn't take a genius to work out you're not exactly wild about the place.'

'That's not strictly true,' he said thoughtfully. 'I love it, I just – well, I don't have a massive ancestral pull towards it

164

like the girls do. I feel like I'm missing some essential Fraser gene.'

Rilla looked at him sideways, thinking about what Beth had said. 'Are you worried it'll end up like a massive millstone round your neck?'

He nodded. 'More than that – imagine having children and basically telling them at birth, look, one of you is going to have to live here – no matter what plans you might have. It feels like the weirdest, most prescriptive thing.'

'You could pass it on to one of the girls.'

He looked uncomfortable. 'That's – well – it's complicated.'

'Don't tell me you don't think women should inherit family property,' Rilla bridled, feeling her temper rising.

'Oh god,' Lachlan started to laugh. 'Do I look like a bloody dinosaur?'

'You don't,' she conceded.

'It's complicated. Weirdly so. Right now, I just want to get the place sorted, then we can work out what to do about it.'

'It'll be easier when I'm out of your hair,' she found herself saying. Half of her felt a strange pull towards Applemore. For the last few weeks, she'd felt for the first time in her life like she belonged somewhere. But it was only temporary – in January she'd be off. She didn't want to get tied up in something. That had always been her motto when it came to relationships – keep things light, and have an exit plan, even if her heart was telling her something very different.

'I don't want to think about that right now.' Lachlan stopped at the entrance to a little alleyway and caught both of her hands. He kissed the side of her cheek. She closed her eyes, losing herself for a moment, then opened them, gazing up into his face. He lifted an eyebrow slightly. 'Deal?'

'Deal.' She nodded. There was nothing to stop her enjoying the moment for what it was. 'Anyway,' she said, keeping her tone deliberately light, 'About this paint...'

A couple of hours later, having loaded up the trailer with the supplies Lachlan needed and some bits and pieces Rilla needed to finish off the van, they strapped everything in place and wandered down towards the river in search of lunch.

'It's funny how Christmas takes over the second Hallowe'en is out of the way, isn't it?' Rilla sidestepped to avoid a harassed-looking woman rushing past in her work uniform, her hands full of shopping. She was clearly grabbing the chance to get as much done as she could in her lunch break. The streets were packed with shoppers, and the windows filled with tinsel and Christmas decorations. A busker was playing carols on a penny whistle, his black and white dog lying patiently at his feet. Rilla hoped that Hugh was okay back at Applemore House with the other dogs, then felt a wave of apprehension. She'd had a call from the rescue kennels the other day, asking if she was still happy to carry on fostering him. Try as she might to stay carefully detached, she knew that she was falling for Hugh. And he wasn't the only one...

Lachlan squeezed her hand gently. 'Penny for them?'

'Oh sorry,' she shook her head, breaking her reverie, 'I was just thinking about Hugh.'

'Weird that nobody's come forward to claim him, isn't it?' Lachlan glanced left and right before they stepped across the road. 'I wonder if he belonged to a traveller.'

'Perhaps.' Rilla was glad nobody had come forward. But there was a tiny nagging voice in her head wondering what was going to happen when January came… the same voice that had her thinking that no matter how lovely this was – wandering the streets of Inverness hand in hand with Lachlan – there was no way it could carry on. She sighed and tried to focus on something else. 'So what's this restaurant like?'

'Gorgeous. They do amazing seafood. You'll love it.'

The restaurant was cosy and welcoming – the décor cool and eclectic, with original artwork hanging on the dark green walls. A waiter showed them to a table in the corner of the room where they could look out of the window at the river and watch the people passing by.

Rilla excused herself and popped to the loo, checking her lipstick and brushing her hair. When she returned, Lachlan was reading the menu and drinking a glass of water.

'Shall we have a glass of wine?'

'Definitely.'

They ordered and were sitting chatting when a tall, very slim man with an expensive suit appeared behind Lachlan, tapping him on the shoulder.

'Lachlan.'

He turned, looking surprised.

'I knew it was you. Recognised that scruffy mop anywhere.' The man gave Rilla a conspiratorial grin. 'You'd think he'd at least shave before taking you out to lunch.'

Rilla looked back at him, feeling slightly bemused.

'Felix,' said Lachlan, giving him a nod and a smile. 'What are you doing up in these parts?'

'Got a dream place on the market – there's a couple from London arriving on the 3.30 flight to view it, so I'm just killing time. I've just had an early lunch – the langoustines are amazing, if you're looking for a recommendation.'

'We've ordered,' Lachlan said, 'but maybe next time. Rilla, this is my old university friend Felix. Felix, this is Rilla – she's an old friend. She's staying at Applemore for a couple of months.'

Felix reached across and shook her hand. He was so tall and slender, it was like shaking hands with a praying mantis.

'Hello,' said Rilla.

'So when am I getting to come over and get your place moving? Have you finished the patching-up job yet?' Felix looked hopeful.

Rilla looked at Lachlan, who cleared his throat and fixed his friend with a very distinct *not now* expression.

Felix's eyes widened almost imperceptibly, and he gave the ghost of a nod. Just at that moment, a waiter arrived with drinks, and Felix took this as his cue. 'I don't want to be getting under your feet, especially when the food's so good here. Enjoy,' he said, directing his words at Rilla with a smile. 'And I'll give you a buzz,' he added to Lachlan.

The waiter returned with their plates. Rilla sat back to give him space to set everything on the table, then put her elbows on the table and balanced her chin on her folded hands.

'So.'

Lachlan looked back at her. 'So.'

'This looks delicious,' she said, still looking directly at him. 'But what I want to know is what your friend Felix is talking about.'

Lachlan picked up a bread roll and broke a piece off, buttering it but not eating it. He held it in his hand and looked at her for a long moment.

'Lachlan?'

'Felix reckons I could sell Applemore and be left with a decent enough profit to be able to hand over a chunk of money to each of the girls.'

'You can't sell it,' Rilla exclaimed, trying to imagine an Applemore House without the Fraser family in it. She shook her head. 'It's your home.'

Lachlan looked at her for a moment, a thoughtful expression on his face. 'I thought you might get it,' he said, his brow furrowing.

'But it's… I mean, it's your home. The girls' home. It's…' Rilla thought about all the summers she'd spent there, and Beth's flower farm, and Charlotte working hard to make the holiday-cottage business work, and… 'Polly's just in the middle of setting up a farm shop. You can't just pull the rug out from underneath all of them.'

'Rilla,' Lachlan said, calmly, 'I know all that. I also know that the place costs tens of thousands to run, and that the repairs I've done are basically like putting a sticking plaster on the Titanic and hoping it won't sink.'

'But…' Rilla was cross at herself for feeling tears springing to her eyes. God, why was she getting so emotional about something that didn't even belong to her?

'I know. There's a million different things I need to work out – how I could divide up the estate so Charlotte could keep going, if we could somehow sell the place with Beth's flower farm staying intact with her as a sitting tenant, and that's not even getting started on Polly and her farm shop idea.'

'Beth needs that place,' said Rilla, passionately. 'It's the only security she's…' She stopped, realising what she was saying.

'What d'you mean?' He looked at her for a moment.

She took a mouthful of food and chewed it thoughtfully, stalling for time.

'Rilla? What d'you mean about Beth? Has she said something to you?'

She shook her head. 'It's nothing.' God, she hoped he wasn't going to grill her. She'd always been hopeless at lying because she had no poker face whatsoever. 'I just know it means a lot to her, that's all.'

'Of course it does.'

Phew, she'd got away with it.

'But the reality is I need to work out the best thing for everyone. If I keep going the way we have, I'm going to run the place into the ground, then we'll be forced to sell anyway, but this way they might actually do okay out of it.'

'You don't actually have to think about that,' she said, looking into his eyes. They were darker than normal, his expression thoughtful.

'I don't, in theory. But can you imagine if I just turned around and went "thanks very much for my inheritance, sod the lot of you, I'm off"?'

She shook her head. 'That's not you.'

'It is not.' He speared a piece of asparagus. 'So I need to work out what to do for the best. And that might just mean doing the unthinkable.'

He'd clearly been agonising over this for some time. She hated to think of him dealing with it alone.

'I get it,' she said, reaching across the table and putting her hand over his. 'You're in an impossible situation.'

'Impossible-ish,' he said, making a face. 'I mean it's not exactly ideal, is it?'

'Not really.'

'I don't want to talk to Beth and Polly and Charlotte

about it until I've worked out some more of the practicalities.'

'I won't say anything, I promise.'

'I feel like a complete shit, encouraging Polly with this farm shop idea when it might all come down around our ears.'

'You said yourself it's given her something to focus on.' Polly had been completely absorbed in the plans. Even now, when she was lying in bed feeling dreadful, she'd been messaging Rilla with ideas she'd come up with to make the farm shop popular with the locals.

He nodded. 'It has. She's been at a bit of a loose end since Dad died.'

'Well then,' Rilla said, rallying, 'I think we have to work on the assumption that something will work out, somehow, and keep encouraging her to make a go of it.'

'You're very zen,' he said, laughing.

'Only with other people's lives,' Rilla admitted. 'But being here has helped a lot. I've really loved it.'

'So you're not going to say anything?'

'Not a word. When is this Felix guy wanting to come and look at the house?'

'Oh, we haven't arranged anything like that. Right now I just want to get past Christmas and…' He stalled, narrowing his eyes slightly and picking up his glass. He looked down into it. 'I'll think about what I'm going to do in January.'

Neither of them said anything more, but the atmosphere shifted slightly. Despite the fact that they had a lovely, romantic lunch sitting overlooking the river and a drive home together through the purple-streaked dusk, the subject of what was happening in January wasn't mentioned again.

CHAPTER 16

There were two missed calls from Gus when Lachlan finished dealing with the builders. A couple of weeks had passed, and the scaffolding was coming down with a cacophony of clattering and clanking, which was setting the dogs off barking every two minutes. He whistled them from the kitchen door and they jumped to attention. Maybe he'd just take them down to the cottage and see how Rilla was getting on with the van, and that way the builders would get some peace from the incessant barking.

In the outhouse, Rilla was painting the cupboard doors they'd fitted earlier that week.

'What d'you think?' She looked pleased with herself.

'It looks amazing.' The van was almost done, which left him with a lot of feelings that he didn't really want to address. Half of him was green with envy that Rilla was going to pack her things, throw them in the back and head off on her travels. The other half was mainly wishing she wasn't going, despite the fact that he was still trying to tell himself that this was nothing more than a slightly extended holiday romance.

Rilla wrinkled her nose at him, making him laugh. 'What are you thinking?' She climbed out of the van, putting the paint-covered brush down on a piece of plastic sacking.

'I'm thinking you look like you could do with a shower. And I'm thinking I could scrub your back, if you wanted…'

She twined her arms around his neck and kissed him. 'I've still got another two cupboard doors to do.'

'Boring,' he teased.

'What are you supposed to be doing?' She put her hand on the flat of his chest, holding it there for a moment.

'I've missed two calls from Gus. I'm really hoping this new brewer hasn't messed up again – we had two barrels blow up last week. The last thing we need is a reputation for being unreliable.'

'What happens when they blow up? It sounds a bit dramatic.'

He shook his head. 'Someone needs to go and deliver replacements, which is a pain in the backside if it's after working hours, which inevitably it is. But it mightn't be that – I'm just looking on the dark side.'

'He might be calling to tell you you've won some major brewery competition or something.'

'Always the optimist,' he said, taking her hand and lacing his fingers through hers.

'Always,' she said, laughing. 'Have you seen how Polly's getting on?'

'I was coming to do just that.'

'Not to see me?' Rilla teased.

'To see you,' he kissed her on the tip of her nose, 'and to

check on Polly. D'you want to come and see how she's doing?'

'Give me a sec and I'll meet you over there.' Rilla put the brush in water.

Over at the barn, Polly had worked miracles. The walls had been whitewashed from floor to ceiling, so the place looked bright and inviting. The shelves she'd ordered had arrived and lined the back wall, with hand-painted signs hanging above them. There was an old table which she'd painted to use as a shop counter, and a set of scales and a second-hand cash register she'd bought online.

'These paintings look amazing.' Lachlan had to hand it to her – she'd done a brilliant job.

'They're all for sale. They're by that woman who lives in the little croft on the road out of town – the one with the black and white horse in the field?'

He nodded. 'I know the one you mean.'

'So I'm thinking if you can cut me down a tree, I can decorate it for the official opening, and we can make it all Christmassy and lovely. I've got someone who'll be baking bread every day, and cakes, and we've got milk and cream from Roger at the dairy farm, not to mention all the hand-made stuff which I think will sell like hot cakes with the holidays coming up…'

He felt a stab of guilt that his sister had been working so hard on something he might well be going to completely sabotage and turned away, gazing out of the front door and across the yard. He could just make out the shape of Rilla, who was climbing out of her overalls.

'You've done brilliantly,' he said, turning back to Polly. 'I'll get the chainsaw and take the trailer up to the woods later. What size d'you want?'

'As big as possible.' Polly beamed. 'I think this place is going to make us our fortune, y'know.'

Lachlan gave her a slightly awkward smile. Fortunately, Rilla arrived then, full of ideas and enthusiasm, and the moment was lost.

Later that afternoon they headed up to the house, taking Hugh and a bottle of wine Rilla had bought earlier that day at the shop. The weather had changed – winter was definitely in the air, and the trees had lost their leaves and were etched dark against the low sun which hung in a pale, opaque sky.

'Polly's going out. I'll make dinner, you can chill and keep me company and drink wine. You deserve it after all your hard work on the van.'

Rilla, who had managed to get most of the paint off her hands, examined them thoughtfully. 'D'you know, I think I'll actually miss being covered in paint when all this is over.'

'I don't think I'd recognise you without it,' he said, laughing. 'Oh, look—'

Standing on the side of the drive was Joan, her short grey hair just visible under a slightly terrifying-looking purple woollen hat.

'Hello!' She waved as Lachlan opened the window, and peered in past him. 'Rilla, it's nice to see you looking so rosy-cheeked and healthy. What a difference from the pale thing you were when you arrived.'

'How are you, Joan?'

'Oh just grand, thank you. Looking forward to seeing Polly's little farm shop up and running. I've told her if she needs a hand just to shout.'

'I'm sure she'd love that.'

'She's an independent wee thing,' Joan said, nodding wisely. 'Nice to see her having something for herself, isn't it?'

'It is,' Lachlan agreed.

'And of course it's a good thing to have a bit of a business going on. I've been watching a programme all about a country estate in England and apparently diversification is the way forward.'

Lachlan could feel his eyebrows raising slightly. 'I think that's her plan.'

'Well, we're all rooting for her in the village. With the shop closing, we need somewhere that'll be the heart of the village, and the shop always was that for me. I need my wee gossip catch-ups every morning when I pick up my bread and milk.'

God, everyone had an opinion. It was nice, he supposed, that they all felt part of Applemore. Not so nice if he turned around and sold the place to the highest bidder... it was clear that if he did, he'd have a lot of explaining to do. Sometimes it felt like he'd inherited not just a house, but a whole community. He envied Rilla and her free-spirited travels. Right now it felt like he was being drawn even more tightly into the clutches of Applemore and he was never going to get out. He said goodbye to Joan and headed home.

'I better give Gus a ring,' he said when he walked back into the house and his phone pinged three times with voice-mail notifications.

'It's fine,' Rilla said, 'I'll just sit here and relax with the dogs. No rush. Do you want me to chop some onions or something?'

'That would be amazing. Thanks.'

He left her in the kitchen and headed for the little study, where he sat, feet up on the desk, looking out of the window. The pine trees that surrounded Applemore loomed in the darkness. It never ceased to amaze him just how dark it got out there at night, and the evenings were so long now – one minute it was daylight and the next, pitch darkness.

'About bloody time.'

'Sorry, I was out of signal. What's up?'

'We need to talk.'

'Sounds ominous. Go on.'

'Not on the phone.' Gus cleared his throat. 'Think this is a conversation we need to have face to face.'

'Okay, now this sounds even more ominous,' Lachlan said, trying to make a joke of it. What the hell was up with Gus?

'It's nothing ominous.'

'No more exploding barrels?'

'Not one. I think that was just a one-off bad batch,' Gus said, sounding more like his old self.

'How's Lucinda?'

'Hrmm.' There was a pause. 'Good. I'll explain all when I see you. When can you make it down? The sooner, the better.' He sounded tense and distracted – quite the opposite from his usual laid-back approach. It must be serious, Lachlan decided, scanning his calendar to check there wasn't anything he needed to reschedule.

'There's no reason why I can't come down on Friday.'

'Not tomorrow?'

'I've promised Polly I'll cut a tree down for her.'

'Obviously.' Gus laughed.

'I'll head down first thing. Should be with you by lunchtime.'

'Excellent. I'll take you to the new bar on George Street that's just started taking our stuff. They do a really good burger.'

'That's a deal.'

Gus hung up, which surprised Lachlan. Not only was his

friend unusually tense, but he was normally so garrulous that Lachlan was desperately trying to get him off the phone forty minutes after he'd called, with Gus still rambling on about the rugby match he'd watched the night before or something that had happened when he'd been sorting out social media stuff for work. No, there was definitely something up.

Lachlan looked around the study, which was still lined with his dad's old books and papers. A black and white photograph of his dad, together with Lachlan and his sisters, hung on the wall. He frowned at it, wondering what his dad would make of all of this. He'd never spoken about the weight of responsibility he must have felt with four children to bring up and Applemore to run – no wonder, then, that he'd ended up in a state of genteel chaos. Lachlan wasn't doing much better.

The next morning, having had a lovely evening together, Lachlan dropped Rilla back at the cottage. He had a tree to chop, some grant paperwork to sort and a friend in need waiting. She'd told him not to hang about when he'd told her how strangely Gus had been acting on the phone, so he'd rung him back that morning and said he'd be down later that evening. There was no point leaving Gus stewing on whatever it was for another day.

He was just slinging a bag into the back of the Land Rover when Beth appeared.

'Hello, stranger,' she said, giving him a wave. She was pushing an empty wheelbarrow. 'Polly said you were off to Edinburgh.'

'Yeah, not sure what's going on with Gus, but I'm half expecting to get down there and find out Lucinda's pregnant or something. He was really cagey on the phone. Not like him at all.'

'Weird.' Beth put down the wheelbarrow to scratch the end of her nose, which was pink with cold. She'd clearly been out in the walled garden all day.

'Where are the babies?'

'Still with the childminder. I'm just about to go and get them.'

'And Simon?'

'Work, I imagine.' Beth picked up the wheelbarrow handles again. She didn't quite meet his eye.

'You okay?' Lachlan remembered Rilla being a bit elusive when he'd asked about her the other day.

'Yeah,' Beth said, still looking down. 'I'm fine. Why d'you ask?'

'Oh nothing,' he commented, casually. 'Just feel like we've hardly seen you of late, which is bonkers when you only live two miles down the road.'

'I've got toddler twins and a business to run,' pointed out Beth, reasonably. 'I don't see anyone. My entire life is taken up with wiping noses and planting things.'

'As long as that's all it is,' Lachlan replied, as she started to trundle the wheelbarrow back towards the walled garden.

He was torn between the urge to probe further – because he knew his sister well enough to recognise that there was something – and to leave her be, because he knew that she was like him and didn't really like sharing how she was feeling. But Rilla had changed all that, with her open, sunny nature. She'd asked about his feelings about this place, about his dad, about losing their mum…because of that, he turned around.

'Beth?'

She turned back. 'Yeah?'

There was a tear running down her cheek.

'What's going on?'

'You need to get off.'

'Not this second,' he said, leaning back against the bonnet of the Land Rover. 'I'm not going anywhere when you're upset. What's the story?'

And it all came out – everything she explained that she'd already told Rilla, who'd kept his sister's confidence. He felt his heart expanding with love for her on realising that – it would have been easy for her to just dump it all on him the moment she'd seen him, but instead she'd listened to what Beth wanted and kept it to herself.

'I can't believe you've spent most of this year keeping all this quiet. How the hell didn't you say something?'

Beth shrugged. 'I didn't want to look like a failure.'

He shook his head. 'How could you ever be a failure? You're bloody amazing.'

Beth looked at him. Now, knowing what he did, he could see just how tired she looked. She had bruised purple shadows under her eyes and she'd clearly lost weight – her cheekbones were prominent and her jeans hanging loose. He'd been so wrapped up in his own worries that he hadn't even noticed how shit things were for her.

'I'm sorry. I need to go and sort whatever it is that's going on with Gus, but I'll be back tomorrow and, when I am, we're going to sit down and work out what we're going to do. There has to be something we can do to help, even if it's taking it in turns to look after the babies.'

Beth gave a sigh. 'I would really like that.'

'Okay. It's a deal. Meanwhile, what are you up to this evening?'

'Simon's coming over to see the twins.'

'I can't believe he moved out and you didn't even say anything.' He had to rein in his fury. He'd never really warmed to Simon, for a reason he'd never been able to put his finger on.

She shrugged, looking slightly embarrassed. 'It just – I didn't know where to start.'

'Well, I'm glad you have now. We'll sort it.' He grinned at her. 'I'll even figure out how to change a nappy, if it helps.'

'I'm holding you to that.' Beth laughed. She picked up the wheelbarrow again. 'Now I really must get going.'

'Okay. We'll sort this tomorrow.' He got in the car, and wound the window down. 'And Beth?'

'Yeah?'

'Tell the others. Seriously. We're supposed to be a family. That's what we're here for.'

CHAPTER 17

'I think we should celebrate,' Polly said to Rilla, standing in the farm shop looking at the tree Lachlan had chopped. It was seven o'clock at night and the two of them had been working hard decorating the tree with countless buttery-yellow fairy lights. The shop floor had been swept clear of pine needles and the place looked absolutely gorgeous. All it needed now was the stock on the shelves, which was the final stage. Rilla had to admit Polly had done brilliantly.

'Actually, I think we should celebrate *with Beth*,' said Polly, thinking about it. She stood back with her arms folded and admired her handiwork.

'I'm not sure she's going to be that much in the mood for celebrating, given everything.'

Lachlan had stopped in on his way to Edinburgh to say goodbye, quickly explaining that he'd spoken to Beth and she'd told him the whole story. He'd taken Rilla's face in both hands and looked at her with an expression she couldn't quite read, shaking his head slowly.

'What?' she'd asked.

'Just you.' He'd kissed her.

'Just me what?'

'You didn't have to do that.'

'I didn't do anything. I just listened.'

'You're lovely.' He'd kissed her again. 'I'll show you how lovely I think you are when I get home tomorrow.'

'That's a deal,' Rilla had said, laughing. Then she'd watched as he strode across the yard and into the farm shop, where he'd briefly updated Polly on what was going on. When he'd driven off, Polly had found Rilla in the van, where she was scrubbing paint off the hinges of the doors.

'Bloody hell, I can't believe it.'

'I know.' Rilla had straightened up.

'I'm going to nip down and see Charlotte and tell her what's going on.'

Rilla had privately wondered how it would feel to have a whole gang of siblings suddenly close ranks when you'd been surviving for so long – a bit overwhelming, she suspected. But maybe that was what families did. She'd waved goodbye to Polly, who'd promised to return later on.

And now they were here, with Charlotte on the way.

'Why don't you come into mine,' Rilla suggested. 'I'll make dinner.'

With that, the sisters swooped into action. Charlotte drove to Beth's place, collecting her. Polly gathered the dogs and brought them down, 'so they don't miss out on all the excitement'. Rilla lit the fire and made the sitting room of the cottage look as tidy as she could – it was a far cry from the huge sprawling sitting room at Applemore, but there were flowers on the mantelpiece, and when the fire was lit and the lamps were on, the place looked sweet and cosy. She put on some music and stirred the Bolognese she'd made earlier. She'd been planning to have it for dinner the next night when Lachlan got back, but they'd just have to have something else – it was nice to think of a girly night out... or in, even. It wasn't something she did particularly often.

'Right,' said Charlotte's loud, clear voice as she opened the door. 'I have procured one Beth, one piece of parmesan and a loaf of ciabatta. Oh –' she put her hand into the bag she was holding '– and one bottle of very nice red.'

'I've got two bottles of probably not very nice red here. I got it from the village shop closing-down sale.'

'We'll drink mine first. Hopefully by the time we get to yours we won't even notice the taste.'

'We can always put clothes pegs on our noses,' said Beth, coming into the kitchen. 'Thanks for this, Rilla. It's really sweet of you.'

'It's the least I could do. You've all been so lovely to me.'

'This place is so cute,' said Polly, appearing from the sitting room. 'I wish we lived in a house like this instead of Applemore.'

'You do?' Rilla looked at her quizzically, thinking how relieved Lachlan would be to hear that.

'Not really,' Polly admitted. 'Well, yes and no.'

They drank the first bottle of wine in what felt like moments. Charlotte, who had decided she was in charge of driving, sat back on the sofa drinking lemonade and making comments about how virtuous she was.

'I've been virtuous for bloody ages,' said Beth, opening a second bottle. 'Babies and breastfeeding and boredom. All the Bs.'

'Well tonight you can let your hair down,' said Polly, disappearing into the kitchen to check on the saucepan of water they'd put on for the spaghetti. 'And tell us why on earth you decided the best course of action was to pretend your marriage wasn't imploding.'

'Oh god,' Beth groaned, 'stop. How on earth was I supposed to know what to do.'

'Tell us?' Charlotte looked at her with a mock chastising expression. 'I mean, I'm not meaning to point out the obvious, but... anyway. You've told us now. A problem halved is a problem –' she counted on her fingers – 'well, not so much halved – you've got Rilla, me, Polly, Lachlan...'

Rilla was touched to be included. Once again, she felt the bittersweet sensation of being accepted and feeling like she really belonged with the sharp reminder that in only a matter of weeks she'd be gone.

'I feel like a complete idiot,' admitted Beth.

'You're not,' chorused Polly, Rilla and Charlotte in unison.

'You're going to be okay, you know?' Polly sat down on the arm of the chair next to Beth, who nodded. 'We can take it in turns to look after the babies. And I can even learn how to do flower stuff, if it helps?'

Beth rolled her eyes. 'I think you should focus on the shop. The last time you tried to help me with the flower farm, you hoed an entire bed of seedlings to death.'

'Oh my god, I forgot that,' said Charlotte, snorting with laughter.

'I can laugh about it now,' Beth said, 'but, my god, I was cross.'

'I remember.' Polly giggled.

Rilla pulled her legs up so she was sitting cross-legged on the sofa. She'd left a framed photo of her dad, herself and Sally on the mantlepiece and Beth followed her gaze, noticing what she was looking at.

'I think our dads would be pleased to see us all hanging out, don't you?'

'Definitely.' Rilla nodded.

'How's the camper van coming along? I keep meaning to come and have a look.'

'I'll show you if you like,' said Rilla.

'Ooh yes please. Bring the wine, Poll.'

The four of them trooped out into the night.

'Bloody hell, it's freezing,' Charlotte shuddered, wrapping her arms around herself.

'It's November.'

'Nearly December. This year's gone past so quickly.' Polly stood out of the way so Rilla could reach the light switch.

'Here we are,' said Rilla, with a little flourish.

'Oh my god,' said Beth, as Rilla pulled open the side door, 'this is so cute!'

'It's got a bed and everything.' Polly patted the mattress they'd put in the other day. It had been sitting in the spare room of the cottage, barely used – and it fit perfectly. It felt like it was meant to be.

'Can I try it?' Beth looked at Rilla.

'Of course.'

Beth hopped up onto the bed and sat on it, legs crossed, holding her glass of red wine. 'You've got a cute little stove and a sink and everything.'

Rilla – feeling proud of her dad's handiwork – switched the stove on. The gas lit with a tiny *pop*. She'd hung the cupboard doors with Lachlan's help, and now everything was painted white, it looked bright and cheerful even in the dim light of the single overhead bulb in the outhouse.

'So d'you think you'll go off adventuring in January?' Charlotte opened and closed a door, experimentally.

'Well,' Rilla felt a knot of something like regret in her stomach, 'I've got a contract for three months' teaching in Paris first. But then I might… I could travel a bit and pick up some casual teaching work. I guess with the van I can go wherever I like.'

There was a sharp bark from inside the cottage.

Charlotte laughed. 'You'll be missed, though. You're the best foster mum he could have asked for.'

'Oh god, don't. I feel sick when I think of leaving him.'

'Just him?' Beth looked at her sideways.

Rilla shook her head, laughing.

Polly did a little mock swoon. 'It's so romantic.'

'Come on, let's go back inside,' said Beth, jumping down from the bed, 'and we can give Rilla the third degree on her intentions towards our brother.'

'I don't have any intentions,' protested Rilla, laughing.

'I think he has some towards you,' Polly said, as they headed back inside.

They worked together, dishing up the dinner and setting it at the little kitchen table. The dogs lay under their feet, hoping for crumbs.

'It's a shame you've met again and now you've got to leave,' said Beth, with a sigh. 'It'd be nice if at least one Fraser family member had a successful love life.'

'You've got the rest of your life ahead of you,' said Charlotte, kindly. 'It might not feel like it now, but I promise, Bethy, you'll meet someone nice.'

'Right now that's the last thing I want to think about.' Beth nodded as Polly offered her the bottle of wine.

'That's just because Simon the Shit has made you feel so bad. I never liked him.'

'Charlotte!' Beth burst out laughing. 'You never said.'

'Of course I didn't,' replied Charlotte, twirling spaghetti onto her fork. 'You loved him, and you were happy. It's not my place to tell you who you should be with, or to venture an opinion. Not until he's well out of the way, in any case.'

'That's very loyal of you,' said Beth, shaking her head. 'Loyal or bonkers, I'm not sure which.'

'That pretty much sums up Charlotte,' said Polly. 'How come you're such a relationship expert, anyway, Char?'

'I've had my fair share of disasters,' admitted Charlotte. 'Don't you remember Robert McArthur?'

'Oh god, Robert who always smelled slightly of cows?' Beth put her hand to her mouth, trying not to laugh.

'That's the one. He was lovely—'

'If you liked the smell of cows,' said Beth.

'What happened with him?' Polly rotated her wine glass between her fingers. 'He always seemed quite nice.'

'I got the ick.'

'Ohhh,' said Rilla, nodding in understanding.

Both Beth and Polly looked at their sister as if she'd lost the plot completely.

'The ick?'

'Rilla gets it.' Charlotte gave a snort of laughter. 'You know when you're with someone and you sort of like them, then one day you realise they chew really loudly and it makes you feel queasy?'

'Or they talk with their mouth full or they're rude to waiters.' Rilla nodded.

'Or – well, it could be anything really. But, basically, it's like someone turned off a switch. I didn't even mind the fact that he smelled of cows. But the way he chewed made me feel like I was going to throw up. I tried to ignore it, but he'd be sitting there going *chomp chomp chomp* and I'd be counting to ten in my head.'

'Poor Robert,' said soft-hearted Polly. 'That seems a bit arbitrary.'

'Oh it wasn't,' replied Charlotte, reasonably. 'I mean,

there was the whole smelling of cows thing, and the fact that he was a bit boring, and—'

'You're not really selling him here,' said Rilla, laughing. It was nice to see Charlotte loosening up a bit.

'Anyway. I decided he could have the old heave-ho and that was that. Then I thought I'd try internet dating, but you can't really do it up here because everyone knows everyone already.'

'My friend told me she saw one of her friend's husbands on Tinder. Well, ex-husband now,' Polly said.

'Exactly,' Charlotte said, sagely. 'Wait – was he an ex-husband when he was on there?'

'Nope.' Polly shrugged. 'He was pretty damn quickly once his wife found out, though.' She looked across the table. 'Oh god, sorry, Beth. That wasn't exactly tactful.'

Beth shrugged. 'It's been months, Poll. I'm past the feeling bad bit. Well, mostly.'

'I can't believe you didn't say anything.' Polly looked at her sister.

'I'm an idiot, I know.' She took a sip of wine. 'Anyway. Enough about me. I want to hear what your plans are, Rilla. D'you reckon you'll stay in touch with Lachlan when you go?'

Rilla looked down at the table, suddenly very interested in the plate of pasta. 'I'm not sure.'

'I've never seen him so happy to be here,' said Beth. 'Normally you can't get him to stay at Applemore for more than about two days before he shoots back to Edinburgh claiming there's some sort of emergency.'

'That's exactly what he's done today,' said Polly. 'Maybe he's reverting to type.'

Rilla frowned. Maybe he was distancing himself, knowing she was going. She needed to get a grip and remember that this was nothing more than an extended holiday romance. 'I think we'll stay in touch,' she said, thoughtfully, 'but really this wasn't anything serious. It was just – well, like laying a ghost.'

Polly giggled. 'Laying several ghosts.'

'I don't want to think about it,' said Beth, making a face. 'I'm very glad you're both happy – for now.'

CHAPTER 18

Lachlan drove the long journey to Edinburgh with the radio on, not taking in a word of what was being said. He was thinking about what to do about Beth, and Polly, and how the hell he'd got into a position where the logical solution – sell the place and move on – was completely tangled up with the emotion of the situation – which was far, far more complicated.

By the time he arrived in the New Town, the skies were dark and it was pouring with rain. Water sloshed across the windscreen in sheets and the lights of the city – the streets still busy, even at nine o'clock at night – were dazzling after the quiet of Applemore. He pulled up on the road outside Gus's place and turned off the ignition. He had such a strong urge to text Rilla and find out what was going on, and let her know he was there safely – but he didn't want to look like, well – a boyfriend. He glanced at his phone for a second, then shook his head and pocketed it as he got out of the Land Rover.

He turned the key in the door of the flat, half-wondering if he should knock. He'd told Gus he'd be there, but things felt different now he'd been up in Applemore for so long. It didn't feel like his place any more, somehow. The dried flower wreath on the door – which had to be Lucinda's handiwork – and the unfamiliar scent of expensive candles that greeted him when he walked into the hallway conspired to make him feel even less at home. He flipped on the light. There was nobody home. It was strange, considering he'd told Gus he was on the way.

In the kitchen, the dishwasher was rumbling quietly to itself. There was a pink Post-it note propped up on the kettle. *Gone to the Dog and Trumpet*, it said.

Lachlan let out a long breath, pushing his hair back from his face. Could he face it? He picked up his overnight bag and headed for his bedroom, deciding he'd shove his stuff in there and think about it. When he opened the door, he found the room had been Lucinda-ed. A brown fluffy cushion sat on its point on top of his pillow, and there was a dark brown knitted throw folded neatly over the end of the bed. One of her headache-inducing scented candles was sitting on the chest of drawers, and a stack of co-ordinating towels were folded neatly beside it. None of his belongings were anywhere to be seen. He opened a drawer – it was empty. What the hell?

Inside the wardrobe, he found two cardboard boxes full of his things. Bloody hell, he thought, I wonder if she'd be in my grave this quickly? He shook his head. Maybe he would have that drink, after all.

'Lachlan!' As soon as he opened the door, Rowan, the bar manager, greeted him with a huge grin of welcome. She cocked her head to one side, which with her rainbow-coloured spikes made her look very much like a cockatoo. 'How's tricks?'

'Better once I've had a drink,' he said, settling down on one of the bar stools and looking around. There was no sign of Gus and Lucinda.

'If you're looking for them, they've nipped over to the Red Lion to check on something, apparently. He said to tell you they'd be back shortly.'

'That's fine.' Lachlan took a sip of beer, grateful that Rowan didn't even have to ask to know what he wanted. 'I've just driven down from Applemore. I could do with decompressing for quarter of an hour before I have to deal with Lucinda.'

Rowan pulled a sympathetic face. 'Not surprised, mate. I tell you what – I'll get another pint ready. You hungry?'

Lachlan shook his head. 'I ate something on the way down.' He caught sight of Gus and Lucinda standing on the opposite side of the road, sheltering under an umbrella. 'But I'll take that pint if it's going.'

He knocked the first one back in a minute.

'Sorry. I needed that.'

'There you are,' trilled Lucinda as they arrived in the bar in a flurry of shaking wet umbrellas and patting of hair. 'I said to Gus you'd arrive as soon as we left. Sod's law, isn't it?'

Gus smiled at her indulgently. 'What d'you want to drink, babe?'

'I think we should have some fizz to celebrate, don't you?'

Gus shot her a look. 'Why don't you pop to the loo. Didn't you say you were desperate?'

Lucinda looked at him as if he'd lost the plot. 'Did I?'

'You did,' said Gus, taking her by the shoulders and steering her gently in the direction of the ladies'. 'You definitely did.'

'Celebrating?' Lachlan looked at his friend, who was looking slightly uncomfortable. 'Gus, what the hell is going on?'

'Can I have a glass of the sauvignon for Lu, and I'll have the same as Lachlan, please.'

Rowan shot Lachlan a sideways glance. 'I'll bring them over. I assume you'd rather a table?'

Lucinda was very definitely not a bar-stools sort of girl. They headed for one of the little tables that was in an alcove. Gus sat down and started fiddling with a beer mat.

'All right, are you going to tell me when it's due?'

'When what's due?'

'The baby. I assume that's why you're freaking out.'

Gus burst out laughing. 'If she was pregnant, d'you think she'd be ordering champagne?'

Lachlan groaned. 'Oh, right. Didn't think of that. So she's not pregnant. You're getting married?'

Gus shook his head. 'Not that, either.'

'Okay, you've got me. What is it?'

'Have you told him?' Lucinda reappeared after what had to be the fastest pee in history.

'I haven't had a chance,' Gus said, dropping his head into his hands. 'Between Lachlan assuming we're having a baby and you reappearing after two nanoseconds, there hasn't been much time for me to get a word in edgeways.'

Lucinda beamed. Whatever it was, she looked like the cat who'd got the cream.

Gus took a deep breath. 'I spoke to someone from the big brewery company the day before yesterday. I tried ringing you to see if you wanted to jump on a FaceTime call, but I couldn't get through.'

'I was probably on the estate – you know what the

reception's like as soon as you get two metres away from WI-FI.'

Gus nodded. 'Anyway, he just wanted to run something past me – well, us.'

'Which was?' Lachlan narrowed his eyes slightly, looking at Gus.

'They want to buy Hedgepig!' Lucinda burst out, earning herself a glare from Gus. She put her hand over her mouth and gave a little squeal of excitement. 'Sorry.'

'I wanted to tell you myself, but apparently that wasn't to be,' said Gus, shaking his head in despair.

'I assume you told them no,' said Lachlan, in a level tone of voice. Inside he was completely rattled.

'Of course not,' replied Lucinda.

Lachlan pressed his lips together to stop himself from pointing out to Lucinda that this had bugger all to do with her. Instead, he took a deep breath, followed by a large mouthful of beer. Rowan caught his eye again and made a face.

'What did you say, then?'

'I said I'd have to talk to you, and we'd have a meeting, and that I'd be in touch.'

They'd built the brewery up from nothing, starting with one barrel and no clues, until the point where they'd developed a good reputation amongst bars across the whole central belt of Scotland. It had been a point of principle for Lachlan, who'd been determined to prove that he could do something that didn't rely on his family background. They'd put in long hours of hard work and sweat – both physical and mental – getting the business to where it was now, where they both had enough money to get by comfortably. He'd known in his heart of hearts as soon as he'd driven north to sort out Applemore that something like this was going to happen.

'I don't want to sell.' He could hear absolutely no expression in his tone.

'You don't even know what they're offering.' Lucinda gave a little squeak of excitement. 'I don't want to sell.'

Gus shot a warning look at Lucinda.

'It's a decent offer. It doesn't mean we'd have to give up – we could start over, try some new stuff.'

'You said retire' said Lucinda, sounding slightly irritable.

'Have you lost the plot?' Lachlan looked at Gus and burst out laughing. 'You can't retire at thirty-five.'

'You can on the amount they're talking about,' said Lucinda, looking pleased with herself.

Lachlan looked at his friend, who was grinning from ear to ear.

'Well, you could certainly take a gap year or two.' Gus took a sip of his beer. 'Now d'you see why she wanted to pop open the bubbly?'

Lachlan sat back against his chair and closed his eyes for a second, shaking his head. This couldn't be happening.

He'd heard of other small breweries being bought up by the big international brewing companies, but the tales of multimillion-pound offers had always seemed about as likely as winning the lottery. The reality though was that he wasn't driven by a desire to make millions – he just wanted to be comfortable and have enough to pay the bills. Lucinda, though, was a completely different kettle of fish. And Gus – well, he came from a comfortably-off family, but he'd always had a fairly easy-going approach to work. It was Lachlan who'd been driven to prove something. Of the two of them, he'd pushed for the brewery to expand and make enough that they could get by. The irony of course was that on paper he looked like the rich one, so he knew that turning this down was going to make him look like a selfish arsehole. But…

'I don't want to sell.' His voice was flat. He put both hands palm down on the table on either side of his beer and looked across at Lucinda, whose sharp little face had dropped slightly, and Gus, who looked somewhat resigned, as if he'd been expecting this.

'I know what you're thinking,' Gus began.

Lachlan puffed out a breath. 'You do?'

'We've put everything into this, it won't be the same, we can't just start again from scratch, yadda yadda yadda.'

'You can't just land this on me and expect me to be all guns blazing,' said Lachlan, taking a drink.

'I think it's a brilliant idea. You can start all over again if you really want to, although, to be perfectly honest, I have no idea why you'd want to spend your time grubbing about in a smelly brewery stinking of hops when you could be relaxing by a pool somewhere counting your millions.' Lucinda pursed her lips. Gus shot her a look. 'What?' she said, indignantly.

'Selling out,' Lachlan said, feeling irritable, 'is just that. Selling out. Do you really want to see our hard work watered down? You know what the big companies do. They'll take our recipe, start making it in bigger quantities, cut down the ingredients month by month until it ends up tasting like gnats' pee…'

'To be fair, mate, it wouldn't be our problem.'

Gus just wasn't getting it. It was about integrity – about something they'd made that actually mattered. Lachlan looked across at the bar where Rowan was pouring a pint of one of their beers, handing it to a customer with her habitual cheeky grin. They'd worked so hard to gain a decent reputation in an industry which was rife with criticism. It meant something – to him.

'I knew you were going to be difficult about this,' said Gus, sounding slightly sulky. It was the first time in all the years they'd been friends that they'd disagreed about anything. Even in the early days when they were starting out and everything that could went wrong and they had to scrabble about for money to pay the rent, they'd managed to make a joke out of it. Now they were being offered enough money that rent wouldn't be an issue, and...

'I'm not being difficult. I'm just saying—'

'Oh for goodness' sake, Lachlan,' shot Lucinda, losing her cool. 'You can't just say no and ruin all our lives because you don't want anyone upsetting the applecart. You're being selfish.'

Gus didn't say anything. Lucinda glared at him, the ice in her drink melting.

A group of rowdy twenty-something lads in football shirts walked into the bar, and the decibel level doubled in seconds. Lucinda said something under her breath to Gus and he shook his head.

Lachlan sized up the situation, downed the second half of his pint and stood up.

'I need some time to think.'

'Take as long as you need,' said Gus, giving him a cautious smile.

'Not too long,' added Lucinda, who just couldn't help herself. 'They might change their minds and buy someone else's brewery instead.'

As Lachlan left, he could hear Gus explaining patiently to Lucinda that, no, that wasn't how it worked, and that she needed to give Lachlan space.

He walked down the road towards Gus's place – it didn't

feel like home, weirdly, any more, with his stuff shunted into boxes by Lucinda (who'd claimed she'd only moved them so she could redecorate). At the last moment, standing at the foot of the steps, he put a hand on the iron railings and thought. He turned, walking briskly up the road in the darkness.

The brewery was set under the railway arches in a part of Edinburgh which had been filthy, run-down and down-right dangerous at night when they'd first taken it on. They'd redeveloped the building, getting funding to make the place sterile and up to the exacting standards needed for drink production.

Lachlan opened the wooden door, relieved that Lucinda hadn't had the locks changed, and flipped on the lights. Everything was as spotless as it had been when he'd left it – Jake, the brewer they'd hired to cover him while he was up in Applemore, was clearly as scrupulous as he was about keeping everything just so. He wandered around, looking at the barrels stacked neatly by the wall.

He sat down on the squashy leather office chair where he and Gus worked, putting his feet on the table and closing his eyes for a moment. He could picture the day they'd picked up the keys for this place as if it was yesterday... and the day the work was done and the spotless new floor and washable walls were installed... and the first barrel of beer they made and drank far too much of in celebration.

Lachlan sighed. Money wasn't everything. The old Gus would have seen that – but now he was wrapped up in this new life with Lucinda where everything was about being seen in the right places, going on expensive holidays and hanging out with an entirely different crowd, he'd changed. If Lachlan thought about it realistically, it had happened over the course of the last year.

God, he wished he could pick up the phone and call Rilla and talk it through with her. She'd be on his side, he was certain – she was the last person to be worried about material things or having millions in the bank. He remembered the other week when he'd helped her with the jigsaw, showing her how to work it as she cut through a piece of MDF to make a shelf. He'd stood close behind her, arms wrapped on either side of her, guiding her hands as he explained how she needed to follow the line of the laser. Her ponytail had fallen to one side, exposing her neck, and he'd been powerless to resist the urge to lean over and kiss it. She'd turned, a smile curving on her lips, and wrapped her hands around his neck. God, he wanted her there.

He picked up his phone, looked at the screen, then shoved it across the desk. No. He needed to work this out for himself.

CHAPTER 19

Lachlan arrived back at Applemore the next afternoon, delighted to hear that Rilla had had a good evening with the Fraser sisters but seeming slightly detached. She figured that he was probably tired after a long drive and gave him a kiss on the cheek, telling him she'd come round to the house later after she'd finished making a curtain for the van.

She'd been quite proud of herself – she wasn't exactly the best seamstress in the world, but with Sally's help via several FaceTime calls, she'd managed to measure, cut and sew a piece of fabric to make a curtain which would divide the cab from the sleeping area of the van at night. It looked pretty good, if she said so herself.

Working in the van in the chill of early December wasn't cold, because the little diesel heater that her dad had fixed into the back pumped a constant supply of warm air. She was growing to love the little space – it felt just right to her, as someone who didn't like a lot of stuff, to have a tiny space where she could keep everything she needed to hand, and there was nowhere to hoard a lot of the useless stuff people tended to hold onto. Travelling had taught her to keep her belongings to a minimum, and she liked it that way. The only trouble she had was the awful, nagging feeling of not wanting to leave either Hugh or – she sighed, cross with herself for having allowed her feelings to get in the way of what she wanted – Lachlan.

Hugh nosed at her hand, looking for attention, as she sat at the little table in the van with the door closed, trying to imagine how it would feel to be driving all the way to Paris. It had been her dream to travel the world, never settling down, always looking forward to the next adventure. So why on earth was she sitting here thinking about how much she wanted to just wander up to Applemore, sit at the kitchen table, drink coffee and soak up the feeling of belonging?

She shook her head. This was ridiculous, and she needed to get over herself, and fast. Maybe the answer was to remind herself how much she liked travelling…

'What are you up to?' Polly appeared from the door of the farm shop, paintbrush in hand. She'd made a sign to hang outside and was looking pleased with her handiwork. All day long, suppliers had been coming back and forth, dropping off the first of the stock for the shop – handmade crafts and paintings, cheeses from the local dairy, huge sacks of potatoes from the farm along the road. The big opening was three days away and Polly was just about in orbit with excitement and stress.

'I'm going to take the van on a trial run,' Rilla said, jangling the keys. She'd fastened everything that was loose inside, making sure that there wouldn't be anything flying around or rattling as she drove around the bendy country roads near Applemore.

'Ooh, I wish I could come,' said Polly, 'but I've got to get organised.'

'Next time,' Rilla smiled. 'I'll be back tomorrow.'

She drove up the bumpy potholed lane to Applemore, finding Lachlan inside the house sitting at his desk in the study.

'What are you up to?' He looked up at her, a pen in hand.

'I thought I'd take the van for a trial run.'

An unreadable expression passed across his face.

Rilla looked at him. 'You okay?

'Just got a lot of stuff on.'

He seemed distracted and not his usual self. Rilla gave him a kiss and left him to it, deciding that perhaps he was just sorting out stuff do to with the house.

At the end of the day, she told herself, this was what you wanted. You don't want to be caught up in all of that. You want this. She pulled out onto the main road out of Applemore and headed north. You want the open road and freedom and no ties.

Hugh sat beside her on the passenger seat, tongue lolling, looking delighted to be there. Well, Rilla smiled to herself, no ties besides a dog.

She paused at the junction, deciding that perhaps she'd pop in on Joan on her way past. She'd been promising to do so for ages, and now was as good a time as any.

'Hello, lovey,' Joan beamed, opening the front door. 'This is a surprise.'

'Do you want me to leave Hugh in the van?'

'No, come away in, bring him with you. He'll be fine.'

'He's a bit muddy and hairy.'

'Nothing a quick hoover won't sort out afterwards. Gosh, your dad would be delighted to see you out on the road in the van.'

'He would, wouldn't he?' Rilla sat down on the sofa.

There seemed to be even more cushions than there had been the last time she'd visited.

'I think so. Now, tell me what's been going on. Polly's going great guns with the shop, isn't she?'

'It's nearly ready,' agreed Rilla. 'It's been lovely watching it grow out of nowhere.'

'She's a determined wee thing,' Joan said. 'Very like her mother.'

'That's funny,' Rilla said. 'Nobody ever talks about their mum. What was she like?'

'Oh,' Joan paused, hearing the kettle click. 'I'll tell you all about her in a moment. Let me just make a cuppa and we'll have a bit of cake. You'll need the energy for the journey.'

Rilla wasn't sure that a twenty-mile drive necessitated a slice of chocolate cake about four inches thick, but she wasn't going to argue with Joan, who handed her the plate and put a cup of tea on the coffee table in front of her.

'So,' Joan said, settling back on her armchair. She sipped her tea and looked thoughtfully at Rilla. 'Jennifer Fraser.'

'They never really mention her.'

'It's a shame, really. I mean, I can understand why – after what happened – but really, it's the old story – families and secrets, and things left unsaid. If there's one thing I've learned, it's that you need to just be truthful. It's always the way.'

'Go on.'

'Well, it starts with your dad, funnily enough. Years and years back, when he first brought you girls up here. He'd not long split up with your mum, and he was muddling along trying to work out how to keep the two of you occupied in the summer holidays.'

'What's that got to do with the Frasers' mum?' Rilla realised she sounded abrupt.

Joan looked at Rilla for a long moment, a curious expression on her face. 'You haven't a clue about any of this, have you?'

Rilla shook her head. 'No. Not at all.'

'Well, I suppose – you know, the funny thing is that now they're all gone, I feel like I shouldn't – but maybe it's right that you should know the truth.'

Rilla put the cake back down on the table. She felt slightly uneasy suddenly, as if she'd opened up an old diary that didn't belong to her but couldn't stop herself from reading what was on the pages. 'The truth about what?'

'Your dad and Hector Fraser hit it off straight away. It was one of those friendships that just blossoms – you know what I mean?'

Rilla nodded.

'Only… well. It was more than that.' Joan looked at her quizzically. 'You really didn't know any of this?'

Rilla shook her head.

'Jennifer was a nice enough girl. A bit stuck-up, if I'm honest – not meaning to speak ill of the dead, of course – but she came from money and when she married Hector, her parents were delighted that she was the lady of such a grand old place.'

'Even though it's falling apart.'

'Even though. Although, back in those days, it was nowhere near as dilapidated as it is now. And she tried her best – she did the garden, and kept the children nice, and even though it was pretty clear she wasn't all that happy with her lot, she went through the motions. I was there every day. I saw it all unfolding.'

'What happened?' Rilla frowned. She couldn't see where this was going.

'Your dad and Hector… it wasn't just a friendship, if you get my meaning.'

Rilla sat up. She looked at Joan's face, not sure if she was misreading the weight in her words.

'But—' she began.

Joan inclined an eyebrow.

'I thought…' Rilla tailed off.

Joan sat back and folded her arms, looking at Rilla as if she had all the patience in the world.

'Dad and Hector.'

Joan nodded.

'Are you saying they were… in love?'

Joan nodded again. 'That they were. Everyone has one grand passion in their life, or so I've been told. Well, your dad and Hector were that.'

'But…' Rilla opened her mouth and closed it again. All those words of love, written in that neat, careful hand. Those letters, folded up and read and re-read until they were soft with age. Her heart contracted. 'How could they be? Nobody told… I mean, why didn't we know?'

'Ah,' Joan said, shaking her head. 'Things have changed a lot in the last twenty-five years. Back then – aye, even then – there was a real stigma attached to things like that.'

Rilla thought of her dad, and how she'd always felt bad for him being alone up there in the cottage. She'd presumed his insistence that he was quite happy pottering about on his own was something he'd said to make her feel better… but all the while he'd had someone who loved and treasured him. Her eyes filled with tears.

'The letters,' she shook her head. 'I can't believe I thought it was you.'

'Letters?' Joan sat up. 'You thought... oh—' She gave a laugh, shaking her head. 'No, definitely not me.'

'I found a whole sheaf of letters when I was clearing out the cottage. I just assumed they were from his past – lovely little notes of love, saying how much this person wanted to be with him and how things would be different in the future, and how they wouldn't always have to creep around in secret.'

'Ah,' Joan said, with a sad smile. 'Isn't that touching?'

'It's awful to think of them having to live a lie.'

She nodded. 'It is. Hector came from a long line of very old-fashioned upright Frasers, and I think that never really left him. The whole idea of passing on the family heritage mattered to him – that's why he'd be so upset that Lachlan has such an antipathy to the place.'

'He doesn't,' Rilla said, defending him. 'He just hates everything it stands for. God, I can see why if he knew that it stopped his dad being happy.'

'Lachlan has no idea,' said Joan, gently. 'The only person who ever did was me – well, and Jennifer, of course. She found out in the worst possible way – came home early from a meeting and found them in bed. It was the final straw for her, I think. I always wondered if she'd been a bit depressed after Polly was born. Anyway, she packed her things and left.'

'And left the children. That must have been so hard for her.'

Joan nodded. 'Mothers do leave, you know. Sometimes they do it because they think it's the right thing to do.'

'But they didn't stay in touch?'

'They did, on and off. But she married someone else and went on to have two little boys with him, and I think it was easier for her to just forget her past.'

'I can't imagine that.'

'It's funny what the heart will do to protect itself.'

Rilla looked away, thinking of her plans to leave in January. 'So, Dad and Hector—'

'All those years. Not a soul knew, apart from me. And they died months apart – I don't think they could have lived without each other.'

Rilla was astonished. She sat in silence for a long while, trying to recall the times she'd seen her dad with Hector. He'd always been warm and welcoming to her, and she could picture him standing with her dad, laughing in the cottage kitchen or chatting outside Applemore House, but—

'Why didn't they just admit it?'

'I don't know. I don't think anyone would have batted an eyelid. Of course, the saddest thing was what happened with Sally.'

'The accident on the loch?'

Joan nodded.

'Your dad and Hector were together when it happened. David always blamed himself, saying that he should have been paying more attention to where you were going.'

'It wasn't his fault.'

'Of course it wasn't. But your mother blamed him. She'd started a new life in the United States by then, and she was more than happy to use it as the excuse she needed to stop you two girls coming back every summer.'

'I had no idea,' Rilla repeated. 'So that's why Dad never fought against it?'

'I think so. He felt he only had himself to blame. I think he was punishing himself.'

Rilla felt tears gathering in her eyes. 'That's so awful.'

'It is, I know. But you can't feel bad about it. The truth is that the two of them had something most people will never have – and that's worth a lot.'

Rilla wiped her eyes. 'I wish I could talk to him – to both of them – and tell them it was okay.'

'You got the chance to spend time with him before he died,' Joan said, leaning forward and squeezing her knee. 'That meant the world to him.'

'I have to tell Sally. And Lachlan. He needs to know there was more to his dad than…'

Joan nodded. 'I think you're right there. He looks at this place and sees it as nothing more than a poisoned chalice.'

Rilla got up. 'I think I might go back and talk to him now.'

'I think that's a good idea. There have been enough secrets in that family. Maybe it's time they found out the truth.' Joan put an arm around Rilla and pulled her into a hug. It felt warm and comforting. Rilla was reminded fleetingly of her own mother and thought about how long it had been since they'd spoken.

'I'll let you know how I get on.'

'You do that. I love those children, you know.' Joan smiled.

'I know you do.' Rilla paused for a moment. 'Have you spoken to Beth recently?'

'Not for a wee while,' admitted Joan. 'She's always so busy with the flower farm and the twins. I must pop by and see how she is.'

'I think that would be a lovely idea.' Rilla didn't want to break a confidence, but she had a feeling that right now Beth could do with one of Joan's lovely warm hugs and some of her chocolate cake, not to mention some mothering.

'I'll pop up there later. No time like the present, is there?'

Rilla nodded. That was exactly how she felt. Lachlan had been in such a strange mood earlier – maybe this might help make things a bit clearer for him.

Rilla climbed back into the van, waiting while Hugh made himself comfortable on the front seat. Turning left to return to Applemore, instead of right to head up to the white sands of the beach, she switched the heating up. It was cold, the sky a faintly purplish grey which looked like the first snow of the year could be on the way. Her fingers were chilly on the steering wheel.

In the field which followed the line of the road, the herd of dairy cows stood huddled together by a stand of dark pine trees, their breath rising in clouds in the freezing air. A tractor rumbled across the far field, pulling a trailer. In the distance, she could just make out the dark shapes of the islands across the water. A fishing boat was setting out to sea.

She turned up the drive to Applemore, passing the cottage. Hugh leapt forward in excitement, thinking he was home. 'Not yet, my lovely,' Rilla said, patting him on the head. The cottage looked pretty in the winter light, a plume of smoke rising from the chimney and the last few roses still clinging on stubbornly around the front door.

She pulled up outside Applemore. A delivery van was just leaving, having deposited a stack of DIY supplies on the step outside the front porch. As she approached, Lachlan pulled open the door from the inside, and his face brightened the moment he saw her.

'Well, this is a nice surprise,' he said, looking at her for a moment before reaching forward to take her hand and kiss her briefly. 'Were you delivered with the bathroom tiles?'

'I wasn't,' Rilla laughed. 'But I decided that maybe we needed to talk.'

'Can we get out of here?' Lachlan looked at the pile of DIY supplies. 'I can't face this lot, and I could really do with escaping for a bit.'

'I was going to take the van for a run out to the beach, if you want?'

'I would love that.'

'You'll have to share the front seat with Hugh. He's pretty much convinced he owns the entire space.'

'I can deal with that. Let me just grab a jumper. It's bloody freezing.'

They drove north, heading for the beautiful white stretch of beach that curved around the headland. Lachlan seemed thoughtful, looking out of the window and not talking for the first few miles. Rilla decided to let him be. Whatever it was that was bothering him, she wasn't going to try to drag it out of him.

'Look, I'm sorry I've been such a bear since I got back from Edinburgh.'

'It's fine,' she said, glancing over at him. Hugh shuffled sideways slightly, leaning his head against Lachlan's arm.

'It's not fine,' he said, making an apologetic face. 'It's just – I've got a lot to try to figure out. I'm so used to just doing it myself without having anyone to talk to that it's just a habit to end up turning away from people and not actually opening up.'

'That makes perfect sense to me.' Rilla took a sip of water from her bottle. 'You don't have to talk if you don't want to.'

They drove along in silence for a long time. Eventually, Lachlan put a hand on her thigh, the warmth of his hand reaching through her jeans, making it hard to focus on anything else. She looked sideways at him.

'What?'

He inclined his head towards her, smiling. 'What?'

'You look like you're building up to say something.'

She felt a weird gnawing sense of discomfort. For every part of her that wanted to fall into his arms and give up the job in Paris and stay here, there was another, like opposing magnetic forces, desperately trying to drag her away. She'd always survived on her own until now. Being with Lachlan felt safe, but it felt terrifying at the same time.

He broke into her thoughts. 'The thing is, when I got to Edinburgh, Gus threw me a massive curveball and I can't work out what the hell I'm supposed to do.'

Her shoulders dropped – she hadn't even realised how tense she'd become. Relieved – although there was an unexpected part of her that was a little disappointed - that he wasn't about to declare undying love, she felt safe to drive, and listen, as Lachlan explained how his friend had dropped the bombshell that there had been an unexpected offer on the brewery for an amount of money that would change their lives.

'The trouble is,' Lachlan concluded, 'I'm not sure I want to change my life.'

Rilla frowned slightly. 'What happens if you say no?'

'I don't know. I mean, the truth is nothing can be the same after this. If I say no, I can't see how Gus and I can carry on working together, because he'd be full of resentment about what could have been. If I say yes, everything changes anyway.'

'D'you think he'd be up for setting up a new brewery?'

Lachlan lifted a shoulder in a vague shrug. 'I doubt it. I

mean, would you, if you had enough money to not have to worry about working?'

Rilla thought about it for a moment, slowing up as they approached a big articulated lorry that was heading north. She checked her mirrors and overtook.

'I think I can't imagine doing *nothing*, can you?'

He shook his head. 'I can't. I'm not the sort of person who could sit around counting my money all day. Not that that's been an issue up until now.'

She laughed. 'Nor with me.'

'But neither of us are particularly driven by stuff like that.'

'Which is ironic, given you're the owner of a gigantic house in the Highlands,' she said, teasingly. He squeezed her thigh slightly. She'd not even noticed that his hand was still resting there – it felt so natural. She shifted slightly, and he moved it away.

'Shut up.'

'I can't help it if you're part of the landed gentry.'

'Not very landed. They kept selling it off to pay off death duties.'

'Talking of which,' Rilla pointed out. 'If you did sell the brewery, you'd solve that problem.'

Lachlan groaned. 'Tell me something I don't know.'

'Have you thought about doing a list of pros and cons?'

'You are ridiculously sensible,' he said, shaking his head. 'But yes, I have. Sort of.'

'Look at the advantages. You know what you're doing. You could start something new. You said you were going to do the gin thing. That could be your new venture.'

'True.' He sounded dubious. 'The weird thing is I went to Edinburgh and for the first time since I moved there for uni it didn't feel like home.'

'Maybe you've finally been bitten by the Applemore bug.' She kept her voice deliberately light, knowing that somewhere inside she'd been thinking exactly that. The thought of it terrified her.

'Don't you start. Polly said that the other day.'

'Would it be so bad if you had?' She could play devil's advocate.

'It's got a lot of… well, I was going to say bad memories, but that's not fair. It's just – there's a lot of stuff tied up with it. I don't want to end up like my dad. That's the turning for the beach, coming up on the left.'

The road down towards the beach was narrow and twisting. Rilla, tongue between her teeth as she concentrated, didn't speak as she focused on steering the big unfamiliar van down the steep hill.

'That was a bit hairy,' she said, pretending to mop her brow when they pulled up at the little car park. It was deserted, with only a sign saying 'leave nothing but footprints' hanging on the fence. They climbed out of the van and Hugh dashed off in search of delicious things to sniff. Lachlan took her hand and they wandered along the path through the dunes.

A few minutes later, they stepped out from the shelter of a huge grass-covered dune and Rilla gasped. The sea was a perfect turquoise frilled with white waves. What seemed like miles of perfect, sparkling sand stretched out along the shore. Gulls wheeled overhead, breaking the silence with their calls. Other than that, the place was deserted.

'This is utterly beautiful.'

Lachlan looked down at her for a moment, a curious expression on his face. She turned away, pushing her hair back as it flew across her face in a gust of wind. Once again, she felt that strangely uncomfortable feeling of being utterly torn, and covered it up with a joke.

'I feel like I want to jump in and swim.'

'You'd jump out again pretty bloody quickly,' Lachlan laughed. 'That water is freezing. Look, even Hugh isn't going in.'

Hugh, who normally threw himself with alacrity into an available body of water, was hovering at the edges, snapping at the waves that lapped at the shore.

'I think that's probably a sign I should stay here.'

Lachlan put an arm around her shoulders. 'I think that's a very good idea.' With his other hand, he lifted her chin, looking at her for a moment before kissing her gently.

'What was that for?' Rilla said, standing close so she could feel the heat of his body against hers. Even with coats and jumpers, it was absolutely freezing cold, and she allowed him to draw her towards him, feeling the warmth of his thumb as he traced her jawline for a fleeting moment.

'To say thank you for listening.'

'I haven't really helped.' She tried to make light of it.

'You gave me a chance to think. The thing is, I could sell Applemore, but…' He gazed into the distance for a moment, looking distractedly over her shoulder. 'It's not just about me. That's the thing. I've got to think about what's best for everyone.'

'Including yourself,' she said. It seemed to her that Lachlan was so busy thinking about what everyone else needed that he'd forgotten his own desires. 'What do you actually want?'

He looked back at her, his eyes darkening as they met hers, and for a long moment he didn't say anything.

CHAPTER 20

More than anything what Lachlan wanted to say was one very simple word. *You*, he wanted to say. *That's what I want.* Instead, he shook his head and lifted his eyebrows. 'I have absolutely no idea.'

It was increasingly clear to him that his feelings for Rilla were getting out of control, and time was passing. The van was ready, Christmas was approaching, and her new job was waiting. He needed to make some major decisions about what he was going to do, but he needed to steel himself and recognise that she wasn't going to be part of the equation, no matter how much he might want her to be.

'Shall we walk?' Rilla put a hand to his cheek. Her fingers were icy cold.

'Are you sure you don't want to go back to the van?'

She shook her head. 'Hugh's been stuck in there all afternoon. Let's give him a run. There's something I need to talk to you about, anyway.' She bit her lip.

God, she was pretty. He shook his head as if to chase away the thought.

'Okay. As long as you're not going to freeze to death.'

'I solemnly promise not to. And if I do, you can take me back to the van and defrost me.'

'Deal.'

She grinned at him.

'So what is it you wanted to tell me?'

Fifteen minutes later, they turned back towards the van, having walked along the edge of the shore while Rilla explained the secret that their fathers had taken to their graves.

'I can't believe it. I mean, I can't believe how stupid I was to miss it.' He shook his head.

'I did too. I think it's not so much that we were stupid to miss it, more that they were careful not to let anything slip, ever.' Rilla took his hand again, having thrown a stick for Hugh.

'But why on earth wouldn't they just admit that they loved each other?'

Lachlan was surprised by just how much it made sense. All those years he'd wondered why his dad seemed content not to meet anyone after their mother had left. All the time he'd spent pottering about companionably with David in his workshop while he built things or repaired bits and pieces. They'd been safe in their own little world, quite happy together.

'I think maybe it was different for my dad – I mean, he mixed in a world of academics when he lived in Edinburgh. It wouldn't have been such an issue for him.'

'But Dad's family were strict Presbyterians. I can't imagine my grandfather accepting their son was gay.'

'Things were a lot different when our dads were growing up. I mean, they're still not great now, whatever people might think. I've got plenty of gay friends and they experience prejudice every single day.'

Lachlan nodded. 'Yeah. It's shit, isn't it?'

'It really is. But if you think about it like that, and imagine being thirty years older than us?'

'I'm glad they found each other, even if they did keep it a secret.'

'Me too.'

'All that time I thought Dad's only focus was Applemore and duty – that he'd stayed because he didn't have a choice. To think he was quite happily living here with someone he loved.'

They walked along in silence, watching Hugh as he raced up and down the beach at a hundred miles an hour. Lachlan thought about his dad and how he'd seemed to just give up fighting after David had passed away. It made so much more sense now – without the love of his life, he'd clearly decided it wasn't worth holding on. He wondered what his dad would have to say about everything. And his mum – his heart squeezed tightly in his chest. How he wanted to be able to tell her that he understood now why she'd left, why staying had been one heartbreak too many.

'I don't know what to think about all of it. It's just huge, isn't it?'

'I'm glad there aren't any more secrets.'

'I am too. It's a shame we can't tell them we'd have given them our blessing.'

'Maybe they didn't need it,' said Rilla, thoughtfully. 'Perhaps they were happy enough as they were.'

They drove back to Applemore, both quiet and lost in their own thoughts. When they pulled up to the cottage, Polly was still working away putting the finishing touches to the Farm Shop, all ready for the opening the next day. She beamed a welcome.

'Did you have a nice adventure? I'm glad it didn't break down.'

Rilla patted the van on the bonnet. 'She was amazing. We had a lovely time, didn't we?'

Lachlan nodded. 'She'll have no trouble driving you to Paris – and beyond.'

Rilla gave a bright smile. 'Exciting, isn't it?'

'I bet you can't wait,' Polly beamed.

Lachlan couldn't meet either of their eyes. He headed into the farm shop to have a look. It looked absolutely amazing. Polly had strung long swathes of golden yellow fairy lights from corner to corner, and the tree he'd chopped down was twinkling with yet more lights and a rainbow of wooden decorations. He lifted one up.

'They're for sale,' Polly said. 'Look.' She turned one over to show a tiny price tag sticker. 'They're made by Ben Lewis from the old croft up on the road to the big loch. He carves them all and hand-paints them.'

'They look amazing,' said Rilla. Lachlan turned to look at her. She'd tied her windswept curls back in a ponytail. She stood gazing around at Polly's handiwork. 'You've made this place look magical.'

Polly's cheeks went pink with pleasure. 'D'you really think so?'

Lachlan nodded. 'It's really impressive, Poll.'

'I'm so nervous about the opening tomorrow, I think I won't sleep a wink tonight.'

'What can we do to help?'

'I thought you'd never ask.' Polly giggled and pretended to faint. 'If you could man the till, that would be amazing. I think I need to be mingling about a bit to start with anyway.

Someone from the local paper said they'll try to come out to take some photos.'

'I'll do whatever,' Lachlan offered. He was so proud of his baby sister he could burst. For a moment, he felt a pang of sadness that his dad wasn't there to see just how much she'd achieved, then he remembered – everything he thought he'd known about his dad and how he felt about this place was altered by what Rilla had shared with him on the beach. It changed everything, somehow. He had a lot of thinking to do.

That night, he took a glass of whisky into his dad's study and sat down in the battered leather chair he'd had for as long as Lachlan could remember. He closed his eyes, trying to think back. Had he missed the clues? Was he really so spectacularly unobservant? If his dad and David had been together for over two decades, how on earth could they have kept their love under wraps?

Lachlan looked up at the black and white photograph of his dad with the children and shook his head. If only he could have five minutes with him, just to tell him how much he loved him and that he'd have been proud of him, happy to stand up and say this is my dad, and this is the man he loves. But – he winced, thinking about it – how his grandfather would have been appalled. He'd been an upstanding, old-fashioned man, pillar of the community, always doing his bit for the people who lived and worked on his estate. But he was also short-tempered, quick to judge and believed slavishly in the old-fashioned rules of the church as he saw it. He'd have considered his son a sinner... His poor dad, growing up believing that was the case.

Lachlan swallowed a mouthful of whisky and shook his head. There had to be something he could do to make up for what had happened... Meanwhile, he had to work out what the hell he was supposed to do about everything. Felix had left two voicemails urging him to call earlier that day when he'd been out of signal on the beach with Rilla. Knowing what he did now, though, seemed to shift the whole world on its axis. If Applemore hadn't been the mill-stone around his father's neck he'd always believed it to be, did that mean it meant something different to him, too?

He stood up, looking around at all of his dad's things. In the past, the study had seemed cluttered and oppressive – a reminder of a duty he hadn't signed up for and one that he resented. Tonight, though, it felt like a warm and comforting reminder of the father he'd lost – and who he missed more today than he had ever before. Everything had changed, and Lachlan didn't quite know what he thought or felt.

The morning of the farm shop launch dawned and with it came the first snow of the year. Even before Lachlan drew back the curtains, he could sense it – there was something in the muffled silence he'd recognised ever since he was a boy. He looked outside to see the black branches of the beech tree outside his window laden with snow, and each of the pine trees that led to the drive iced as if they'd been sprin-kled with fine sugar.

Downstairs, the devastation of toast crumbs, cafètiere and coffee mugs suggested that Polly had been up and was already gone. He looked up at the clock – only 8.30. Once he'd eaten and showered, he'd head down and see what she needed in the way of help.

The courtyard behind the cottage was already filling up when he got there. He spotted the vet's Range Rover, her logo painted on the side. And there was Sally from the bookshop in the village, hair tied back with a piece of tinsel, beaming with excitement as she waved hello to him and made her way into the shop. Polly had done an amazing job again that morning, adding the final decorations of some of Beth's brightly coloured flower arrangements which set off the plain white walls beautifully. There was a huge vat of mulled wine balancing on a camping stove, the scent of spice and cinnamon filling the air.

'Never too early for a mulled wine at Christmas, eh?' Fiona, the vet, gave him a huge wink and laughed, raising her paper cup.

'I think I might hold off a bit,' he said, laughing. He was scanning the room, which was thronging already, searching for Rilla. There she was – dressed in a red shirt and jeans, her hair tied back from her face with a piece of scarlet ribbon. She caught his eye and waved, her face wreathed in smiles. She mouthed *hello* at him before turning to deal with a customer. There was a queue, unbelievably. Polly was skipping about chatting to people and showing them everything that was on offer – and the shelves were stacked with an amazing assortment of local produce.

'Morning,' said a familiar voice. Lachlan turned to see Harry from the hotel grinning at him.

'Shouldn't you be feeding people breakfast or something?'

'Came to check out my new supplier.'

'Polly?'

He nodded. 'She's sorted out a pretty good deal for fruit and veg – and you know I'm all about locally sourced stuff. She's bloody impressive.' He looked across at Polly and gave an approving nod. 'Your kid sister grew up into a bloody good businesswoman.'

Lachlan raised an eyebrow. 'Watch it,' he said, noticing the way Harry was looking at her.

'I haven't done a thing,' he said, laughing.

'Yet.' Lachlan gave him a look. 'The last thing she needs is a broken heart and with your track record…'

'Bloody hell, man,' Harry snorted with laughter. 'Give a reformed rake a chance.'

'I will,' said Lachlan darkly, 'but not with my sister.'

'She's a woman who knows her own mind.'

'Hmm,' said Lachlan.

Harry wandered off. Lachlan watched him kissing Polly hello and noticed how she looked up at him, eyes dancing with amusement as he bent his head to whisper something in her ear. Ah well, he thought, she's old enough to make her own mistakes.

'You okay?' Rilla appeared by his side. 'Have you met Ben? He's the artist who made all the wooden carvings.'

Ben looked more like a lumberjack than an artist. He had a shock of dark hair which stood up in slightly untidy spikes and a heavy beard. He was wearing a thick plaid shirt and jeans with a pair of work boots. He put out a hand in greeting.

'Nice to meet you. I was talking to your sister Charlotte the other day – one of her holiday cottages is just down the road from my place.'

'How are you settling in?'

'I love it here. It's a bit of a change from Lancashire, but I've been doing loads more work, so I'm happy.'

'Not finding it too isolated?'

Ben shook his head. 'I like the space. Gives me time to think.'

Lachlan thought about how busy he'd found Edinburgh when he went down the other day, and how much he'd appreciated the quiet of Applemore when he got back. Maybe the place was getting to him after all. 'Yeah, I know what you mean.'

'You're lucky to have grown up here,' said Ben, looking around at the people of the village who were all standing in little groups, chatting and laughing.

'You know,' Lachlan began, realising as he spoke that he felt it for the first time, 'I really was. It's funny, I don't think I ever actually thought about it until recently.'

'Nice place to bring up kids. Have you got any?'

'No,' Lachlan shook his head. 'You?'

'One daughter,' Ben said, 'but she lives down south with her mum. I'm hoping she'll come up for the holidays. I miss her like mad.'

'I bet.' Lachlan turned to Rilla. 'Rilla used to spend her summers here when she was growing up,' he explained to Ben.

'And now I can't keep away,' she said, laughing.

Lachlan caught her eye for a moment and wanted desperately to catch hold of her, kiss her and not let go. Instead she gave him a quick squeeze of his fingers, then said she needed to get back and help Polly on the till.

'Have you two been together long?' Ben watched Rilla weaving her way through the crowds of people.

'Oh – we're not – well, we're…'

'It's complicated?' Ben laughed.

'Something like that.'

'She seems like a really nice girl.'

'She is.' Lachlan felt a twist of regret once again. Every single day brought them closer to the point where Rilla was going to walk back out of his life, and he seemed powerless to stop it.

CHAPTER 21

'I can't believe how much we've taken in the first two weeks.'

Polly flopped back against the wooden table as Rilla closed the door on the final customer of the day.

Rilla looked around. Once again, the wicker baskets that had been full of home-baked bread and delicious cakes were completely empty. The produce shelves looked as if they'd been raided by a horde of ravenous animals. There had been a run on the pretty handmade Christmas decorations that afternoon, so they'd ended up removing the ones hanging from the tree, which now looked as if it had been decorated by someone who'd forgotten what they were doing halfway through.

Polly switched off the speaker which had been blaring out Michael Buble's Christmas songs all afternoon. 'I think I might have reached peak Christmas.' She puffed out a breath of air, lifting a long strand of her fringe up from her face for a moment before it landed back and was pushed out of the way.

'It's unfortunate that we're going to the Applemore carols round the tree celebration, then, isn't it?' Rilla said, mischievously.

'Don't.' Polly shook her head and checked the time on her phone. 'Shall we just go into the village now and get a drink at the hotel first?'

'I thought you'd never ask.'

Together they did a quick tidy-up of the farm shop – Polly straightening up the things that were left on the shelves and setting up the baskets neatly for the morning, and Rilla sweeping the flagstoned floor with the huge broom. They switched off the tree lights, pulled the door to and headed into Applemore.

A fire was lit in the bar at the Applemore Hotel, and Harry was sitting at a table frowning at his laptop when they walked in.

'Hello, you two.' He flipped the lid of his computer shut. 'Please tell me you're here for a drink and you can give me the excuse I need to stop thinking about stock ordering until the morning?'

'Only if you promise to keep us company at the Christmas tree lighting.' Polly crossed her arms and gave him a mock-stern look.

Harry opened his laptop again, grinning. 'On second thoughts…'

'Don't start.' Polly shook her head.

Harry stood up and nodded towards the bar. 'I'm only kidding. Let's get something to act as an anaesthetic.'

'Oh come on, Scrooge,' Polly said, taking him by the arm and dragging him across the carpet. 'Everyone loves singing carols. It'll get you in the Christmas mood.'

Behind the bar, a red-headed girl was polishing glasses. She looked up, cloth in hand. 'What can I get you?'

'You carry on, Katie,' Harry said. 'I'll sort these two out.'

Rilla and Polly sat down on the bar stools. Polly chatted to Katie, whose elder sister had been in her year at school. Rilla looked out of the window at the little harbour. Twinkling lights had been strung along the metal railings and a group of people were setting up a mulled wine stall beside the huge fir tree which was silhouetted against the midwinter-dark sky. It was only six o'clock, but it was already pitch dark outside.

An hour later, warmed by a whisky, they headed outside into the crisp evening. A crowd had gathered, seemingly out of nowhere, and the air was filled with excited chatter and the cinnamon scent of the mulled wine that was being handed out by the primary school PTA.

Rilla felt a tap on her shoulder. 'How are you getting on with your little rescue dog?'

Rilla turned to see a woman who was well wrapped up against the cold in a red Puffa jacket which was zipped up to her chin, with a thick scarf and woolly hat covering most of her face. It took her a second to realise it was Kerry, the dog groomer.

'He's an angel,' she said, fondly.

'No sign of the owners reclaiming him?'

Rilla shook her head. 'No, and there's still no space at the rescue kennels – not that I'd want to send him there.'

'Sometimes dogs come into our lives for a reason.'

Rilla sighed and gave a small smile. The thought of handing Hugh over when she left filled her with a horrible sense of guilt, not to mention sadness at the thought of not waking up to his warmth as he lay curled up at the foot of her bed.

'Sometimes,' she said, trying to sound non-committal.

'No sign of Lachlan?' Polly returned from the hotel loo, pulling on a pair of gloves. 'God it's cold, isn't it? Feels like it could snow.'

'Not often that happens,' said Kerry. 'Anyway, I better get back over there – I've left my husband with the boys and they're liable to try to throw themselves in the sea or something when his back's turned.'

'Were you expecting him?' Rilla turned back to Polly.

'He said he'd be here.'

'Ladies and gentlemen,' said a woman with a loudhailer, which then squealed so loudly that everyone jumped. 'It's lovely to see so many of you here this evening – this chilly evening – for the annual Christmas tree light-up celebration.'

There was a flurry of clapping. A small child in a pushchair shouted, 'When's Santa coming?' making everyone laugh.

'As you'll know, we're hoping to raise some money for new play equipment for the primary school, so after the lights are on and we've had a little singsong, we'll be passing round the bucket, so have your loose change ready. Don't you go sneaking off, Donald,' she continued, as a man headed off towards the bar. 'I'll be in the bar personally afterwards emptying your wallets.'

'That's Mrs Drummond, the head teacher,' Polly said, leaning close to Rilla so she could be heard as the woman carried on giving a list of instructions. 'She's a bit of a dragon but she's turned the school around, so everyone loves her – it was doing terribly until she turned up. But once she gets hold of that loudhailer…'

'She's hard to stop?' Rilla lifted an eyebrow in amusement.

'I swear she needs to have it prised out of her hands. Oh look, she's finished talking at last.'

Rilla giggled.

'One more thing,' said Mrs Drummond, lifting the loud-hailer again, to a small but definitely audible groan from the crowd, 'we've got a special guest coming this evening, so keep your eyes peeled, boys and girls.'

Singing 'Away in a Manger' on autopilot, Rilla tried to tell herself that *she* didn't have her eyes peeled, looking out for Lachlan, who she hadn't seen for a week. He'd been down in Edinburgh helping Gus with a beer festival, and she'd had to focus very hard on not missing him. It had worked, almost. She screwed up her face, thinking about it. Well, it had sort of worked. That was good enough. It was perfectly natural to miss someone, after all, wasn't it? When she left places she'd taught before, she'd always missed the friends she'd made along the way. It wasn't as if he was the first good-looking man she'd had a relationship with, either—

'Rilla?'

She jumped as Polly put a hand on her arm. 'Sorry, I was miles away.'

'Joan says she'll give us a lift home, so I can have another drink. D'you want a mulled wine?'

'Yes please.'

Mrs Drummond picked up the loudhailer again, and after a rousing version of 'We Wish You a Merry Christmas', accompanied (badly, but very endearingly) by a small boy playing a trumpet, she began the countdown.

'Four... three... two... one!'

There was a moment of silence and some muffled swearing.

'Not in front of the children, Donald,' Mrs Drummond

admonished. The loudhailer gave a squeal of disapproval and then a second later the huge tree was lit up with a thousand tiny pinpricks of light. The whole village of Applemore seemed to gasp with delight at the same moment.

'Isn't it pretty?' A little girl with a missing tooth looked up at Rilla, who nodded. Her dad put an arm around her shoulders, turning her round.

'And who's this?'

Rilla followed their gaze. Coming down the main street in a cart pulled by two huge Clydesdale horses, their bridles sparkling with tinsel, was Father Christmas himself. He pulled the horses to a halt and handed the reins to Harry, who'd left the pub and was standing with a thick grey jumper on underneath his Applemore Hotel apron. One of the horses rubbed its nose on him, making everyone laugh.

'If all the children want to make their way over to Santa, he's got a little present for each of you.'

Polly returned with their drinks, looking highly amused.

'What's so funny?'

'That.' She inclined her head towards Santa, who was now surrounded by a sea of small children. He was laughing as he handed out presents from a huge red sack, and when he caught them looking, he gave a brief salute in their direction.

'Do you know who it is in the Santa suit?' Rilla frowned in his direction, trying to work out if she could recognise the face underneath the huge fake white beard. The hat had slipped down over one eye, and the costume had clearly been designed for someone considerably rounder of stomach. 'Has he got a pillow stuffed up the front of his coat?'.

'He has.' Polly giggled. 'George Mackay who normally does it came down with a stomach bug earlier this afternoon, so the PTA needed someone to take over. I happened to be chatting to Mrs Drummond when she came up to the farm shop, so I thought maybe my big brother should do his bit.'

Rilla put a hand to her mouth, bursting into peals of laughter. 'That's Lachlan?'

Polly gave him a little wave, waggling her fingers teasingly.

'Yes it is.'

Half an hour later, he found them in the corner of the bar, defrosting by the fire. The crowds had dissipated and all the children – high on the sweets Lachlan had given them – were being dragged back to bed by their parents.

'I am going to kill you, Polly.'

Both Polly and Rilla snorted with amusement.

'You made a very good Father Christmas,' Rilla said, as he sat down beside her. She leaned across, removing a piece of white fluff from his woollen sweater. 'Although your beard appears to be shedding.'

'Nice to see you lot out having fun.' Joan, wrapped up against the cold, appeared from the little corridor that led through to the restaurant.

'Hello,' said Lachlan, leaping to his feet and giving her a huge hug. 'How are you?'

'All the better for seeing you three.' Joan gave Rilla a squeeze on the shoulder and leaned across, kissing Polly on the cheek. 'I had dinner booked with a friend, completely forgetting the tree lighting do was on this evening or I'd have been out to watch.'

'You missed Lachlan making a star performance,' said Polly, elbowing him in the ribs.

'I did?'

'Someone,' he glared at her, trying to look cross and failing, 'decided to volunteer me for the role of Santa.'

Joan burst out laughing. 'Well now, that is priceless. I'd have skipped my main course to see that if I'd known.'

Lachlan closed his eyes briefly as if to forget the horror of countless shrieking children all clamouring at his feet. 'I don't think I'm cut out for primary school teaching, let's put it that way.'

'Nonsense,' Polly said, laughing. 'He was so good I've heard they're already planning to have the suit taken in for next year.'

Lachlan shook his head. 'I've got plans for next Christmas.'

They stayed longer than they'd planned – Lachlan sticking to Coke, Rilla and Polly drinking one too many of Harry's Christmas cocktails. When they drove home, half of Rilla wanted to invite Lachlan to come back to the cottage, but she steeled herself. The spectre of New Year, and the thought of leaving, was never far from her mind. She could feel herself doing what she always did – starting to slowly extricate herself in the weeks before she left.

One evening, though, Lachlan turned up at the cottage unannounced.

'Come on, Cinderella,' he said, laughing. He handed her a bottle of champagne.

'What's this for?'

'Later,' he said, simply. 'But for now, unless you've got any other plans, I'd like to take you out for dinner.'

'Of course I don't have any other plans.' Rilla looked at her shirt, which was dusty with flour from a delivery of cakes they'd had that afternoon.

'Good.' Lachlan nodded. 'I'll pick you up at seven, then.'

When he knocked on the door a couple of hours later, she was glad she'd made an effort. He was clean-shaven, his still hair falling in damp spikes over his forehead. As he leaned in to kiss her, she took a breath in, smelling the fresh, lemon-woody scent of his aftershave.

'You look gorgeous.'

She hadn't packed for winter nights out – but the velvet dress she'd worn for the Hallowe'en party – which Polly had insisted she kept - had turned out to be the perfect thing for a Christmas evening out. She'd twisted her hair up in a French knot, but curls were already falling down around the sides of her face. She'd taken more time than usual with her make-up, putting on dark smoky eyeshadow and a rose-pink lipstick. She caught a glimpse of her reflection in the mirror by the front door of the cottage.

Lachlan caught her eye in the glass. 'I mean it.' He caught her chin in his hand, running his thumb gently along the edge of her cheekbone.

'Shall we go?' Rilla felt suddenly uncomfortable with how much she wanted him.

Harry had saved them the best – and most private – table in the restaurant. Candlelight gave the little alcove an intimate feeling, and once the waiter had poured their wine and taken their order, it wasn't long before Rilla had forgotten there was anyone else in the room. Lachlan had a way of focusing on her when he was talking so that she felt like nothing else mattered.

He poured some more wine into her glass as the waiter took away their starter. Rilla cupped it in one hand, looking down into the dark red depths.

'Rilla.' Lachlan put a hand on her wrist. She looked down at the still tanned arm scattered with dark hairs, which was such a contrast to her pale freckled skin. 'I wish—'

Rilla shook her head. 'Don't.' She couldn't bear to hear him say anything he might regret in the cold light of day.

'Okay.' He picked up his glass. 'Tell me something that's been happening with you – apart from working your fingers to the bone for my slavedriver little sister.'

'The weirdest thing, actually.' She looked at him over the top of her glass. 'I rang my mother last night. You know how rare an occasion that is.'

He nodded. She'd explained to him that the thread that held them together was a very distant one. 'What inspired that?'

'Not Christmas,' she said, motioning to the sparkling fairy lights that were hanging over the top of the painting on the wall beside them, 'but all the stuff with our dads. I thought about it, and I wondered if she knew. I didn't want to ask her outright, so I just sort of vaguely alluded to it.'

'And?'

'She picked up on it straight away. Said she hadn't known for years, but not long before he died, they'd had a long conversation where they'd cleared the air.'

'I wonder why she didn't tell you?'

'I think perhaps she felt that it was all better left in the past.'

'D'you feel better for talking to her?'

'Ish.' She shrugged. 'I don't think we're ever going to be the best of friends, but I'm glad we cleared the air a bit.'

'I wish I could have done the same with mine.'

'I'm sorry.'

'Don't be. It's good you got the chance to.'

The waitress came over, bringing their main courses.

Rilla leaned back slightly, letting her put down the plate of risotto.

'That looks amazing.' She picked up her fork and tasted it. The food at the Applemore Hotel was unbelievably good – Harry had found an exceptional chef, and word was beginning to spread. Almost all the tables were full, which for a Wednesday night in a tiny Highland village seemed an impressive feat. 'Have you thought any more about what to do about the brewery?'

Lachlan shook his head. 'Still mulling it over. Fortunately when I was down for the beer festival, Gus and I had a chance for a decent chat because Lucinda was at work. The offer's on the table, and I just need to work out what I'm doing about it.'

'No pressure, then,' she said, smiling.

'Exactly.'

It was a lovely meal, but there was so much hanging unspoken in the air that Rilla felt slightly awkward. Lachlan was still attentive and romantic, taking her outside afterwards and kissing her in the harbour under a sky blanketed with stars, but she knew she was distracted by the fears she was having that she felt more for him than she wanted to admit to herself. She'd been travelling for the whole of her adult life, and Applemore seemed determined to ensnare her, somehow. It wasn't a feeling that she was used to, and she wasn't sure she liked it.

On Christmas morning, though, it was as if everything had returned to normal just for one day. Rilla stayed over the night before at Applemore House, and they stayed up – Beth sleeping in one of the many spare rooms with the babies – far later than they should have, drinking whisky and playing charades by the fire in the sitting room.

The next morning, feeling slightly delicate, she and Lachlan went downstairs to find Beth in pyjamas and the twins sitting in matching high chairs eating toast, which they were holding in their tiny podgy fists, their faces beaming with delight.

'I'm enjoying the last Christmas before I'm woken at five in the morning by tiny despots demanding presents,' laughed Beth. 'D'you want coffee? I've just made a pot. You look like you need it, Lachlan.'

Rilla watched as Lachlan, wearing jeans and a dark grey T-shirt, yawned and stretched hugely, his T-shirt lifting so she could see the fine trail of hair that led from his stomach downwards. She lifted her eyes to meet his, and he gave her the ghost of a wink. God, he was ridiculously gorgeous. It stood to reason, therefore, that she was leaving the best thing she'd ever known to go and work in Paris with a load of wildly unenthusiastic language students. She shook her head slightly as he turned away.

'Morning,' sang Polly, waltzing into the room with a tinsel halo on top of her blonde head. 'I've decided the secret to a hangover is just to start drinking, so who's for breakfast mimosas?'

'Oh go on then,' said Beth, standing up and getting glasses out of the cupboard.

'I'm in,' said Lachlan, pouring coffee for himself and Rilla. He passed her mug over, having added cream and sugar without asking. She sipped it and smiled a thanks.

Half an hour later, Charlotte arrived.

'I would have been here earlier, but – quelle surprise – the nightmare guests from Lochinver Cottage were on the phone at half seven this morning telling me they couldn't get the heating working. Turns out they'd messed around with the settings so much they'd managed to wipe the entire programming.' She rolled her eyes. 'Yes, I will have a drink, thank you very much.'

'Can you take this one,' Beth said, depositing a plump toddler on Rilla's lap, 'and I'll change this stinky monster before we open presents.'

'You look quite at home,' teased Polly a moment later as she wandered into the room. She'd changed out of her pyjamas into a pair of purple dungarees and a striped T-shirt and tied her hair up in a loose ponytail.

'You think?' Rilla looked down at Lucy, who was chewing happily on a wooden train toy.

'I do,' said Polly, giving Lachlan a pointed look. 'Look what you could have won,' she teased.

'Thanks for that,' said Lachlan, drily. 'Can we have one day when we're not reminded that Rilla's waltzing off to travel the world and leave us here?'

Rilla bit her lip. It was good that they could joke about it, of course, but, God, she was going to miss all of this. Not just Lachlan – when she looked at him, she felt a dull ache in her heart which she was trying very hard to ignore – but Polly, Beth and Charlotte, too. Growing up, she'd always felt like the odd one out in her family, but here she seemed to fit in perfectly. Applemore felt like… well, it felt like home.

Lachlan prepared a rib of beef – everyone having agreed previously that they could happily never eat turkey again – and Rilla and Polly prepared the vegetables. When everything was in the Aga, they all collapsed for a while in the sitting room, flopping by the fire and watching a Christmas movie while the babies had a nap. Rilla sat curled up on the sofa, Lachlan's arm wrapped around her shoulders, breathing in the smell of him. When the film ended, she told herself that the tears she was shedding were for the characters, not for her.

Over lunch, Lachlan and Rilla took it in turns to explain the whole story of their dads, and the secret that they'd taken with them to the grave. It was a lovely, strangely funny meal which was full of tears and laughter, where they toasted their late dads and talked about how different things might have been.

While they were washing up the dishes, Lachlan stopped and turned around.

'I've been thinking about this – and it might seem a bit weird, but I was wondering if we could do some sort of memorial. We haven't done a headstone for dad, yet, but…' he looked at Rilla, picking up her hand. 'You said your dad was cremated?'

She nodded. 'His ashes are still in Edinburgh. I didn't know what to do with them – I couldn't very well take them travelling, and I haven't been back there since… well, since…' She tailed off.

'We could do something for the two of them.'

'Oh god, I love that idea. Two fingers up to the establishment and everyone who stopped them from admitting the truth.'

'I don't think the establishment minds that sort of thing these days,' said Beth, mildly.

'I don't know,' said Charlotte, 'I think you'd be surprised. Anyway, I think it's an amazing idea.'

'Like a headstone with their names on?' Polly suggested.

'Exactly.' Lachlan nodded. 'Only – well, you'll need to talk to Sally and see what she thinks, of course.'

'I suspect she'll be fine with the idea.' Sally – who always seemed so strait-laced and conventional – had absolutely revelled in the story when Rilla had told her. 'She thought the whole thing was incredibly romantic.'

'Okay. Well, I'll look into it when things open up in the New Year.' He caught Rilla's eye briefly, and neither of them said anything. She knew exactly what he was thinking and turned away, taking a slow, careful breath.

The rest of the day passed in a hazy, lazy whirl of chocolate and whisky and delicious food. Once everyone had gone to bed, Rilla stood by the Aga, warming herself, not wanting the magic of the day to end. Lachlan told her to stay there and keep warm while he let the dogs out.

'I was thinking,' he said, when he came back inside, 'That we should have one night away in the van to christen it. You've done such an amazing job finishing it off.'

'I couldn't have done it without you.'

He stood in front of her, putting one hand on either side of her so she was trapped – but deliciously so – against the bar of the Aga. 'You could have,' he said, kissing her on the temple, 'because you can do anything.' He kissed her again, lifting her jaw to trail kisses all the way to her mouth. She reached up and pulled his body against hers, feeling the hardness of the muscled chest and the heat of his skin against the thin fabric of her shirt.

'If I can do anything,' she said, her mouth close to his, 'am I allowed to make requests?'

'I think that's definitely part of the deal. Now let's get upstairs to bed before I do something completely inappropriate in a family kitchen.'

CHAPTER 22

'The forecast is terrible, you know,' said Polly, looking out of the window. 'You're going to be absolutely bloody freezing.'

'I don't care,' Lachlan growled. 'It's not like we're planning to bag a Munro. We're going to go for a drive and enjoy one of Rilla's last days before she goes.'

'All right, grumpy.' Polly rolled her eyes at him.

He knew he was being like a bear with a sore head, but he couldn't help himself. He had Gus nagging at him – and still no real idea what to do about the brewery. He had Rilla packing her bags – when he'd gone to the cottage two days after Christmas he'd realised that the little place already felt like something was missing, despite the fact she was still there. And he had another two missed calls from Felix, who didn't seem to grasp the concept of a holiday season. Whatever it was he was wanting, it could wait. He picked up the bag he'd packed with food and drinks and slung it over his shoulder. 'I'll see you later.'

'Have fun,' said Polly, not looking up from her phone.

'Poll,' he said, pausing in the doorway for a moment.

She looked up. 'What?'

'Sorry.'

'S'all right.' She gave him the sunny, open smile that told him he was forgiven for being so moody.

Outside on the drive, Rilla was waiting in the van. She was wearing her dad's huge old sweater and a scarf wrapped twice around her neck and still managed to look impossibly cute.

'Is the heating broken?'

She shook her head, laughing. 'No, but it hasn't warmed up yet and by the time I'd fiddled around filling up the water tank and sorting stuff out, I was freezing.'

'Come on, you,' Lachlan said, opening the door so Hugh could jump out. 'I'll take him inside. Two secs.'

'Back already?' Polly was standing at the kitchen counter breaking eggs.

'No, I'm just delivering a temporary house guest.'

'Ahh,' said Polly, delighted to see Hugh. She bent down, scratching him behind the ears. 'Hello, gorgeous boy, how are you?'

'See you later,' Lachlan called as he left.

'So where are we going?'

'I thought we could go up Ben Achill.'

'You want me to climb a hill?' Rilla snorted.

'I do not.' He shot her an amused look. 'I am well aware of your feelings about climbing hills.'

'I'm just of the opinion that they're for looking at and they look perfectly nice from ground level, that's all.'

'Which is why I thought we might drive over the pass and you can see it from a different perspective. There's a little layby in the woods where we can park and go for a walk.'

Rilla raised an eyebrow and put the van into reverse.

241

'A level walk,' he continued, laughing.

'Okay,' she said, turning the van around. 'This is the last trip before...' She paused for a moment and he watched her gather herself. 'It's a trial run. Let's hope nothing falls off.'

'It'll be perfect.'

The rain Polly had threatened started about half an hour after they'd left Applemore. The sky was leaden, with no sign of relief anywhere. The windscreen wipers were going at full pelt and even so were struggling to keep up.

'D'you think maybe we should stop for a bit?' said Rilla, pulling into a little clearing in the forestry.

'I thought you'd never ask.'

They made coffee on the little gas stove and curled up together on the bed, sitting with their backs against the door, watching the rain pouring down the windows. Rilla shifted slightly, feeling the weight of Lachlan's arm around her. It should have been the perfect romantic moment, but her heart felt so heavy that she half expected to hear a thud as it crashed through the floor of the van and onto the muddy ground below.

'Did you ever think this time last year you'd be here?' Lachlan said.

She shook her head. 'Weird the way life turns out.'

'Where were you last New Year?'

'I was working in Marrakesh for a friend who owns a language school out there.'

'I've never been.' Lachlan took a sip of coffee. 'Always wanted to.'

She could feel his breathing and the regular thump of his heartbeat and snuggled in closer to him, enjoying the feeling of being cocooned against the world. He stroked a hand down her hair.

'It might not be as exotic as Morocco, but I'm glad we're here.'

'Me too.' She lifted her face to his, meeting his kiss. She slid her hand inside his jumper, feeling the heat of his skin and the muscles of his back. He pulled her close, kissing her again.

'Give me that coffee cup,' he said, taking the empty mug out of her hands and reaching across her to put them down on the little shelf that hung above the bed. He rolled over, putting his arms on either side of her body, holding himself up and looking down at her.

'Hello,' she said, hooking her arms around his neck, trying to make a joke of the situation. The expression on his face was so tender and loving that she closed her eyes against it, allowing him to kiss her on and on until she forgot the storm that raged outside.

Rilla woke, several hours later, to discover that the sky had cleared. Pale midwinter sunlight filtered through the trees. Lachlan lay fast asleep, one arm thrown carelessly across her. She traced a line through the dark hairs that covered his wrist, turning his hand slightly to check the time on his watch. It was almost half past three. She didn't want the day to end. Making love to her, he'd murmured 'I love you' so quietly in her ear that she'd half wondered at first if she'd imagined it, but he'd taken her face in his hands and looked at her, his eyes dark, and nodded once, as if to confirm it. Her heart contracted with pain. She breathed out, long and carefully, and turned to look at his sleeping profile, his jaw etched with dark stubble.

I love you, too, she thought. But that just makes this harder.

He stirred, drawing her close in his drowsy, half-awake state, and kissed her on the top of her head. In another time, this could have been perfect.

CHAPTER 23

Lachlan had hated watching Rilla drive back to the cottage. A gnawing feeling of foreboding had been growing in his stomach the whole journey back, and when she dropped him off at Applemore, he'd wanted to hold on to her and not let go. But his phone – back in range of signal for the first time that day – had gone off like a rocket, and he'd torn himself away, reluctantly, and headed inside to deal with reality.

By the time he'd spoken to Gus, who was clearly making a supreme effort not to push for an answer, and dealt with a sash window which had swollen in the storm and wouldn't shut so it was rattling in the wind, it was pitch dark outside and he was ravenous. He wandered into the kitchen to make something for dinner, finding Polly curled up on the armchair by the Aga reading a book. The dogs all wagged their tails lazily, not getting up to greet him.

'Nice time?' She glanced up, briefly.

'Yeah,' he nodded. He didn't want to talk. Neither, it seemed, did Polly. She got up, yawning, and said she was going to go and have a bath and an early night. It was only as she was heading out of the door that he realised Hugh was still there.

'I completely forgot he was here when we got back.'

'Oh,' said Polly, lightly, 'it's fine, I said to Rilla we'd just keep him overnight. No point in disturbing him.'

He gave her an odd look as she disappeared rapidly out of the door. Rilla had always been assiduous about making sure Hugh was with her – and she'd said that she didn't enjoy being in the cottage on her own overnight. Lachlan shook his head, frowning. He'd nip down first thing and drop him off.

The next morning was the sort of chaos that came with a big family. Lachlan woke at seven to find Polly had her things spread across the kitchen table and was making plans for the farm shop. Heading blearily for the kettle, he made coffee, standing barefoot by the Aga watching her scribbling away.

'I'm going to nip down and drop Hugh off,' he said, yawning widely. 'Once I've had this coffee, anyway.'

'It's a bit early, isn't it?'

'You're up.'

'Yeah, but I've got an empire to run. It's the Christmas holidays, you don't need to be leaping out of bed and rushing off first thing.'

'Atlan!' The door swung open and Beth appeared, hair tied up in a scruffy bun, looking harassed.

'Hello, Eddie,' he said, as the twins toddled into the room, beaming with delight at seeing their favourite uncle. He bent down, picking one up in each arm.

'Morning,' Beth groaned. 'Polly said there might be breakfast on the go?'

'I'll make bacon sandwiches for everyone, shall I?'

He put the babies down beside the dogs, laughing as they patted them with wide-open hands. He got to work, cooking some of the local bacon Polly sold in the farm shop, slicing a loaf of bread, putting butter on the table after clearing a space.

'You don't need to take the entire table up with all this,' he said, laughing.

Even Charlotte turned up, complaining that the guests from hell were still proving difficult. They sat around the table, chatting and laughing, and Lachlan leaned back against his chair and surveyed his family. Without thinking, he'd sat in his dad's place, and he wondered how it had felt for all those years to keep a secret so precious, and to have known happiness but not be able to share it. If he... if things were different, he'd want to share what he had with Rilla with the world.

He closed his eyes thinking about yesterday afternoon in the van. He hadn't meant to say the words aloud, but in a strange way he was glad that he had. Not that it was going to change anything – she was still leaving, but, well, for once he'd been completely open. Right now, though, the old saying about *better to have loved and lost* was going round and round in his head and it made him want to yell with fury at the top of his voice. There was nothing good about this.

He stood up. 'I'm going to go down with Hugh,' he said.

Hugh looked up, hearing his name.

'Come on, let's get you back to your foster mum.'

Polly shot Beth a glance.

Charlotte put a hand on his arm. 'D'you want me to come too?'

He looked at her and frowned. 'I think I can probably make my way down the drive on my own.'

'Okay,' she said, and an odd expression flitted across her face.

He jumped into the Land Rover, Hugh sitting bolt upright beside him on the passenger seat, full of enthusiasm. They bumped their way along the drive, dodging the potholes almost without thinking, and he pulled into the courtyard behind Applemore Cottage.

The moment he climbed out of the car, Lachlan sensed something was different. The place looked dark – no light was shining from the little kitchen window. There was no smoke pluming from the chimney. He fisted his hands, closing his eyes briefly and taking a deep breath in. He knew, almost before he realised, what had happened.

He walked around to the front of the cottage, which looked as if it had lost the light from within that had been there for the last few months. Petals from the last roses that had hung on until now were scattered across the front step, beaten down by the storm. He remembered the look on Rilla's face that first day she'd arrived, exhausted and pale with jet lag, bashing the door in a desperate attempt to get in. His legs propelled him towards the front door and almost mechanically he lifted the doormat, knowing what he'd find. The two keys – the small, shiny Yale and the huge, old-fashioned dark metal one – lay on the stone of the front step. He took a step backwards, looking inside the cottage, seeing nothing but darkness. Rilla had gone.

He headed back to the house on autopilot.

'Hey.' As soon as he opened the kitchen door, Polly rushed across the room, putting her arms around him.

'You knew.'

She nodded. 'It's the worst thing, I'm sorry.'

'She didn't say goodbye.'

'She couldn't.' Polly pulled back from the hug, looking at him. Her expression was sombre. 'You knew she had to go. She couldn't bear it – and I don't know what happened yesterday, but something made her decide she just had to do it.'

He chewed the inside of his lip, not saying anything. He'd blown it by telling her how he felt. If he'd kept his trap shut, they'd have had a few more days together and he'd have had a chance to say goodbye… but that would have been just as bad. The reality was that there was no way of dealing with their situation that wasn't going to hurt like hell. He took a deep breath.

'I get it,' he said, squaring his shoulders. 'I know why she did what she did.'

'I've told her we're keeping Hugh.'

As if he knew what was being said, the spaniel pushed up at Lachlan's hand, nudging him for attention.

'Fostering?'

Polly shook her head. 'It's not like we haven't got plenty of room for another dog. He loves the girls, and he fits in perfectly. As long as he's not going to make you too miserable reminding you of Rilla all the time.'

Lachlan smiled, bending down to scratch Hugh behind the ears, just where he liked it. 'I think having him here as a reminder of Rilla is a good thing, don't you?'

Polly nodded. 'I'm sorry, Lachlan. It's shit.'

'It's fine,' he said, not feeling it. 'We both knew that she was leaving.'

His brain and his heart seemed to be on two entirely different tracks. Logically, he knew why it had happened. But it seemed his heart hadn't got the memo. He felt like he'd been hit by a ten-ton truck and then rolled over several times for good measure.

A second later, there was a cacophony of barking and all three dogs shot off from their habitual position by the Aga and towards the door of the boot room, crashing through the half-open door and into the courtyard.

Polly looked outside. 'There's a very shiny Range Rover out there. Are we expecting guests?'

Lachlan groaned. 'I bloody hope not. I couldn't be less in the mood for people.'

'Morning,' said Felix, brightly. He unfolded himself from the driving seat of the Range Rover, all long limbs and expensive country clothing. One of the dogs leapt up at him, leaving muddy footprints on his ginger cords.

'Fe,' said Lachlan, in surprise. 'Mabel, get down. What the hell are you doing here?'

'Well,' Felix said, glancing at the Range Rover, 'you didn't return my call, and I thought well, sod it, nothing ventured, etc, etc. I was 99% sure you'd be here for Christmas, so here we are.'

Lachlan peered at the darkened windows of the Range Rover. 'We?'

'I have got you the dream buyers. Sol and Grace Harroway. They're from New York State. He's a venture capitalist, she's a philanthropist. Let me introduce you.'

Lachlan, so stunned that he couldn't find the words, stood in the courtyard as they climbed out of the Range Rover.

'It's so sweet of you to let us have a first look at Applemore before it goes on the open market,' said Grace Harroway, extending a slim, manicured hand. Lachlan shook it, politely.

'Wow,' said Sol, 'this place looks like a fairy-tale castle, doesn't it, honey? Look, it even has turrets, just like you wanted.'

'It's amazing,' Grace agreed.

Lachlan turned to look at Felix, eyes widening with shock.

'*What the hell?*' he mouthed.

Felix cocked an eyebrow at him.

'Hello,' Polly, came out into the courtyard. She'd pulled a thick sweater over her pyjamas and was wearing a pair of too-big wellington boots. She looked, Lachlan realised with grim amusement, like the epitome of the eccentric country house owner. Grace and Sol would probably want to throw her in as part of the package.

'Hello, Poll,' said Felix. 'Long time no see. How's tricks?'

'Um,' said Polly, looking from Felix to the American couple and back to Lachlan, 'good. I think?'

'Excellent.' Felix seemed unperturbed by their confusion.

Grace and Sol wandered around the side of the house, and he followed them.

Polly turned to Lachlan. 'Are you going to tell me what the hell is going on?'

He dropped his head into his hands. 'Have you ever had a massive decision to make and not known what the solution was until it was staring you in the face?'

'Probably?' Polly looked confused. 'Why are these people here, and why is Felix dressed up like that?'

'It's his country house estate agent garb,' said Lachlan, flatly. 'And they're here because he wants me to sell them Applemore.'

'What?' Polly's shriek was so loud that it brought Beth, who'd been watching kids' TV in the sitting room with the toddlers, rushing to the back door of the house.

'Is everything okay?'

'Everything is not bloody okay. Did *you* know Lachlan was planning on selling?'

Beth looked at him. Where Polly had looked furious, he saw nothing but hurt on his sister's face. 'You said months ago that wasn't an option. Were you lying?'

He shook his head. 'I didn't know what to do, Beth. Back then, this place just felt like some sort of curse. But the last few months, with Rilla here, and finding out about Dad and David – it's changed everything.'

He looked across at the sweep of shaggy lawn, and the pine trees that led down towards the field full of sheep grazing in the distance. The dogs were careering around, chasing the scent of rabbits, and the air was crisp and fresh. He heard Felix explaining to Sol and Grace that they'd have an opportunity to make this place something really special, and in that second he knew the answer he'd been looking for.

'Felix.' He beckoned him over.

'Any chance we can give them a tour of the interior? Don't worry if it's a bit of a state, they've got all sorts of plans for redeveloping the place. Grace is an interior designer.'

A vision of Applemore House decked from top to bottom in swathes of expensive tartan fabrics flashed before Lachlan's eyes and he shook his head. 'No, sorry.'

'Really, I promise you – they're not expecting *Homes and Gardens*. I told them turning up on spec meant they'd have to take you as they found you. They're a lovely couple – very down to earth.'

'No,' said Lachlan, shaking his head again. 'I'm not selling.'

'I thought you wanted shot of the place.' Felix, ever the

salesman, sounded slightly curt at the prospect of the commission he'd lose.

'I said I might,' Lachlan replied, as Beth and Polly came to stand on either side of him. 'But things have changed. Well, I have.'

Polly put a hand on his arm and gave him a fond squeeze, which gave Lachlan all the motivation he needed.

'This is home. It might be falling apart and cost a bloody fortune, but it's ours. And it's been in the Fraser family since it was built. I'm not selling.'

'They're willing to pay over the odds. You won't get a better price,' insisted Felix.

'I don't need a better price.'

Felix sighed, recognising that he was beaten. 'Fine. Your loss.'

'On the contrary,' Lachlan said, turning to look at the house, 'I think it's definitely my gain.'

Having seen off a disgruntled Felix and a bemused Sol and Grace, they headed inside. Beth was relieved to find the babies still staring fixedly at Peppa Pig. Once dressed, Polly, sensing Lachlan wanted some time alone, disappeared in her beaten-up car down to the farm shop to do some tidying before it opened up the next morning.

Lachlan picked up his phone.

'Morning.' Gus had clearly been for a run. He was pink-faced, standing in a sweat-soaked T-shirt in the kitchen of his Edinburgh flat. 'Good Christmas?'

Lachlan puffed out a breath. 'Good and bad.' He put the thought of Rilla out of his mind. 'You?'

'Great. I mean, we screwed up dinner – turns out neither of us can cook a turkey to save our lives – but we drowned our sorrows in champagne instead, so all's well that ends well, and all that jazz.'

'I've thought about it,' Lachlan said, the words coming out in a rush. 'And it's a yes.'

'You're shitting me.' Gus sat down at the table, so all Lachlan could see was the sweat mark on his T-shirt. A moment later, he adjusted the screen so his face was visible again. 'But you don't want to sell.'

'I'm saying yes.'

'What about integrity? And our beer getting watered down to gnat's pee and all that stuff.'

'Don't care.'

Gus looked at the screen, frowning. 'Who are you, and what have you done with my mate Lachlan?'

'I'm still here.' Lachlan gave a short laugh. 'I've just realised that there are some things more important in life. I guess I had to go home to realise that.'

'You're staying up there?' Gus's face fell. 'Not coming back?'

Lachlan shook his head. 'It's home,' he said, simply. 'I think I fought it for so long that I didn't realise how much it mattered. But things have changed.'

'Rilla?' Gus looked at him through the screen.

Lachlan shrugged. 'She's gone.'

'Shit, man. I'm sorry.'

'It's okay,' Lachlan lied. 'We knew it was going to happen.'

A month later, the deal was done. Over an expensive lunch in Edinburgh, Lachlan and Gus signed over the rights to the brewery, their designs and their recipes.He felt a complicated mixture of sadness, guilt and pride. Afterwards, they stood on the street, both too stunned to talk. The money was in their bank accounts. Gus and Lucinda were planning a trip to the Maldives for a month. Lachlan, on the other hand, climbed back into his beaten-up Land Rover and headed north, driving in silence through the Highlands until he reached home.

Applemore House rose out of the trees, sparkling in a heavy frost which hadn't lifted for days. It looked breathtakingly beautiful, and with the money he'd accepted he'd be able to secure it for the family for generations to come.

When he walked into the kitchen, he was surprised to find all three sisters sitting there waiting for him. Polly was in her habitual spot, cross-legged on the kitchen worktop. Beth was helping the twins to do a wooden puzzle. Charlotte was stirring something on the Aga.

'Everything all right?' He looked from one sister to the next, puzzled.

'Yep,' said Charlotte. 'We're just staging an intervention.'

'A what?' He rubbed his jaw.

'Someone needs to knock some sense into you, you great idiot,' said Beth, 'and we've given you a month and you seem to be determined to blow the one good thing you've had in your life.'

'Rilla,' said Polly, helpfully, 'in case you hadn't worked out what we're talking about.'

'What about her?' She'd haunted his dreams every night since she left. He'd had a message from her when she arrived in Paris, with a photograph taken from the balcony of her little apartment, saying that she'd loved their time together and that she hoped he'd forgive her for disappearing, but that she hated goodbyes more than anything.

'You love her,' pointed out Charlotte, simply. 'And we can't bloody live the rest of our lives watching you pining away missing her when she loves you back.'

'She's in Paris,' he said, realising as he did how stupid he sounded.

'They've got these amazing things called planes these days,' said Polly, as if she was talking to one of the babies. 'You jump on, and they fly you through the air and you end up in another place. Like Paris, for example.'

'Where the person you love who loves you is waiting,' added Beth.

'What if she doesn't?' He thought back to their last time together in the camper van, and how he'd said I love you to her and she'd ducked her head, kissing his neck and not saying anything in response.

'Well, what's the alternative? You spend the rest of your life wondering?'

CHAPTER 24

Paris in January should have been a dream. When she wasn't working in the little school by the river, she wandered along the banks of the Seine, watching couples walking hand in hand, whispering and giggling as they fastened padlocks to cement their love onto the metal railings. She'd thrown herself back into teaching, taking as many hours as she could and offering tutoring outside school hours, in a desperate attempt to keep herself from thinking about what she'd lost. Driving away from Applemore that cold December night had been the hardest thing she'd ever done.

She'd walked into the cottage and collapsed on the sofa, her heart aching in a way she'd never experienced before. It had taken everything she had not to look into Lachlan's eyes and tell him that she loved him back, that she'd fallen in love with him years before and always carried a torch for him which had reignited with a fire she'd never expected when she came back to Applemore. But all she'd been able to think about was the pain of parting, and how she'd always been a solo traveller, and how she couldn't work out how on earth she was supposed to carry on living the life she always had with him in one place and her in another. What she hadn't realised – not until she'd packed the van late that night, and locked up the cottage and said a last goodbye to her dad in her mind – was that something fundamental had changed. She'd taken a long last look at the little cottage in the darkness – the windows reflecting the black of the starless sky, as it stood surrounded by the tall pine trees in the silence of the Highland midwinter. She'd said a final farewell to her dad, remembering the sunny, happy days they'd spent each summer, and wiped away a tear – not just for him, but for everything she was leaving behind. Her heart ached at the thought of Hugh, lying curled up fast asleep by the Aga at Applemore, not knowing she wouldn't be back the next morning to pick him up. She'd thought of Lachlan the first day she'd arrived, wondering how she'd ever not recognised his face. And then she'd shaken her head, as if to clear her memory, and turned away from all of it, and towards the future. The long drive down through Scotland, pausing for a sleep somewhere near Stirling as the sun came up, and then down, down – through England, across the sea, and over the changing landscape of France – had given her the time to think she both needed and didn't want. All her life had been focused on moving on, finding something new, never settling down. This was what she did. She'd prided herself on travelling light, not needing people or things, reliant only on herself.

She'd arrived in Paris, parking the van with an old friend on the outskirts, and made her way to the little apartment that she'd found to rent. There – determined not to weaken and contact Lachlan – she'd unpacked her meagre belongings, placed the black and white photograph of her dad on the window-ledge, and resolved to forget. But it was hard to forget the love of her life in the most romantic city in the world, so she worked harder and harder until she collapsed into bed every night, only to spend the night tortured by her subconscious which seemed determined to force her to relive every second of her time back in Applemore.

Her three o'clock student had called in sick, meaning the afternoon she'd expected to be tied up with an intensive two hour conversation lesson was free, which given the circumstances was a blessing in disguise. There was still a lot to do. All she could think about was how everyone was doing back at Applemore. Polly had messaged regularly, keeping her up to date – which was lovely and awful in equal measure. She'd been proud of Lachlan for making the choice to sell his share in the brewery, knowing how much it had meant to him.

She turned the corner, pulling out the keys for her apartment from her bag, and looked up. For a second she thought she must be hallucinating. Sitting on the step outside her building, leaning back against the metal railing, was a tall, dark-haired man. His long legs clad in battered dark jeans were stretched out on the pavement, sturdy boots planted on the floor. He turned at that moment, dark hair flopping over his forehead. Her heart thudded unevenly against her ribcage. Rilla stopped in the street for a split second, hardly able to believe what she was seeing. He stood up, pushing the hair back from his face in an all-too-familiar gesture, and she thought her heart might burst with happiness. A second later, his long strides had eaten up the distance between them. She wrapped her arms around his neck, feeling the solid wall of his chest pressing against her body and the achingly familiar scent of his skin as she buried her face in his neck. The wool of his sweater scratched against her cheek and she lifted her face and in that moment his mouth met hers for the briefest, sweetest kiss.

'Hello.' His mouth was on hers as he spoke. Her heart thudded wildly in her chest and she pulled back, gazing at him for a moment, taking an unsteady breath.

'Are you going to invite me in?'

CHAPTER 25

Lachlan watched as Rilla fished in her bag for her keys, pulling them out after a moment and dropping them on the pavement. He leaned down, picking them up, looking at the little wooden carved keyring she'd brought from the Applemore Farm Shop. She blushed and looked down at the ground, shuffling her feet and smiling.

'I wanted something to remind me,' she said, taking the keys from his outstretched hand.

He watched her climb the steps to the little apartment. It took all of his self-control not to pull her into his arms then and there on the cool stone stairs, but he followed her, watching as she put the key into the lock, giving in to his need as the door swung open. He drew her towards him, feeling the curve of her waist under his hand. He groaned as she snaked her arms around his neck, feeling soft skin as her shirt rode up, pushing her back against the door so it closed with a heavy thud.

'I had something I wanted to tell you,' he said, one hand tangling in her hair, tipping her head back slightly so she was looking at him with her eyes wide. Her lips were parted slightly. The cold had lent a rosy flush to her cheeks, and he thought in that moment that she'd never looked more beautiful. It was now or never.

'That's funny,' she said, and she stood on tiptoe, reaching up so he kissed her again. He ran a hand up so her coat slid off her arms and onto the floor, and together, somehow, they were moving along the hall, still kissing as if they'd been starved of each other for years, not weeks. He took a ragged breath inward.

'I had something I wanted to tell you, too,' Rilla murmured. She pulled his hands to lead him into the little room which was bathed in late afternoon sunlight. It took a moment before he realised that the room was bare, and that beside the little blue sofa was a familiar looking, slightly untidy pile of bags. He looked at her for a moment, frowning slightly. She nodded back at him.

'I forgot to tell you.' She took an unsteady breath. 'I love you, too.'

'I know.'

'I thought you might.' She ducked her head, looking pleased and coy at the same time.

He cupped her face in his hands and looked down at her.

'But I don't understand. Where are you going?' He indicated the cases.

Rilla shook her head, looking at him with such love that he wanted to wrap her in his arms and keep her there forever. 'I've given in my notice. I was coming home to Applemore to tell you I realised the moment I left that I'd made a mistake.'

His heart contracted at the word *home.* He watched as she took his hand from her cheek, lacing her fingers in his.

She pulled back slightly and looked at him, biting her lip for a moment, suddenly vulnerable.

'I mean – if that's what you want?'

'You are what I want.' It was that simple. Nothing else mattered. 'I came to tell you that I loved you and I wanted to be where you were. That's all.'

'Me too.'

He tucked a stray curl behind her hair, pulled her close, and kissed her, knowing that wherever they might go, they'd found the one thing they'd been missing.

The skies over Paris were velvet dark and sprinkled with stars when they looked up again, long hours later.

EPILOGUE

Three months later

'For two people who wanted to be anywhere but here,' Polly grumbled, trying to squeeze past the huge armchair where Rilla was sitting perched on the side, her legs draped across Lachlan's, as he drank a cup of coffee, 'You're remarkably good at getting in the way when I'm cooking.'

She picked up a wooden spoon, looking at it for a moment and frowning. A moment later she pulled the heavy dresser drawer out and retrieved a different, slightly bigger wooden spoon, and gave a satisfied nod. 'That's the one.'

'For someone who hardly ever cooks,' countered Lachlan, laughing, 'You make a bloody big fuss every time you do.' He put the coffee mug down on the side of the Aga. Polly cracked some eggs into a Pyrex jug, swearing as a piece of shell disappeared into the depths.

'We're not all natural chefs,' said Polly, sticking her

tongue out at her brother. She fished the eggshell out with her fingers.

Rilla leaned across, kissing Lachlan on the cheek, and wriggled off the side of the chair. Hugh stood up, looking at her quizzically. He'd been delirious with happiness to see her, and Rilla had cried with joy into his silky spaniel ears until he'd turned and licked her face, making her laugh.

'I'm not going anywhere,' she said, reaching down to give him a gentle pat on the head. 'Polly, d'you need a hand?'

Polly shook her head. 'Nope,' she said, tipping a heap of chopped onion and garlic into a saucepan so it sizzled gently in the melted butter, 'I'm good. I've developed amazing cookery skills in your absence.'

The room filled with a delicious scent. Polly put her hands on her hips. 'See?'

'I can,' said Lachlan, sounding impressed. 'Nice to know that your repertoire has extended beyond cheese on toast.'

'And beans on toast,' said Rilla.

'Don't forget spaghetti on toast.' Charlotte walked into the room and kissed Rilla hello.

'I'm glad you're back,' she said, gruffly. 'You look a lot happier than you did the last time we saw you,' she said to Lachlan.

'I am.'

'Glad you sorted that out.' Her tone was dry, but her eyes were twinkling with amusement. 'So can we assume you two have got the travel bug out of your system and you're going to take the reins and be responsible adults?'

The van was parked outside in the courtyard. Two big overnight bags, a cool box, and a pile of washing in a black bin bag were sitting on the kitchen table.

'Responsible, yes,' Lachlan said, patting his lap so Hugh jumped up and curled up beside him. 'Adult?'

'Never.' Rilla finished his sentence, laughing.

Lachlan and Rilla had hung out in Paris for a couple of weeks, exploring the city and enjoying each other's company, spending long lazy mornings in bed and afternoons watching the world go by in tiny cafes. With the brewery money through, Lachlan had decided that perhaps it was time that he took some time out for the first time in his life, and together they headed off in the van around Europe for three months, sleeping and eating and spending their days together. It had been an amazing adventure, but they'd both been excited to get back to Applemore where Polly had been holding the fort.

'There's a lot of stuff to do to get this place sorted. But at least we've got the money to pay for it now,' said Lachlan, unfolding himself from the chair and walking across to the window where Rilla was looking out, gazing at the countryside that stretched down to the shore. Somewhere behind the walls of the garden, Beth was working hard in the greenhouses, getting everything in order for the spring that would be along before they knew it.

'We've been thinking about turning one of the fields into a wild camping site – we saw loads of them when we were travelling,' Rilla said, turning back to look at Polly who was frowning into the saucepan.

'Bugger,' she said, crossly. 'I'm sure it's not supposed to look like that.'

Charlotte peered into the pan, her darker blonde head joining her sister. 'It's fine, just give it a quick stir. They're catching, that's all.'

'You'll be on MasterChef before we know it,' Lachlan said, laughing.

'Not sure I'd go that far. Anyway, this camping idea – it sounds really interesting.'

'Well, it'd sort of compliment the holiday cottages. We'd get people from the North Coast 500 coming off the track a bit, hopefully, and it'd bring in business for the farm shop.'

'You've got it all figured out,' Polly said, looking impressed.

'Not sure I'd go that far,' Rilla said. 'But it's an idea, anyway.'

'And there's the gin,' Lachlan added.

'The gin?'

'Applemore Gin.' Rilla looked at him and they shared a smile. 'We just need Beth to grow the right herbs and things –'

'That's the technical term,' Lachlan teased her.

'Herbs and *botanicals*,' Rilla continued, shaking her head and laughing.

'Anyway, watch this space. You can be our first taste tester.'

'Excellent.' Polly beamed. She leaned over, kissing Rilla on the cheek. 'I'm just bloody glad he went to Paris to find you.'

Rilla put an arm around Lachlan's waist. 'Oh, I was coming back to find him, anyway.'

She looked across the kitchen of Applemore House, her eyes landing on a photograph Polly had discovered while they were gone. In it, their two dads were standing side by side beside the cottage, dogs sprawled at their feet. They were looking at each other and laughing as if they hadn't a care in the world. Polly had framed it, and it was hanging in pride of place on the kitchen wall.

'I think they'd be happy with the way things turned out, don't you?'

Lachlan followed her gaze, then pulled her close, dropping a kiss on her temple. 'I do.'

ACKNOWLEDGMENTS

Writing The Winter Cottage in the middle of summer has been the loveliest escape I could hope for. As soon as the idea for a series of books set in a little village in the far North West of Scotland came to me, I couldn't wait to get to work.

What made it even more exciting was that we took off in our newly-finished camper van which we converted during lockdown and headed up to Scotland on a research trip, where we discovered the huge white beaches and gorgeous scenery I've written about here. Like most authors, I can't help but sneak bits of life into my stories one way or another, and so I couldn't resist giving Rilla a van of her own to have adventures in. I also sneaked in our dogs, Mabel and Martha, because they I decided they deserved a starring role in a book given how much time they spend keeping me company while I write.

Enormous thanks and all my love as always to my writing friends – the Book Camp gang and the Word Racers, and to Alice, Caroline, Hayley, Josie, Keris, Melanie and Miranda for keeping me relatively sane in the midst of life and deadlines and everything else in these strange times.

Special thanks and vast amounts of cake and champagne to Kirsty Greenwood, Holly Martin and Tasmina Perry, all of whom have been hand-holders and cheerleaders extraordinaire this summer.

Thanks also to Amanda Preston, agent and all round wonder, and to Hayley Webster, my brilliant editor. A very special thank you to Cressida McLaughlin, too, for a last minute brainwave which made all the difference to the story. And to Diane Meacham, who created the beautiful cover for this book - thank you!

To my children – Verity, Archie, Jude and Rory – who seem to have made it almost all the way to adulthood relatively unscathed, despite the general chaos that comes with having a mother who spends most of her time staring into space and daydreaming about stories - I love you all.

Last of all to James, who taught me about running a brewery (any mistakes are mine, and he'll never read it, so don't tell him) thank you for making me laugh every single day. I love you.

COMING SOON

THE FLOWER FARM

Next in the Applemore series… a gorgeously romantic will-they-won't-they tale of love and friendship from bestselling author Rachael Lucas.

Beth Fraser has spent the last few years growing her business from scratch. She's turned the walled garden at Applemore House from an overgrown jungle into a beautiful and productive flower farm. A sudden change of circumstances means she has to find a way to make it pay more - and fast.

Jack McDonald arrives in Applemore determined to make his outdoor activity centre a success - working with troubled teenagers is something that means a lot to him. He gets off on the wrong foot with Beth, and life in the little village of Applemore is proving far from idyllic. Can he prove that what he's doing is worthwhile, or will the villagers continue to hold him in suspicion?